ADVANCE PRAISE FOR *UNDERWORLD DREAMS*

"Daniel Braum has done it again with another unforgettable book. In the pages of *Underworld Dreams*, you'll find devastatingly beautiful stories that carry you away like a seemingly serene yet dangerous sea. There's horror here to be sure, but it manifests itself in so many different ways: in the uncanny, in terrifying landscapes, and most of all, in the depths of human loneliness and alienation. This is an absolutely gorgeous collection and one that you should add to your reading list immediately."

GWENDOLYN KISTE, AUTHOR OF *THE RUST MAIDENS* AND *BONESET & FEATHERS*

"Haunted men, dangerous women, and enough unearthed treasures to sink a ship: Daniel Braum writes with the same gritty and salt-sprayed flair as coastal-town masters like Kem Nunn and Lucius Shepard, but with a spirited voice all his own. *Underworld Dreams* is a wild, noir-infused ride that's well worth taking."

ROBERT LEVY, AUTHOR OF *ANAIS NIN AT THE GRAND GUIGNOL*

"To read a Daniel Braum story is to [step] . . . [walk] into another room, through a doorway not present a second bef[ore] . . . [feel] familiar, comfy—but don't get too comf[ortable] . . . strange discrepancies, in this place Braum [has made?] u[nreadable] might be tempted to stop reading and close the [door?] . . . [w]here you felt safe. But Braum is too good a writer [to let you not?] step further into the other room... And besides, if you did turn around, who's to say the way back would even be there?"

JAMES EVERINGTON, AUTHOR OF *THE QUARANTINED CITY*

"In these deeply melancholic stories, Braum writes of relationships with all the skill of our best realists, but always punctuates and torques his observations with a suspicion of the strange and the unreal. *Underworld Dreams* is an original high-wire act that deftly walks the thin line between genres without ever slipping."

BRIAN EVENSON, AUTHOR OF *SONG FOR THE UNRAVELING OF THE WORLD*

"In *Underworld Dreams*, Braum takes the reader though a series of mystical vignettes packed with strange occurrences, intense emotion and, yes, flat-out horror. Unsettling, violent and heartbreaking, this is a collection that weaves the supernatural into real characters and emotions so effortlessly it'll linger in your head and your heart, like a nightmare you don't recall having survived."

PHILIP FRACASSI, AUTHOR OF *BEHOLD THE VOID*

PRAISE FOR DANIEL BRAUM'S WRITING

"Daniel Braum is a true storyteller. By that I mean he spins tales of wonder that grasp at ideas and themes that human beings have been pondering since our brains become up to the task. These stories will also make you laugh, cringe, and damn near weep. This is such a big-hearted and wide ranging book and Daniel Braum is the real deal, a writer to treasure."

VICTOR LAVALLE, AUTHOR OF *THE BALLAD OF BLACK TOM*

"Tales of music, magic, tortured spirits, desperation, and even hope await you in The Night Marchers. Braum presents our world through a lens that reveals the wonderful and the horrifying with masterful, elegant prose. *The Night Marchers* is a stunning debut from a writer who's been adding to the field of darkly weird literature for years, but who's name is only now beginning to emerge, and it's about time!"

LEE THOMAS, AUTHOR OF *DOWN ON YOUR KNEES* AND *BUTCHER'S ROAD*

"Daniel Braum is among the best short story writers we've encountered. When you start reading *The Night Marchers*, it's readily apparent that you've discovered something special, possibly even transcendent."

SHANE DOUGLAS KEENE, *THIS IS HORROR*

"The stories are full of sadness, beauty, and unprecedented wonder. Two cups literary dark fiction, a heaping scoop of magical realism and urban fantasy, and a tablespoon of horror."

CHAD STROUP, *SUBVERTIA*

"Braum has a real knack for writing engrossing and deep stories that defy genre categorisation. He creates rich settings and relatable and interesting characters whilst not falling into the trap of stereotyping. Simply put, If you're a little tired of reading the same old, same old then you need to give Daniel Braum's stories your time. One of the biggest compliments you can pay a writer is by saying he/she writes like no other, well, Daniel Braum writes like no other."

ADRIAN SHOTBOLT, *THE GRIM READER*

"In looking for the perfect word to describe this work I decided upon divergent; it's true these tales are unlike anything else I'm reading today. Bold, adventurous, strange, and totally enjoyable."

FRANK ERRINGTON MICHAELS, *HORRIBLE BOOK REVIEWS*

"The stories are a Lemarchand's puzzle box for the reader to try to solve or to just sit back and enjoy, in awe of Braum's fantastic imagination and well written, fast moving, captivating creations. There are moments when the author's deep feel for humanity leaves a longer lasting impression upon the reader than the story itself."

DAN STUDER, *TALES OF AN ECLECTIC READER*

"I give very few quotes. I only make exceptions when a novel or collection knocks me out. So... short and sweet: buy Dan Braum's *The Night Marchers*. It's good, damn good. This man has one hell of a career ahead of him, and you get to be at the party before everyone else."

JACK DANN, AWARD WINNING AUTHOR AND EDITOR OF *WANDERING STARS*

UNDERWORLD DREAMS

DANIEL BRAUM

LETHE
PRESS

Published by Lethe Press
lethepressbooks.com

Copyright © 2020 by Daniel Braum

ISBN: 978-1-59021-583-8

Library of Congress Cataloging-in-Publication Data
available on request

Cover design by
Staven Andersen

Interior design
by inkspiral design

CONTENTS

INTRODUCTION
BY THE AUTHOR

LONG AGO THE words *"sogni del mundo sotteraneo"* were the only words I knew in Italian. At the time I had no idea that those words would come to embody, unify, and signify "my kind" of stories for me.

I'll explain.

"Sogni del mundo sotteraneo" means "Underworld Dreams" or "Dreams of the Underworld" in Italian. Armed with just passable Spanish, and bits and pieces of working knowledge of other languages I reached out and made friends with fellow travelers when I was on the road in Central America in the 1990s. Because my knowledge of Italian consisted merely of the words *sogni del mundo sotteraneo* my enthusiasm and very limited skills led to me thinking that some of my first traveler-friends were in Central America to explore caves. Caves. Underworld. Underground. And so on. Of course I was wrong. My friends were *not* cavers nor spelunkers as I had convinced myself. I should have known.

As years went by, and friends and travelers reunited on different journeys and as we all became more fluent, I realized I had not only been wrong about my friends and caving, I realized I had been wrong about entire conversations. Facts and memories simply were *not* as I had originally thought they were. In addition being a lesson in humility and a good laugh, the experience of my misconceptions felt like something more... I thought I had touched on something inherent about life and the stories that make up our lives. It dawned on me that what I had been certain were real stories were figments of my imagination and misconceptions because I had not grasped or been aware of the truths and meanings that were in plain sight all along.

In the decades that followed I became a storyteller. I wrote and published the stories that came to populate my first two story collections *The Night Marchers and Other Strange Tales* and *The Wish Mechanics Stories of the Strange and Fantastic*. I came to learn how subjective many aspects of a story can be. Once published, what any given reader comes away from a story with can be intended, or not, by the author. In general I think meanings born of misunderstanding are not what authors strive for. However, the possibility of heightened understandings, unexplored meanings, alternate interpretations, and resonances due to what an author might intend and craft into a story and or from what a reader might bring to or take away from a story are things that excite me to no end.

Stories with controlled ambiguities in them and stories that are intentionally open to interpretation always captivated me. There is something… interactive going on, in addition to the storytelling. As I wrote and published and explored and learned I came to find my place in the world of fiction, where once upon a time (when I was just a young traveler misunderstanding Italian words), I had thought there might not be one. I dove deeply into learning about the different labels and conventions and genres that encompassed the stories I loved. I learned an important lesson, that no matter what the label or category, these stories with controlled ambiguities, were a "thing" and not just a "thing" that I had come up with. "My kind" of stories belonged to a category, a genre, a tradition I had not been aware of. With this awareness and sense of belonging came a confidence and an enthusiasm. I wanted to craft more of this kind of work and to dig deeper into the emotional truths, spiritual explorations, and supernatural catalysts the form allowed me. And thus the stories for this volume, Underworld Dreams were born.

In the Kabbalah, the mystical aspect of Judaism, there is a saying "as above so below- as below, so above." The notion is that there is no heaven or hell and that the highest spiritual purpose and achievements are not in an afterlife but in the here and now. The above and below are linked because the higher purpose (or the world above) is to live one's own life (the world below or the "under-world") and live it in the best way as opposed to living a life that gains one entry into another place or a heaven. Without subscribing to one religion or another and without judging any religion or another this notion of "as above so below, as below so above" strikes a chord with me; inherent in the notion that there is no afterlife and that a so called heaven can be here and now is the notion that a so called "hell" can be here and now too. Both these ideas are in fact are the here and now and not some mystical and supernatural other place or state. The notion is that what we tend to think of as this mystical spiritual supernatural thing or place or state is right now in our mundane and earthly and world and lives and successes and struggles.

This resonates with me because it makes me feel like our aspirations and efforts the lives we live, in this here and now, (this underworld that we all live and breathe in, together, every day,) are indeed as important as they feel. The stories, our stories, of this here and now are our connection to each other and maybe even to some greater whole or great beyond or maybe merely our connection to a great nothing and inevitable void. Either way they are the stories I know I want to write.

Whether or not the universe is infinitely expanding or destined to contract and implode; and whether or not there is cosmic significance or only an unresponsive, cold, void, our stories- our dreams are real. I have included story notes telling some of the inspirations for the tales that make up this volume. Joseph Campbell said where we had thought to be all alone we shall be with all the world. My experience with these underworld dreams and the stories that make up this book make me believe Campbell's saying is true. I invite you now to dream with me. Come dream with me and with these stories in this beautiful and fearsome underworld.

-   Daniel Braum, Delray Beach January 2020

HOW TO STAY AFLOAT WHEN DROWNING

Montauk, New York

I FIGURED SLIPPING away to the bar would be a good way to escape the table's cringe-inducing conversation, but I can still see Uncle Roy and Alison, laughing it up with the Client and our hired boat captain among the litter of cracked lobster shells and half-eaten fish platters.

The bartender sees me coming and is ready with another rum and coke. The night wind blows a gust of clean ocean air into the dock's aroma of fried food and cigarette smoke.

"Enough fishing talk for you, buddy?" the bartender says over the miasma of tables full of high-season out-of-towners here for something the fast-paced Hamptons can't offer.

He knocks on the wooden bar top and collects the dollar bills pinned under the tea light burning in a thick shot glass.

"I prefer my meals without talk of buckets of blood and guts," I say. "Thank you very much."

From over my shoulder a laugh joins the murmur of lapping waves audible in the second before the next classic rock song kicks in on the tinny speakers.

The bartender and I both turn to look at the woman on the stool next to me. She's in a long sun-dress and a green army surplus jacket despite June's warmth. There's no make-up on her young face, but she doesn't come across as young; the way her lithe frame is comfortably parked on the bar stool speaks of years. I think there's something unusual about her forehead but it's just the glow from the light strings hanging above the bar flashing on and off her face.

"What's so funny?" I ask.

She's staring past me at the water. I don't think she's going to answer.

"Everyone knows the real way to chum for sharks is to cut yourself from nape to navel and let your guts spill out," she says.

I expect her to laugh again, or at least smile. She doesn't.

The bartender winks at me and steps over to serve an old Italian man who has come up to the bar.

"We're uh, talking metaphorically here, right," I say. "Spill as in, spill into life? Your life, my life? Not into the water, right."

"Sure. Yeah sure," she says, blankly.

I feel like I've disappointed her and she's searching my face for a hint of the answer she wanted me to say. I know I should be uncomfortable with the way her gaze remains on me but I'm flush with excitement.

"Come on, you know what I mean," she says.

I *don't* know what she means but I smile like I do.

"I'm not really one for chumming," I say.

"But you're bleeding all over the place."

There's a splash from baitfish jumping below.

"*You better look out… there may be* sharks *about…,*" I half-sing.

It's her turn to smile at me with no idea of what I'm talking about.

"Sorry. My singing's terrible, I know," I say. "The real lyric is *dogs* not *sharks* though… never mind."

"I get it," she says. "Sharks smell blood like some people smell weakness."

At the table the Client and Uncle Roy are pretending they're holding rifles and aiming into the air.

I try to fight away the memory that comes. I'm surrounded by a mob that's pulling a six-foot thresher out of surfer-crowded waves and I'm squeezing Nina's hand.

"Fear isn't strength, it's just...thrashing," I mutter.

"Strength is in truth. The real kind of truth vulnerability brings," she says.

"Not too many people feel that way or would even comprehend that."

"You do," she says. "But you're here to hunt?"

I'm not here to hunt. There's no way I'm going out with Alison and them in the morning. There's no way to tell her without spiraling into everything I don't want to talk about. I almost say 'I'm just here to get through the day'; but even that intentionally-casual answer leads to unwanted paths.

"I'm only here for my family," I say.

She laughs again.

"What?"

"Tell me something true," she says.

"That is true. That's my sister sitting over there with my Uncle Roy. She runs the surf apparel distributorship our parents founded. The guy next to her is the purchaser for a big group of stores. So yeah, the point of the weekend is to land his business. The other guy is the boat captain my sister hired to take us out tomorrow. He told us his full name but he insists we call just him Captain Mike. He's a *bit* too serious about the Captain part of it too, if you ask me. Boring stuff."

"Then tell me something else."

"I don't know, like what?"

"Do you surf?"

"Never been on a board. Yeah and my family's business is surfing, go figure."

She swirls the ice in her glass, slides a few cubes through her lips then covers her mouth as she shifts her lower jaw. I think I hear a little pop.

"I... lived out here one summer," I say. "Feels like a lifetime ago. It was."

"What *was* it like?"

"Nothing like now, the town's grown up so much since—"

"No. What was it like for you?"

"Me? I was young, though I didn't feel young at the time. I felt alone and far from home. Then I fell in with someone. We were sort of engaged and… what can I say, we ran away together. That's what it was like."

"Almost sounds romantic," she says.

"I wish it was. It should have been. It wasn't."

"Are there really any good places left to run to?" she asks.

"We found a place in the middle of nowhere. Costa Rica. They have bats down there we wanted to see. This kind that grab fish right from the water. We had to take buses, and a little plane, and then a boat. The boat had to go… well the whole thing was a mess. Did you know whirlpools were a thing? I never knew they were real. And a thing to worry about when you navigate into the mouth of a river from the ocean. That's how I know. For a while there we thought our boat was going down. I'm not the praying type but I swore if we got out of it alive I'd never leave sight of land again."

"Wow, careful," she says.

"Don't worry. I'm not going out tomorrow. No way."

"I meant careful, keep being honest and vulnerable like that—"

"…and I don't know what I'll attract."

"I guess that too," she says. "I was going to say careful, you might get used to it."

We stare past the diners and drinkers at the crescent moon and the red dot beneath it. I wonder if she's going to speak. I like that she isn't about small talk; that she dives right into the heart of things.

"Can I get you another drink?" I say. "Better yet, I'm dying to get out of here. You up for a change of scenery?"

"It's late."

"Yeah, the days start so early around here. How about just one more?"

"It's not that," she says. "I'm here for my family too."

I want to ask *her* to tell *me* something true but it feels like the moment to ask that has passed.

"If I stay I'm going to have to go back to that table and talk about fishing and brand name wet suits," I say. "So I'm gonna walk these drinks off. If you're feeling like company and want to walk and talk with me, just say the word."

"I've already stayed too long. I have to find my sister."

She stands. I awkwardly wish her good night and mumble something about how I understand family comes first instead of asking her name and if I could see her tomorrow. She weaves through the tables and disappears into the door leading to the inside part of the restaurant and the parking lot and road beyond.

The bartender returns and shakes his hand like he's just touched an oven.

"Now that's a keeper if I've ever seen one," he says. "For a second there I thought you were going to reel her in."

I pay my tab and ask him where else is open around here this time of night.

"You could count the places on one hand," he says, then tells me.

I return to the table. Captain Mike and Uncle Roy are lighting cigars. Uncle Roy implores me to join them.

I politely decline, remain standing, and announce that I'm hitting the hay.

Alison whispers in my ear as I peck her cheek and wish her goodnight.

"You look pale. You okay?"

I nod and smile to let her know that I am.

"Goodnight," I say to the table. "See you all in the morning."

I don't mind lying to them though I'm kicking myself for not having the presence of mind to ask the woman for her name. I hope it's not too late to catch up.

Headlights from the road briefly light up the neighboring dock as I make my way through the tables. One of the busboys is standing on the shore having a smoke.

Somewhere in the dark a night bird calls.

THE DOCK WHERE I spent so much time with Nina isn't far from here. Salt air smells the same ten years on and isn't easily forgotten. I try to conjure the feel of her hand against mine. I'm not sure which memories are of real sensations and which are just fabrications dulled by the years. Wind rustling the sea grass brings the sense of vast open stretches of sand back to me. The night bird's honking cry echoes over the water...

THE OCEAN BREEZE has tussled Nina's black bob into a wild tangle framing her sun-touched face. I can smell her last cigarette, though she swears she's quit. She leans in and rescues our melting ice cream cone with a well-timed lick followed by a big sloppy smile that transforms her. She ceases to be the depressed soul who thinks and talks so much about Art School but never paints. I no longer see the street-wise girl, running away from school, from the city, from what she calls 'conformity and everything' but instead she is an ethereal, sensual, carefree being, here watching the waves and afternoon surfers with me. Me. The would-be surfer who's never stepped on a board. With the afternoon sun warming my shoulders through my t-shirt and her sticky hand around mine I think maybe this is all life is, pairing up and running away from whatever it is you are running away from. Together. Like this.

The end of the pier is crowded with people fishing, holding hands, and wave-watching like us. The break isn't so hot but there are still surfers out there hoping the left will develop.

Someone in the water is yelling. Nina and I push over to the railing to look with everyone else. A young man has hooked a thresher shark on a line. The panicked fish spins and spasms as it is hoisted from the waves. A half-dozen people have their hands on the line helping bring it up. The shark swings and manages to smash itself into one of the concrete support pylons. The people pull and pull and bring it up all the way to the rail. A woman leans over and gets her arms around it. Someone holds her waist and pulls her in. The crowd grabs hold of the shark, lifts it over the rail, and drops it on the pier. It flops and twists, its open mouth revealing a maw of dangerous teeth and the steel hook that snared it protruding from its lower jaw. No one wants to go near it now. A widening circle of space forms around it as everyone backs up. The woman who first grabbed it emerges, brandishing a baseball bat. Her blow connects with the shark's side, right under its dorsal fin. It flips, landing on the steel hook, driving it deeper. The woman slams the suffocating thing again, then the mob is all over it. This isn't fishing. This isn't protecting anybody.

Our ice cream splats onto a puddle of blood and salt water. The shark is beaten into an unrecognizable shape. I realize Nina has never seen tears in my eyes. In the chaos of kicks and bat swings and skin and scales it dawns on me we're drowning. We're drowning here.

"Let's go," Nina says.

"I'm with you."

"No. I mean it. I mean let's really get out of here."

"Anywhere you want," I say. "Anywhere at all."

THE SILVER SETTING reminds me of a wave curving around the small blue opal and two tiny diamond dots. The plan is to ask her to marry me at the lodge, at night, after we see our first fishing bat.

"Maybe I'll draw a bat while were down here," Nina says, all the bouncing on the dreadful road making her voice vibrate funny.

The awful bus ride doesn't dampen her spirit and she kisses me as we lug our bag from the bus stop to the shore. The roaring ocean and clean air are so welcome. We're warned by the two boatmen not to go in while we're waiting for all the passengers. After ten minutes or so they decide there are no other passengers. There's water in the bottom of the wooden boat. The older man pushes off the beach and jumps in. The boatman on the motor guns it as we crash through the wave line. The boat catches air and lands with a heavy thunk. The older boatman leisurely bails water with a half of plastic jug.

We motor to the estuary at the mouth of the river which is the only way to the lodge. Swells lift and drop us. I don't like the look of the waves we're going to have to pass through nor the way the boatman are bickering in Spanish.

"It's rough," the younger boatman says to me. "We may have to go back and try again tomorrow."

"But it's almost dark," I say. "Where are we going to stay?"

"Don't sleep on the beach," he says. "The sand flies are not very nice."

The men speak to each other in Spanish.

"We're going to try?" I ask.

The boatman guns the engine. I grasp Nina's hand. The water in the bottom has soaked our packs. The older boatman is bailing in earnest now.

A big swell lifts and drops us. We spin and spin and wind up with our port side facing land. The boatmen men yell at each other as the boat is dragged along parallel to shore. Waves hit from all sides, the water fills up faster than the old boatman can bail.

"Can you swim?" the boatman asks.

"What's happening?" I ask.

"Kiss your wife and pray."

The older boatman stops bailing and throws a small wooden crate overboard. Then a full jug of something, motor fuel maybe. Then a bag of oranges he has fished out of the calf deep water. He grabs my pack and I stop him. We watch the jettisoned stuff spin away in the current. Large dark shapes are moving beneath the surface; I spot a lone dorsal fin heading toward the crate.

Nina is perfectly calm though she is squeezing my hand as hard as can be. Behind her a big wave is coming up on us sideways. Her look of resignation inspires a burst of sadness and anger. The boatman guns the engine. The wave slams us. We're soaked but somehow we don't go under and emerge from the blinding spray shooting towards the shore.

THE SWEET WOMAN who runs the lodge escorts us to our cabin which is on a secluded rise nestled into tall palms at the edge of the rainforest. Through the big window taking up most of the far wall we can see the water that almost dragged us down. There is an assortment of pots and pans, a hair dryer, a small electric radio, towels, a flashlight and a can of bug spray lined up on the counter next to the sink in the kitchen area. A thick extension cord runs through the front window bringing power. The shower runs on rain water. We thank her and flop our bedraggled selves onto the big bed. When the woman leaves Nina cries softly. We fall asleep in our soggy clothes; the distant sound of waves no comfort.

We wake in the night. The waves have quieted. The tide has receded. A coral reef and fish are visible in the clear water, their tropical colors illuminated by the full moon. The balcony outside the window is bigger than my apartment. A metal tub, a coal grill, and bucket are the only things on it. We peel ourselves out of our clothes, heat up buckets of water, and fill the metal tub.

From our bath we watch the fish in the water below and spot bats flying by grabbing insects. I rub Nina's shoulders gently and whisper "we made it." This inspires a fresh round of sobs.

"What is it? What's wrong," I ask.

"People don't get it."

"Get what?"

"They don't understand the only thing that's real is how we treat each other. Nothing we do is going to be remembered."

Nothing I say comforts her.

After an hour I decide to trek down the cliff to the main area to see if I can find ice cream or anything that might cheer her up.

I RETURN TO the cabin and notice the big window is open and the power cord is running through to the balcony. Nina's stopped sobbing. I don't like the low-pitched buzz coming from outside.

"Nina?"

She's motionless in the tub. Her head's tilted back, staring at the sky with that same awful resignation that came over her on the boat. I'm confused at why the cord is out here until I see the submerged hair dryer. A blue arc jumps from Nina's bruised skin joining the pink and orange bolts that crackle over the water every second or two. The awful sound is coming from the radio floating by her feet. The reek of ozone and burnt hair hits me and I understand that what she has done was no accident.

I TOLD MYSELF a lot of nevers that night. Never leaving sight of land is the one I've kept. I must not have truly meant the rest. I spot the woman from the bar on the bend of the dark road up ahead. I walk faster to try and catch up.

THE SHAPE I thought was the woman is not a person at all but a big owl perched on road kill on the shoulder where the road turns onto Main Street just past where a bunch of cars are parked. The owl sees me, opens its wings and silently lifts into the air.

A man ambles out from behind the nearest car and crosses the road. There's something wrong about his face. He stumbles into the brush and beach scrub on the other side. I realize there's a path to the beach there and I follow him.

A dozen surfboards are half-buried in the sand forming a circle around a small bonfire. Dozens of people, surfers, are drinking and smoking and milling about in the fire-glow. The man stumbles towards them. In his path, I see the woman from the dock standing just outside the ring of light.

I run over.

"Holy shit, you scared the hell out of me," the guy says.

The woman is nowhere to be seen. I spin around looking for her on the beach and in the crowd of surfers.

DANIEL BRAUM

"Sorry. Uh, hey, did you see which way the woman who was standing right there went?"

"I didn't see anybody," he says.

His face is a patchwork of healed-over burns and scars.

I point to the sand. There's an indentation that's much too big for footprints. It looks like a person or two had been laying there.

"She was right there."

He shrugs and fishes a bright pack of cigarettes out of his pocket. He takes one out, lights it up and pulls deeply. I introduce myself and ask if I can bum one.

He hands me the pack and motions for me to take. Words on the wrapper say *Busa Buka Baki*. The cigarettes are cloves, wrapped in thin white paper. In what far-away place were these purchased? What a life he must have. They all must have.

I scan the beach looking for her again. I spot another of those big indentations in the sand a few yards away.

A tall surfer breaks away from the pack by the fire and comes over.

Every inch of his lean swimmer's build is sun tanned. His hair is bleach blond and he's wearing board shorts and a T shirt like the rest of the young people but the lines on his face show he is older than me.

"Everything alright?" he asks the scarred guy.

"Yeah, sorta, this guy scared me but everything's cool."

"This is a private party," the surfer says to me. "Do we know you?"

"No. And sorry, I didn't mean to crash. Or startle anyone. I'm just looking for my friend."

"You see her?" he asks.

"No. But maybe I can have a look around? To be sure."

A big splash at the shore carries through the darkness before he answers.

"Hey, Danny, I think someone's out there," someone by the fire calls.

The surfer and the scarred guy go to look. I palm the pack of smokes and slide them into my back pocket. I used to lift smokes the same way for

Nina; even though I didn't want her to smoke, I knew she would and we couldn't afford it.

There's no one there, just the sets of waves coming in. People are leaving the fire-lit circle to check it out anyway. There's no thrill being here for me. I've come so far from the time I so desperately wanted to be a part of something like this. I return to the road and trek back to my hotel room.

Despite the hour, I cannot sleep. I wish I had told the woman at the bar that I didn't come to hunt; I came for Alison. I did think there'd be something here for me. That I'd be full of memories of Nina. The ache is so dull and far away it is almost not real.

I take a clove from the pack and smoke it. When it burns down I light another one. Nina thought stealing was wrong so I never told her where the smokes came from. I sit and smoke and imagine what it would be like to connect a swing of a bat into the sides of each of the surfers out on the beach. I know it's terrible but I don't care. Nina thought killing the shark was wrong. She'd probably think it was wrong to beat that mob who did it in. I never had the chance to tell her how I much I longed to do that.

I USED TO believe there would always be good places left to run to. Now I'm not so sure. Determining if there are any good places left to come back to seems more important.

OUR WAREHOUSE WAS in Hauppauge, less than two hours away when the traffic's right. It was more like home than our house ever was...

THERE'S A HINT of saw dust and vanilla pipe smoke in the air, which means Dad's in his workroom shaping a board. Mom is gathering all signs of our domestic activity in the conference room the four of us have made our de-facto dining space and finding hiding places to obscure them from visiting eyes.

"Go get your father before you leave for class," Mom says. "The buyer should be here any second. Tell him it's the Professor, he'll know who."

The whine of the motor on Dad's wonky power sander grows louder as I walk through the rows and rows of stock, shelved wet suits and shoe boxes, towards the corner of our warehouse Dad has claimed for his personal workspace.

I push through the hanging plastic barrier into Dad's world. Remnants of past projects, experiments, and abandoned works in progress fill the small, square space; a test section of planed hardwood, a rack with two shaped but unvarnished boards, dozens of fins.

Dad's at the machine in the center of the room grinding a piece of wood that will one day be a surfboard. His long, dirty-blonde hair is tied back. Oversized safety goggles mask his clear blue eyes. He clenches his stubble-covered jaw in concentration.

The fins fascinate me the most. Dad could easily make standard designs. Easy sells to buyers but he makes all kinds of crazy boards with all sorts of fin positions.

"What kind is this one going to be," I say to announce my presence. "Single fin or double?"

One style is all the rage right now but I can't remember which.

"Neither. When it's done, I'll know."

"Mom says someone's here for you."

"A buyer? This late?"

"Mom said you'll know who."

This inspires Dad to stop the machine. He flips his goggles off.

"It's almost done, want to try it with me?"

"Now?"

"No better time."

"I dunno. I'm heading to class. I'll walk with you up front."

I know he's not pushing. He's trying to instill in me the notion to take on the world, on my own terms and at my own time. I grew up with him telling me you don't know if you can surf until you try and I love him all the more for it.

He shuts the lights and the power and together we walk through the rows of inventory towards the front. He's muttering to himself as we walk.

"When you are taken by the undertow, if you are lucky you realize you are but a river in this dark sea," I discern him saying.

"What's that?"

"Something for this meeting."

"What's it mean?"

"It's something surfers say."

"Come on, tell me."

"If I could I would."

Mom has transformed the conference room back into showcase for our business. I grab my book-bag and leave Mom and Dad talking about waves.

As I'm getting into my car an old gray fiat with an empty surf board rack on top pulls up.

"Going to school, young man?" the man in the car, who I take to be the buyer, says through his rolled down window.

"Yes, sir."

"Good," he says. "All my best surfers do, I like that."

WHEN MOM AND Dad did not show for work the next morning Alison and I realized they were gone.

The police and the insurance investigators pointed out that the bank accounts were untouched and no valuables, personal items nor a single piece of inventory was missing. Except for whatever Dad was working on. His surfboards and parts and experiments were the only things unaccounted for.

Alison kept the business going fueled by the belief they'd be back. Later that summer, right around when Uncle Roy showed up to help her, I left. I'd only gone out East, but the East End might as well have been the ends of the earth when it came to the warehouse and my sister.

KNOCKING ON THE door wakes me.

"Come on. Time to go," Alison is calling from outside.

I get up and crack the door. Morning light leaks in.

"I'm staying behind, sis," I say, pretending my best to sound ill.

"You okay?"

I open the door more so she can see my face, to let her know that I am. The door pushes inward; the security chain stretches taught preventing it from opening. It's Captain Mike.

"That's not how you treat family, son," he bellows. "Get your ass out here. Your client is waiting down at the dock."

Alison maneuvers him out of the way.

"It's okay, I got this," she says.

I'm about to say thank you when I realize she's talking to Captain Mike.

"Can I come in?" she asks.

I let her in. We sit on the edge of the bed. She takes my hand in hers and I know she is asking me to come on the boat.

"I'm not leaving sight of land," I offer as an explanation. "I promised myself after…"

"I know," she says. "It must be so hard for you to be back here."

"I'm fine," I say.

"The Client won't go without you," she says.

"Why the hell not?"

"How am I supposed to know, he just won't. Bad luck. Superstition. Misogyny? All of the above?"

"Tell him to fuck off."

"Believe me, I want to. The point of this weekend is to land his business though."

I realize how little I know of her. I know who she *was*. When we were a family. Before I left. From the few times we spoke I remember she'd broken someone's heart or had her heart broken, maybe both. Her life, as far as I know now, is keeping the business alive. And I don't think there's much else.

"Are you going to be okay if he doesn't sign with you?"

She shakes her head, no.

"Uncle Roy thinks I should give up, cash out, and sell the business."

"Why'd you even invite him to come?" I say.

"I wasn't sure you would."

We sit in silence.

"Where's the Client now?" I ask.

"On the boat, with Uncle Roy, waiting for us."

I grab my clothes and take them into the bathroom to get dressed.

The sensation of being pulled sideways in waves comes over me while pulling my shirt over my head. I stumble into the shower curtain.

"You okay in there?"

"Yeah, I'm okay. I'm coming. Just give me fifteen minutes to get coffee."

"MAYBE YOU'RE NOT a pussy after all," Captain Mike grumbles under his breath as I leave the room.

"Does your boat hold water?" I ask in reply.

"What the fuck kind of a question is that," he says to Alison. "Where's he going?"

"To get coffee," she says.

I head for the diner Nina and I used to go to on Main Street, next to Lisa's bait shop. Most of the fishing boats are already out. There's no break and the waves are free of surfers. I turn onto the street and join the early-riser tourists walking leisurely from storefront to storefront. The only vehicle traffic is the knife-grinder truck crawling along, announcing its presence with a song on its old-fashioned bells. The truck gives a gentle honk as it passes the hardware store, which I'm amazed is still open for business. I see old Harvey Levitin behind the wheel and give him a wave. He returns the wave without any expression of recognition. A young mail guy is delivering to businesses that have sprung up since I was last here.

The diner next to Lisa's has been replaced by a frozen yogurt shop. It doesn't sell coffee. I wonder how long it will take me to find some and make it to the dock. I look to see if a new place has opened up and see the woman from last night walking my way.

"Hello," I call.

She doesn't respond. I walk over and match her pace.

"Hello. Good morning," I say. "I'm so glad I ran into you. I went looking for you last night. Right after you left. I didn't ask your—"

Her mouth opens into a smile revealing a maw of jagged, triangular teeth. They are sharp and pointed and much too big. The edge of each tooth is serrated with small barbed notches.

I stop and squint, her face now showing no sign of the sharp-toothed monstrosity. She continues walking. I watch her pass the bait shop then double back and go around the side. She's not the woman from last night. Her hair is slightly shorter and she holds herself differently, otherwise she looks exactly like her.

An ambulance turns on to the road and speeds towards us; lights on, siren silent. It gives a brief chirp; the tourists move the minimum distance to give it space. The mailman crosses the street to my side after it passes. I walk to him and ask, "What was that all about?"

"Someone was killed," he says.

"What? Here?"

"Late last night. Beach's full of cops."

"What happened?"

"Who knows? We'll know when they tell us, right?"

We watch it turn left towards the beaches and docks and the path I came upon last night. I want to follow the ambulance. I want to follow the woman. There is no time for either.

The Captain's forty-foot convertible, the Lady Luck, is the only fishing boat remaining at the dock. An American flag attached to one of the antennae on its cabin tower flaps in the breeze. Alison, Uncle Roy, and the Client are on deck watching me approach. I can see Captain Mike inside the open cabin fiddling with the gear and switches on the console.

I step off the dock onto the boat's weathered rail, then onto the cushion of one of the built-in seat benches, then the deck.

"Hey, coffee boy," the Client says. "What happened, no coffee?"

His playfulness is grating. He's so chipper I wonder if he's still drunk. Uncle Roy puffs on a cigar, watching for my response. Is he wanting everything to fail?

"Who needs coffee when we've got eels," Captain Mike says saving me from having to speak. He exits the cabin hauling a white five-gallon bucket in each hand.

"Ready to land some Stripers? Don't let anyone tell you they like squid. This is my forty-first summer doing this and I know the bass love this eel."

The edge is absent from the Captain's voice when he directs us to help by untying the ropes holding the boat to the dock. I think he might actually be trying to be pleasant.

"Hold onto your hats," he says. "It's a fine day for fishing."

I hope it is. The Lady Luck leaves the inlet and speeds into the Atlantic.

I'm not happy when the last glimpse of Long Island disappears from view.

The steel gray ocean water is mercifully calm. The sky is clear. The sun is warm. I imagine it is a fine day for fishing. Captain Mike has classic rock playing on the radio. We can hear him singing along over the sound of the engines and gulls hitching a ride in our aerial wake.

He spots something on the fish finder and stops the boat.

He secures our rods in metal holders attached to the rail and helps us bait them. We're told we're over a school of striped bass. Within minutes I

DANIEL BRAUM

watch Alison land the first fish, then every few minutes someone is pulling a two or three-footer from the water.

Captain Mike brings two coolers from the cabin to the deck. One is for storing the fish. The other is full of iced beers. Uncle Roy and the Client each crack open a can. Alison waves her hand-held video recorder in front of them asking them what they've caught. They raise their beers proudly and hand one to me and the Captain.

Captain Mike declines because he is driving the boat and "on duty." I make a show of drinking one with them though a hundred beers aren't going to help me feel any better.

Captain Mike steps in front of the camera.

"I was driving the boat that pulled the world record 70 pounder out of the Sound. There are seventy pounders out there. Who wants a world record?"

We boat farther and farther out following schools on the boat's fish-finding sonar. The Client tells us stories of how his family brought him fishing when he was young and he doesn't seem like that much of a dick. Uncle Roy joins in by telling stories of how much Mom and Dad loved to surf and fish and finally pulls his weight by working in how they were such geniuses in business.

After we fish the next school Captain Mike adds heavier rods and reinforced line into the holders.

"Ready for more or ready for lunch?" he asks.

"We're drinking our lunch," the Client says.

They are such children.

"I suggest you put some grub in your stomach as there's no yakking on Lady Luck," Captain Mike says.

He breaks out the sandwiches he has packed. We sit on the deck benches eating his deli meat sandwiches wrapped in wax paper and foil and throwing bait to the gulls who grab it in the air. The boat rocks in the gentle swell. Alison seems carefree. For a second I almost forget how unhappy I am to be here.

SOMETHING STRONG IS pulling on the Client's line. His rod has bent into a shepherd hook.

Captain Mike scrambles from the cabin.

"Pull 'er in, pull 'er in," he gloats.

"I'm trying," the Client says.

His reel is spinning.

"Okay, give it some, give it some. Let her take it. Wait for her to stop."

About half of the line goes out.

"Now crank," Captain Mike barks. "Want me to take a turn?"

Captain Mike and Uncle Roy and the Client take turns giving line and pulling in.

The client insists Alison take a turn. She passes me the camera. I get a shot of Uncle Roy against the rail trying to spot the fish.

About fifty yards out something jumps from the two-foot waves. A shark. The unmistakable dorsal remains above water for an instant before disappearing.

Captain Mike yells a mix of "hell yeahs" and indiscernible hoots before he switches to English.

"That's a ten-footer, out there," he hollers. "At least."

He instructs the client to take over the rod and reel from Alison.

"You want this fish?" he says to the client.

"Yes," the client says.

"Then dig in, this is going to take a while."

"You want this fish?" he asks to Alison and Uncle Roy in turn.

"Then put down that camera and get ready to fight," he yells. "Now we're fishing."

The damn guy is actually trying to give Alison her money's worth.

The client yells a pathetic imitation of Captain Roy's hooting.

"Now we're fishing," I whisper.

THEY'VE WRANGLED THE tired shark up against the side of the boat. Each section of rail is five feet long so we know the fish is over ten feet.

The shark is sleek and streamlined. The silver skin of its pointy head has a blue sheen from the sun and sky.

"Keep your hands away from its mouth," Captain Mike says.

He produces two sticks that look like broom handles tipped with a sharp metal barb. He drives one hook into the side of the shark and instructs the client to hold it. He sinks the other in the fish a few feet away and puts Uncle Roy on it.

"Hold it there. Just a few more seconds."

He lifts the cushioned top of one of the built-in seats and retrieves a short-barreled shotgun.

The shark slaps its tail sending up a spray of ocean water. I taste the salt on my lips.

He pushes the barrel down, drops in two slugs, and pumps barrel back, chambering the first shot. Then he places the gun about a foot behind the shark's black eye and tries to hold it steady. The gulls on the tower take to the air in a noisy cloud when he fires.

MY SHOES ARE soaked with blood. All of our shoes are stained dark red. If Nina could see me now I would tell her I would do anything for Alison just like I tried to do anything for her.

When we reach the mouth of the inlet we can see the small crowd of people from the newspaper and fishing rags waiting at the dock. A crew of two men and a crane-necked hoist help Captain Mike get the Mako from the side of the boat onto the measuring gallows. It is almost twelve feet. The people from the papers are taking photos of the Client and Captain Mike with the shark hanging behind them.

I'd kiss the ground, for real, if everyone wasn't around. The Client is on cloud nine and thanks Alison for it, so at least I didn't break my word for nothing. The guy operating the hoist gives me the business card of his brother who is a butcher and the card of a friend who is a taxidermist. The small town doesn't feel as small as it used to.

A police car pulls up in the lot. Two officers get out and walk directly to us. They ask if they can speak with Captain Mike in private and escort him away from the hubbub to the soda vending machine under the extended roof of the shack that houses the restrooms. I watch the excitement of the day vanish from his face as they speak. Then he doubles over and drops to his knees. The officers help him up. One of them tries to embrace him. He pushes the man away and tries to hide his tears as he runs to his truck.

THE SURFER KILLED last night was Captain Mike's son. Someone opened him up the middle from neck to navel. The area on the beach where they found him is still an active crime scene. The Client insists on taking us to the bar and grill on the dock again to celebrate the catch anyway.

The place is less crowded than last night. A thing like a death is not going to stop people, mostly out of towners like us, from eating and drinking on weekend summer night. Uncle Roy and the Client are drinking and smoking and holding court at the table for the seemingly endless amount of people who want to congratulate them on their catch over lobster and shrimp cocktails. The Client is flanked by two women he brought to dinner. He says they are his cousin and her friend on summer vacation but they are obviously two escorts from the city. Uncle Roy is in hog heaven. The bartender has named a cocktail for the occasion; he told me he did it under orders of his boss. Alison's downed several of his Mako Madnesses and I don't blame her because she's the one who is really stuck in the shit show.

I escape to the bar, again, to fetch another cocktail for her.

"Too bad it isn't September," the bartender says. "That fish would have won the shark derby for sure."

"How many sharks do they land in the derby?"

"I dunno. A lot. Real shame about Mike's son. I'm not fond of his Dad but Danny was a good guy. I hate what his stupid beach parties do for business but when he's here he always tips proper. Way back when he taught my kid to surf."

"Was he tall and blonde?"

"Like every other surfer, right? No surprise to anyone he was forty-one and never settled down. Speaking of which, whatever happened with that young lady from last night?"

"Oh, I never caught up with her."

"That's a shame."

The Client and Uncle Roy get up from the table, receive a few last back-claps and handshakes, and then depart with the two women. Alison joins me at the bar and lets out the biggest sigh.

"He's going to sign," she says. "Thank you."

"I'm going to celebrate with a clove," I say.

"Cloves. Where'd you get them?" she asks.

"All the surfers smoke them," I say.

"I'll join you."

We go over to the busboy who's taking a smoke break on the beach where the neighboring dock begins.

"Off the record, Captain Mike is a dick," the busboy says as we smoke. "Harsh to hear about his son, though. There's a memorial bonfire going on tonight."

"Want to walk?" I ask Alison.

"Sure," she says. "I'm going to need a week to decompress from this."

We head away from the restaurant lights into the dark. Alison takes off her shoes and walks in the wet sand.

"Thanks for today," she says.

"I'm glad it worked out."

"He's happy as can be. This trip might become an annual thing, but I'll take that as it comes. You okay? You've been thinking about Nina all weekend?"

"Strangely no, something else. Something Dad once said to me."

She doesn't ask what. I don't blame her. It's been a hell of a long day.

"Need any help back at the warehouse?"

"Sure," she says without hesitation. "I'll need the help more than ever now."

"I've been thinking about sticking around. Count me in for Monday morning then."

I don't ask if she ever feels like she is sinking. She's too busy moving and keeping everything going to contemplate such a question.

"You ever wonder why Dad's stuff was the only stuff that went missing?" I ask.

I spot the bonfire up ahead. Even more people than last night are silhouetted in the glow.

"I still have Mom and Dad's boards," she says. "Their personal ones, from the house."

The smell of smoke and sound of rock and roll reach me together.

Someone between us and the fire is walking our way in the wet sand. We step away from the shore to allow her to pass by us easy. She changes course to keep right toward us. A woman. I recognize the elegant contour of her face. Is it the woman from last night? Or this morning?

The woman's lower jaw drops. In the dim light I discern those horrible teeth much too big for her mouth. Her arms do not end in hands but tapered triangles.

I push Alison towards the road. "Go," I say. "She's coming for me."

"What the fuck?"

"Go."

She sees my fear and takes a few steps.

The woman veers for Alison. I try to get between them and I trip on uneven sand.

The woman continues for Alison with only a glance at me. Her skin is rough and grey and full of texture. Someone emerges from the darkness.

D A N I E L   B R A U M

For a second I think I am seeing double and that there are two of the same person standing before me.

The first woman tries to side step around the second, but the second woman matches her step. She pushes Alison's attacker preventing her from getting around her. She is the woman I met last night.

"Go, get out of here," the woman from last night says to me. "This is my sister."

Her sister lunges for me. All I see are teeth.

THE TWO SISTERS step side to side, their grappling an almost elegant dance. Alison reaches the end of the beach and disappears into the sea grass and dunes.

"I want her meat," the sister says. "Let me—"

"No," the woman from last night says. "Blood from sea for blood from land is not what we do."

The sister tucks her head and throws herself at her sister.

The woman from last night darts aside and her sister thuds down on the spot where she had been standing a second ago. She reaches for her sister's legs. Her thrashing throws up sand and shells and a spray of liquid that I hope is water.

I'm not certain of what I'm seeing; they are two women fighting but their shapes are not right, something more than the almost darkness. I am sure the woman from last night is easily evading her sister's wild swings and thrusts, and that she's speaking, almost singing as she does. With each heave and thrust and bite the two of them wind up closer to the sea. When they reach the wet sand the fighting has stopped. The singing has stopped and I'm watching the two women walking into the water side by side. The receding tide pulls one of them out, leaving the other standing there, watching. I run to her.

"You saved me," I say.

I reach my hand around her back and pull her to me to kiss her. She pushes me away with one hand. The force causes me to stagger backwards and fall. She retreats from the water and stands over me looking down with only disdain on her beautiful face.

"I'm not here for you. I told you I'm here for her," she says. "To stop her from making a mistake."

Her face is the most beautiful I have ever seen. Her sleek, pointed head. Round black eyes. Silver skin with that hint of deep sea blue.

"I understand now."

"What do you think you know?" she says.

"Everything. Life. The currents. Tides. You showed me—"

"I showed you nothing," she says. "There is only one thing I want you to know…"

She takes my hand to her face and places my right index finger just inside her thin lips. A quarter inch slit opens in my skin where I touch her human incisor.

"…always remember the sharpness of our teeth."

Something jumps from the water at the wave line. A fish. A shark? The shape is larger than I have ever seen in the shallows.

She moves her face close to mine. A raised notch pushes through the skin between her eyes. I try to look away. A single spiny antenna unfurls from the center of her forehead.

THE SPINE ENDS in a pleasing shape, a fascinating shape, the shape of something to eat, a source of soft, gentle light in the darkness I cannot look away from.

I see water and waves; there are surfboards in the waves.

V-shaped gills open in a long, elegant neck. The mob carries a shapeless bloody carcass from the pier to the beach. Nina's face, happy and unblemished, dissolves into soft, yellow light, then all fades to darkness.

DANIEL BRAUM

I WAKE UP on the beach in the middle of the night. Sometime later, Alison finds me and helps me back to my hotel. I'm overcome with an aching emptiness, I don't know what from. There is only the terrible yearning, so terrible, but I don't know what for.

Monday morning, I show up at the warehouse as I promised. I get myself an apartment out East. On weekends I return to the town and watch waves like Nina and I used to.

THE NIGHT WIND blows a gust of clean ocean air into the dock's aroma of fried food, cigarette smoke, and miasma of tables full of people. The glow from the light strings hanging above the bar flashes on and off the face of the young woman sitting next to me.

"Here for the shark derby?" I ask.

"Yeah my husband's going to get a record breaking Mako this time."

"How?"

"I just know it."

Her husband sees us talking and comes over from a nearby table.

"I was just telling him you're going to win the shark derby, honey."

"You a fisherman," he asks.

"Kind of," I say. "I try. What's your secret?"

"You can't ask that," his wife says. "A magician never tells his secrets. He's got the right lures though, I know that for sure."

She plants a kiss on him and runs her hands along his back.

"It's all in the chum," he says.

"Everyone knows the real way to chum for sharks is to cut yourself from nape to navel and let your guts spill out," I say.

They look at me like they expect me to laugh, or at least smile. I don't.

GOODNIGHT KOOKABURRA

1.

A Kookaburra scavenges from a table in the shadows of the tall Eucalyptus farthest away from where the other construction workers and I sit discussing which rivers we've taken to get here and which rivers we hope to travel on. A black goanna cranes its serpentine neck and flicks its tongue but the stocky bird is too smart and too fast to remain in reach. With a flutter of dark-brown wings, it takes flight, light-blue spots catching the evening sun. I've come so far. I want to hear the bird's hallmark laughter. It hops along the rail separating the café tables from the patch of bush in silent indifference to my desire. The goanna crawls into the underbrush, tail dragging; its four, clawed limbs holding its body off the dry, hot ground. The kookaburra returns to the table and resumes poking at a left-behind sandwich with its thick, black beak.

Emilia notices me watching. "Don't have birds and lizards like that back home, do ya?'

"We have squirrels."

"So sad," she says then swigs her Bundaberg. "Kookas are predators. He's supposed to be eating brown snakes. Now look at him."

The bird turns his head, regards us with deep-set eyes surrounded by a stripe of brown feathers. I want to hear it laugh.

Later in the dark of the night, alone with the unbearable heat of my tiny room, I'm on my bed envisioning that beak and those dark eyes.

I wonder what you make of us, Kookaburra.

I imagine I'm hearing its laughing call with my own ears. As I drift asleep I picture the woman back home who told me she saw only nothing when she closed her eyes, no matter what she did or how hard she tried; her naked form half-covered in my bed-sheets, white skin faintly visible in the dark of my room.

2.

"WHERE YOU HEADING?"

The guy sitting across the aisle had at least a decade on me. Probably more, but the smile on his tanned face and easy going way, even when boarding, sure didn't show it.

"Brisbane," I say.

"Smart man," he says. "I'll tell you something else. Sell everything you own. Grab the prettiest girl you can find and a good long board or two, go down the coast, and never come back."

"Is that right?"

"It's what I did. What are you here for? How long you staying?"

"A few months. For work."

"Trust me, you'll wish it were longer. Make sure you enjoy yourself."

With his graying beard and Hawaiian shirt he looks like a hippie but he's sitting in first class too. I fall asleep somewhere above the Pacific listening to songs I created with my friends a decade ago. I search the inflections of my voice for some shreds of meaning, intended or otherwise, and the lyrics for some lesson I might need to relearn but there is only the nostalgia of those captured feelings from days gone by, artifacts of long lost lovers never seen again, and those perfectly-imperfect tones infused with the fearlessness of youth straining to lend permanence to what is by nature fleeting.

A HALF A world and thirteen hours later at the luggage pick up the guy from the plane meets a tall, beautiful woman who helps him retrieve three surfboards in travel cases. He winks at me as they head to the car park.

3.

I DRESS IN a jacket, button-up shirt, jeans, and motorcycle boots and take myself out to a restaurant out on the Turnpike that I'd never been to before for a nice meal and to follow my muse. The woman who could see nothing whenever she closed her eyes mistakes me for one of her corporate clients there for her happy hour event.

"I hope you're not doing work," she says. "It's after hours."

"It's not that kind of work," I say.

"I hope you get paid a lot.'"

"Maybe I will. Maybe I won't."

I shake the ice in my glass and look back down at my notebook.

"Now I absolutely have to know what it is you are writing so intently."

I don't have it in me to explain that I'm not here to share. It was always faster to just say something.

"I'm just getting started for tonight. It's going to be something about how love isn't unconditional. And isn't forever. A song, maybe."

She closes her eyes and just stands there. I like the way her tall form fits in her cream pants-suit and how it brings out a hint of color in her smooth, white skin. Her red hair hangs just above her shoulders. I can see the straight places where it's recently been cut. I don't remember what color her eyes are. She keeps them shut longer than I expected.

"What are you doing?" I ask.

"Trying to picture what you said."

"What, unconditional love? What does it look like?"

"I don't know," she says. "I was trying to picture a time when I believed in it. I thought it might help."

"With what?"

"I can't see anything when I close my eyes."

"Anything?"

"Nothing at all."

"You can't or you won't," I ask.

"When I close my eyes I see only black. What do you see?"

"Forget about me. Close your eyes again. Try this. Think of the Statue of Liberty."

"Nothing," she says.

"Can you see the faces of your children?"

"How do you know I have children?"

"Lucky guess," I say.

It wasn't. She takes good care of herself but she can't hide that she's seen things. There's a story in every tiny line.

"Keep 'em shut. Can you see me? What color are my eyes?"

"Blue," she says. "But I remember. I'm not seeing them."

She sighs and opens her eyes. "Since you're so keen on teaching me mister-I'm-not-here-to-work. *You* close *your* eyes."

I do.

"What am I supposed to see?"

"Whatever you want, no, picture a moment when everything was good."

That's easy. The dark of night on a beach replaces the color-spotted dark of my shut-eye void. In the moonlight, I see where the sand meets the sea. The asymmetrical shape of stacked chairs stowed for the night. Lights from a ship on the horizon blurred in the humid air; I feel its warmth on my sun-touched skin. Hear the rhythmic chirp of geckos calling. Taste the salt air and a hint of my ex-wife's lips on mine.

"Come back to earth now, don't get lost on me. What'd you see?"

"Maybe I shouldn't say. It's personal."

"The way you got personal without hesitating is why I'm still here talking to you."

And to think I was trying for the opposite. But now I want to know. If she's telling the truth. And if I can teach her.

"You don't look it but you're different than everyone else," she says.

"You only say that because I'm not here to drink myself silly."

"Speak," she says.

"Alright. There was one night. Down on an island I used to know. I had a room by the beach with my ex. She was the only woman I ever loved. No, she was the only woman I ever truly knew how to show that I loved. I'm just outside our door on a chair. She's inside sleeping. It's Carnival. I can hear the festivities from miles away carrying over the water. There's a cruise ship nearing shore, all lit up too. And a couple of cargo ships just floating there, barely visible in the dark. I'm curled up in that wooden beach chair reading the best story I ever read by the light of a mosquito candle. And listening to the night and the sound of lapping water. Of course, none of it lasted. None of it could. But for that moment...nothing could be better. Nothing ever has. When I close my eyes. I'm there. I always can be. Just for a second."

She stands.

"Did you see any of that?"

"No," she says, straightens her suit, and takes her purse from her bar stool.

"No? That's it?"

She leans close, putting her face next to mine. I feel the swell of her breast against my arm. Her skin is unblemished and free of make-up. There's alcohol and cigarettes on her breath.

"No, that's not it," she says. "It was a good try. I'm not done with you but I have to get back to work, you know make sure everyone here has a good time. Let's try again when this ends, later. Maybe you'll be done working by then, mister."

Later is three hours later. In the parking lot she follows me to my car and tells me to take her to my place. I don't want to bring her to my house. I don't want to bring anyone. Yet I don't want the night to end. I don't want to be alone. I thought writing at the restaurant would be enough.

As we park our cars sensors I installed pick us up and turn the house lights, illuminating my two-story home. I designed every last detail to fit in just right on the wooded lot.

"Wow, nice place," she says.

"It's not mine," I lie. "I'm only house-sitting."

"A shame," she says.

"What?"

"Nothing," she says.

Right inside the door she surprises me with a kiss. She pulls me to the sofa and pushes me down.

"I'm sorry," she says with heavy breath. "Let's take this slow."

She removes herself from me and looks around my living room, examining the framed photos on my shelves. My books.

"Looking for something in particular?"

She ignores the question and approaches me and I think she's going to kiss me again.

"What I want you to do is to go upstairs, take a cold shower, and come back down," she says.

When I return all the lights are off. She is nowhere to be found. I search for her and I wonder if I'd done something stupid bringing her here. I open the door to my room. Her clothes are a dark shape on the floor, her body a shape under the covers in my bed.

I walk to her, silently. She pulls me the last few inches to an embrace and tells me to close my eyes despite the dark. Tells me things to see. Tells me to tell her what I'm seeing. I know I should be on fire but I'm contemplating the shape of where her thigh meets her hip, how it fits into the pale ghost of a woman I see now that my eyes have adjusted, instead of losing myself.

She's lost in what she thinks is our connection and I'm thinking how could I be so numb? There is an absolutely beautiful woman naked in front of me and I'm contemplating how the dark gives things shape instead of letting the mindlessness of sensation take over. I tell myself I'm feeling something that is part of life. Part of the process of moving on. Growing up. Getting old. Being an adult. But no, it's just me traveling down a fork of in the road that should not be. The quiet echo of the tragedy that was my divorce. Long past the part of knowing everything is wrong and long past the part of having the faintest idea what to do. There is the newness of this woman's touch. The for-now, pattern-less rhythms of her kiss. The sweetness of her skin, which is so, so soft. Each a fingerprint. Snowflake. A Retina-burnt-image unique as the way we vibrate together from the inside out and gasp with the endorphin rush. Even these highs are a novelty, temporary, ephemeral like everything else. There's an unexpected, small comfort in that.

I SLEEP IN fits. She wakes me. Once demanding we go again. Twice more telling me long stories about the men in her life that hurt her as I drift in and out of sleep. The final time she gives an order to simply watch her with her eyes closed and to think about something for her to visualize, and not to speak it.

When I wake in the morning she is gone. I didn't know how to teach her, but I know how to remember her. I close my eyes and revisit her shape in the dark. I know I will forget the color of her eyes and every clean cigarette-tinged breath she kissed into me, but that desperate sadness I mistook for passion, I know is etched into me.

4.

EMELIA AND I stop for a beer at the Uni café after work like we always do. The skeletal frame of the building looms over the patches of bush lining the walkways.

Two Kookas are among the birds hanging around the outdoor tables. One has its feathers puffed up, like it is cold, like it is drying itself. The other hops and dances around it.

"What's that all about," I ask Emelia.

"Mating season," she says. "Kookas mate for life. Mating ritual."

"Odd."

"You know, birds and their food. She's pretending to beg for it and he feeds her."

"They really mate for life?"

"Yeah."

"Why?"

"Don't know. You ever been hitched."

"I was. How about you?"

"I was when I lived down in Bondi. I used to plane boards with my partner. Came up here to get away. You ever think you'll get hitched again?"

"I don't know. I'd like to think so. I'd like to think there's some significance to it all. That there's some meaning to everything that's happened to me."

"But you're not sure."

"Right."

"What are you doing here? And don't say work. There's plenty of construction I imagine back in the states and you're the only Yank I've ever seen on the job."

I designed the new hall were putting up. It was easy to get on the crew. But I'm not telling her that.

"I don't know. Maybe I'm on walkabout."

"You Yanks and your stupid walkabout."

The male Kookaburra has scavenged the meat from a sandwich and is stuffing it in the female's open beak.

"I didn't say I was. I'm here welding structural steel. And watching Kookaburra, like you."

"Better be. Yanks get some stupid notion of walkabout in their head. Go out in the bush or desert, thinking they can handle it. And nobody ever sees them again."

"That almost sounds like you're worried. Who are you going to show around on our day off if I'm gone? You'd miss me."

"I'd miss your pair of hands. We've got steel to weld."

The Kookaburra swallows the offering. Ruffles her feathers, opens her beak, and demands more.

5.

EMELIA HAS FAMILY all up and down the Gold Coast all the way to north of Brisbane. She grew up surfing Australia's waters and bushwalking in places like these. She tells me that I'm bound to hear Kookaburras on this Eucalyptus tree laden route she's taken me hiking on. There's no path. Nothing marked. We've stopped on the side of the road somewhere she's decided that looked good.

"Lookout for the drop bears out there," she says.

"What?"

"They're small and grey and slow moving. But are really fierce. They like to drop down from the trees on unsuspecting passersby and bite their necks."

A few minutes in I see one of her drop bears. A koala high in the branches of a tall Eucalyptus, feasting on long tapered leaves.

"There's one," I say "Very funny."

The copse of trees with the koala in it overlooks a gulch. Emelia leads us down the brush-choked side. It's a dried-up river bed. All trace of water gone with the baking Australian summer heat. I notice a set of clothes caught in the tops of a barren sapling. A child's clothes. I can't tell if they are a boy's or a girl's. I'm not sure if Emelia sees them but I think it is very odd that they are there. Probably left behind by a family bathing in the river. We hike a few minutes further. Emelia stops. There are a child's shoes tied together and slung in the low branches of a Eucalyptus tree ahead of us. Tied up in the way my parent's generation used to tie outgrown shoes and throw them over power lines.

"You saw the clothes in that tree back there too, right?" I say.

Emelia nods. I can tell she's trying to make heads or tails of the shoes.

"I thought maybe they were left behind or something but this beds been dry for months," she says.

"Are we being chicken?"

"No," she says. "Something's not right. Let's turn around."

With her words birds take to the air from the top of a Eucalyptus. The raucous cloud of Kookaburra, Gullahs, Magpie, and Cockatoos fills the bush with chatter. Only with their din did I realize the forest was so silent.

"No problem with me," I say.

We hike as fast as we can back to the car.

At the last bend before the road, a tumble of feathers and scales bursts from the brush. A big goanna and a brush turkey roll across the path, a tornado of squawks and hisses and open red-mouthed biting.

"So what do we do? Call the police?" I say.

"Nothing's happened," Emelia says. "This is Australia we don't call the police for nothing."

"I'm an American. Something was wrong back there. I know you know it too."

"Don't let it ruin the rest of your day. Give it a few minutes."

We get into Emelia's car and she drives. Fifteen minutes up the road we turn off onto a dirt road. A few minutes later we are pulling up to a house.

"An old friend of one of my auntie's," Emelia says. "I used to come here all the time when I first moved up. You'll like him. He once was a Yank too."

An old man is sitting in a rocking chair, on the raised porch of his Queenslander with a shotgun across his lap. The clean smell of fresh air and turned over earth greets us along with the tang of potent marijuana.

"Well look what the cat dragged in," the old man says. "And you brought a boy home, too,"

"He's just a friend, Pops," she says.

The house is surrounded on all sides by meticulous rows of fruit trees. A ring of trees, ten, twelve trees deep on all sides before the thick bush. To the west is a low hill. A rounded outcropping of rock, gently sloping towards the sky. I wonder why it is so brown and dry despite the lush green everywhere.

We climb the stairs to the porch.

"We're having friends over for drinks," Pops says. "You just come to do laundry and have a smoke or are you gonna stay?"

An old woman I take to be his wife comes outside with tall glasses of iced lemonade and hand-rolled cigarettes on a tray. I notice the way she looks at the hill and how quickly she moves to return inside.

"Mimi," Emelia says, grabs her hand and brings them together for a hug.

"Come inside, dear," Mimi says.

I hear her whispering as they walk away. "He never leaves the ground. Just plants his trees and minds them."

"Smoke." Pops says.

It's not a question.

"Not a smoker," I say. "But thank you kindly."

"A shame. I don't trust anyone who don't smoke with me. What you doing here with Emelia?"

"We work together. On construction of that-"

"I see right through you. You're not telling yourself the truth. So you're not telling us the truth..."

"About what?"

"How should I know. I barely know you."

A van with surfboard atop it pulls up next to Emelia's car. A noisy bunch of people get out and climb to the porch. One of them is the man who sat next to me on the plane.

His skin is tanner and his beard is longer. I don't see the blonde he was with at the airport among the people who look half his age.

"We'll finish this later," Pops says. "Party's about to begin. Shame you aint gonna stay."

"Hey, it's you," the guy from the plane says warmly when he sees me.

"You made it! I knew you had it in you."

He takes a joint and glass of lemonade from the tray. He offers it to me. I put up my hand. He shrugs and Pops scowls.

"Got a girl?"

"No. Not yet."

"Maybe you find one tonight."

"That would be nice."

"How much time left on your trip?"

"The boy's got work to do," Pops says. "He's got all the time he needs."

That pleases the man from the plane. I don't bother to correct Pops.

THE PARTY HAS broken down according to some unspoken rule of segregation. All the women are inside and all the men are out on the porch, circling the house with drinks and smokes in hand.

I take the stairs down from the porch, wind my way through the herd of parked cars, and into the grove. There are lemons on the branches. Oranges. Other citrus-looking fruits I do not know. A snake is making its way through the aisle. It stops. Rears. Flicks its tongue in my direction and carries on. I hope it isn't one of those brown poisonous ones.

A woman is standing by one of the lemon trees watching me watch the snake. She's in a sun dress (like most of the female party goers) her hair back in a pony-tail or is it a braid, her face is in the shadow of the fruit trees, the top of her head, obscured by darkness.

"Careful," I say. "I think it's one of those brown ones."

I'm annoyed that she doesn't respond.

"Here for the party?" I ask.

"You?" she says.

"I'm here. But I don't really feel here. I don't feel anywhere."

She's moved into the light or my eyes have adjusted. I can see her face a bit better. She has a dark line of make up across her eyes. Or maybe it is just a dark shadow.

DANIEL BRAUM

There's a squawk and a hiss and the snake and some kind of creature tumble across the grove. I recognize the otter-like shape. Has Pops brought in mongoose?

"Oh, the relaxing sounds of the night," I say and wish I hadn't said something so corny.

"What I really want to hear is a Kookaburra laugh."

"In about three months you're going to go home to New York," the woman says. "You'll go to a pet expo and there you'll hear a Kookaburra laugh."

The snake and mongoose pass dangerously close to me but I ignore them. How did she know I was from New York? I step closer to ask her and the realization she is standing too still sends my body into alarm. A fly lands on the sweat on my back. I can't see her eyes. I'm trying to see her face but it is just a play of darkness and shadow.

"You'll take the bird home fancy cage and all. Every night you'll put a cloth over the cage and say goodnight Kookaburra."

There is something terribly wrong about the way she says goodnight Kookaburra. She has formed the words out of sounds not phonetics yet somehow enunciated the language I understand.

"You'll realize you've got it all wrong. But you won't even recognize yourself enough to listen. Does that sound like you?"

"How did you know I'm from New York?"

"How did you know I would be here?" she replies.

"I didn't. Who are you-"

"What do you think happened to the child in the river bed? What river did he take to get here?"

Emelia is calling me from the porch. Another step closer and I'll for certain see the woman's face. I turn and run for the house.

"I found him," Emelia calls. "Hey, who were you talking to?"

There is no one there in the trees. I hear the sound of an animal being dragged away. The victor of the fight? I can't tell if it was snake or mongoose who triumphed.

"I'm too pissed to drive," Emelia says. "We're going to stay the night. Pops says you can't stay in the house unless you smoke with him."

6.

AT SOME POINT in the night the men and women mix together. I see my friend from the plane kissing a young woman. And then another. Quick kisses on the mouth punctuating the bursts of laughter. Pops has his rifle out and fires over the grove into the bush spurring on oohs and ahhs and rounds of murmurs like it is a sporting event.

I even make a show of taking a hit with Pops because I don't want to sleep outside. But I'm relegated to the hammock on the porch as my sleeping spot once the night winds down near dawn anyway.

The night is full of insects. At one point I remove a small snake that has come up from the stairs. I wrap myself in the hammock and give up. A huntsman spider preys on the insects that have come to me seeking moisture.

I turn my head and see the mountain lit up in moonlight. No, not moonlight. The first rays of sun. It is dawn. And I have walked out into the grove. The trees are alive with birds. A Kookaburra hops back and forth on a low limb of a lemon tree.

"What do you think the woman who sees nothing when she closes her eyes sees? Nothing? Darkness?"

Its beak is moving. I do not hear bird sounds. I hear the whispers.

"Maybe she sees in a way you do not see. Maybe it is you, not her that is broken. Maybe it is everyone who is broken."

The bird's eyes are obscured in the line of dark feathers across its cream-colored head. Spots the color of the sun-lit water stand out on its back. The light has not yet hit the grove. I stride away from the tree, away from it.

"Don't you want to know where the boy in the river bed was going?" another bird whispers.

I close my eyes. I see the woman from the grove. Her face no longer cloaked in shadow. She's just a woman but I feel like she is wearing a mask and she wants to take it off and reveal her true face.

"The birds are laughing," she says. "Don't you hear them calling?"

I open my eyes, run through the grove, and into the bush. Dawn has hit the mountain.

Another voice fills my head. Not the bird. Not the woman. Not myself. Nothing I've ever heard or imagined before.

"There are places for those like you to go," says the voice.

The bush is alive with Kookas. I hear them calling and answering. I know the sound should be their laughing call. I only hear whispers. Questions. And answers. And the voice, speaking words made of sounds of the bush, guiding me to the mountain.

THE MONKEY COAT

JUNE WATCHED HER daughter lift the black fur coat from Grandma Estelle's old trunk and hold it up so they could see. Long strands of monkey hair hanging from its arms caught the light, raising a faint iridescence in their inky darkness.

Last week, there'd been a murder. One of their own. In their own suburban town. It made the news but the police weren't giving full details. That always meant it was something bad. June had known the guy. She'd been friendly- well, much more than friendly- with him during her wild time right after David had up and left. Though the storage facility had a security booth with a guard and a well-lit lot, June was uneasy and had waited for a morning when Ivy could come with her after getting off work, even though the divorce was final and she'd had the court order granting her access to the locker for over a week now.

"I'm selling it," June said.

"No, Mom," Ivy said. "*Listen* to your *dear* daughter for a change and go out and paint the town red."

"Sorry, love. I'm selling it," June said. "Hopefully for enough cash to cover your first semester of college."

"Enough, Mom."

"Sorry. I know. I'm glad you came, Love."

Besides Grandma's old trunk the locker had been empty. David had gotten away with everything. She shouldn't have allowed herself to have even hoped for otherwise. Ivy had it right. The jacket *was* beautiful. Vintage. Authentic. And so *chic*. Just like Grandma Estelle. A true original from a by-gone time. On how many of her wild adventures had she been worn this coat?

The waist-length jacket was tight around the bottom where the fur was shortest. Long strands of hair tapered down from the chest and shoulders and hung from the arms forming an elegant fringe. June loved the jet-black color and sheen that even decades of storage couldn't dull. Classic vintage fashion. But it still had that rebellious edge that personified June in her school days, back before working at the shop, marrying David, before Ivy and everything took her and spun her and spun her and never stopped.

June watched her daughter spin the coat around and inspect it.

She had just come from work and June didn't like the low cut of her blouse. Her pinstriped pants suit was nice but much too tight. She was striking, with her father's ivory complexion and green eyes and June's own dark hair and figure that she'd had when she was Ivy's age, but that didn't mean a mother had to like it. She did like that Ivy thought with her heart just like her mom and didn't listen to anyone who told her otherwise. Not that there was anyone who gave a shit anymore.

"It's so you, Mom," Ivy said.

"It's so a semester of college."

"Mom. Stop. I'm fine."

"I don't like you working there."

"I'm only the hostess. It's good money and I don't do any of the other stuff."

"I don't like that you work nights. That you have to."

Times were tough for a third-generation artisan. And things had been careening downhill long before David left. June's Mom had died just as the printed word was transitioning to digital leaving the impossible responsibility of the business solely on her. She loved the big old printing presses but had to let them go when she tried downsizing the shop to stay afloat. Their bulky, pigment-stained hulls had felt like home. Letting them go had been letting go of an anchoring weight. Since then she felt that she, her family, everything was drifting, drifting away. She should have kept them, somehow. She should have found a way, or made one. David always used to say that. June hated that she was thinking of him now. He was off somewhere in his new life, un-caring that Ivy was now a host at the Golden Stallion Sports Club and that she worked as a floral designer at Laine's where she used to buy their holiday arrangements back before her shop went under.

June let Ivy help her into the coat.

"There," Ivy said. "It fits perfectly. I wish we had a mirror."

"Does it? You don't want it?"

"No. It's yours. It's how I imagined you back when you were my age."

"Don't you wonder what your Great Grandmother was like? She was a suffragette, in London. Tell me you remember what that is and don't say Bowie."

"I know, Mom. That's the song you made my ring tone."

June knew Ivy knew the Bowie song but doubted she knew much of the women's rights movement.

"Mom used to tell me all about crazy Grandma Estelle and the wild adventures in Europe she had before moving to New York with your great grandfather."

Estelle had founded E Books. If only she had lived to know the terrible irony of the name. One of Estelle's more colorful adventures had been a stint as a showgirl in Paris but June didn't say for fear of giving Ivy any ideas.

Someone rapped on the roll-up metal door. It was a man in a Self-Storage uniform holding big red-handled bolt cutters.

"I'm here to let you in. But looks like you already are."

"Thanks, Captain Obvious."

"Ivy, be nice," June said.

"They said upstairs we got the court order and you're okay to go in."

"The court's lock was cut when we got here," June said. "I opened the padlock my husb-…, ex-husband and I left on it. Same combination."

"Good thing you remembered then," he said absently, his attention and ability to form words captured by the two female forms before him. "New coat?"

"Yeah, well new to me," June said.

The guy whistled playfully.

June gave a spin. Ivy loosed a cat call and they all laughed.

"Have a nice day, ladies. Holler if you need me."

"See it looks great on you, Mom. Even that guy said. You think it's real fur?"

"There wasn't any other kind back then."

"Ooohhh, Dad would absolutely hate it."

The smile left June's face.

She wanted to say why do you have to bring him into everything but lately it seemed like all she did was harp on her.

"Sorry. It's just I was thinking of him," Ivy said. "You remember when I asked for a stole for my sixteenth? He asked me why I needed a hot enema death wrap around my neck to make me feel pretty."

"Priceless. He said that?"

"You don't remember?"

"He said a lot of shitty things. Mister Hypocrite in his leather boots and leather jacket."

June thought of the long ago day she and David skipped their afternoon classes and snuck onto the roof of the Fur Vault in the Cedar View Shopping Center. He took a steaming whiz into the fresh air intake of the ventilation system. Then they dropped water balloons full of red paint on all the trophy wives on their way out. They'd been so young. And still believed love conquered all.

"Sorry. I shouldn't have said that. Your Dad loves you. At least he did when I knew him. He's got a fucked up way about him. But he loved you."

"He loved you too, right?"

"Doesn't matter anymore if he did or didn't. I'm done. And done talking about him."

She put the coat back in the trunk.

"Yeah, Dad would have hated the coat."

"It's probably why he left it," June said.

"Maybe he forgot to throw it out or take it."

"No, it feels like one last fuck you."

"Enough," Ivy said. "I'm going home to get some sleep."

"It's almost seven-thirty. I have to be at work soon. Thanks for coming with, you."

They exchanged mock European kisses on both cheeks then Ivy left for the elevator. June stood staring at the empty places where she had hoped to find treasures from her life that had been, or at least anything she could sell to get them through.

Ivy was right, June thought. David *had* loved her. Only at some point along the way she had stopped loving him. Now she didn't even miss him anymore. She missed the comfort and stability they'd once enjoyed. She just hadn't figured things would fall apart without him. At least not so quickly and completely.

Yeah, David would have hated the coat. Absolutely hated it. And that was exactly why she was going to go out and wear it.

JUNE WALKED INTO work at Laine's Floral of Five Towns just past eight, wearing her grandmother's fur.

"Oooh la, la," Laine said. "New coat?"

"You like?"

"I *do*. What's the occasion?"

"The occasion is I'm a happily divorced woman and *I'm* going on a date after work."

"You gonna get some?"

"May-be. Don't need an occasion for that."

"Andrew or Randall?"

"Andrew."

"Oh, good for you. You deserve a nice guy. Andrew deserves to get lucky. I like him."

"And maybe he will."

Laine ran her finely manicured hand along the sleeve. A strand of long black fur snagged on the large diamond of her wedding ring and she yanked it free.

"It's not real," Laine said. "Is it? It looks so real."

"Yeah, it's real. Vintage Grandma Estelle."

Laine's expression changed to the one reserved for the male customers who routinely asked if there were any cheaper bouquets and the *goyum* who didn't know not to ask for deliveries on Saturdays.

"Oh, June. You know how they make those things."

She didn't say the rest. She didn't have to. June had heard her say the word, "suffering" so many times before. June didn't live in the neighborhood, like Laine, where everyone kept kosher. Eat no suffering, was the answer Laine gave time and time again whenever asked for the reason she followed the ancient laws. Bring no suffering into your body. June supposed this also included wearing no suffering, apparently.

"Yes, I know how they make them," June said.

What about my suffering, she thought. Who around here really gives a shit about me when push comes to shove? She's never worried over making it to her next paycheck. She goes home to her Jason and their big, paid-for house. Her only worries are making it on time for her pedicures and where the maid misplaced the laundry this time.

"Don't worry, Laine," June said. "Grandma Estelle said these were one hundred percent organic, fair trade, certified road-kill monkeys. No suffering here."

Except mine.

"Bless you," Laine said in Hebrew. "You are so strong. You are strong for all of us."

June hated when she spoke in Hebrew. It reminded her of everything she didn't have. Everything she didn't pass to her daughter. Plus Laine and the rest of her ex-customers used to always lay that phrase on her, usually right before pressuring her to complete their orders on impossible time tables for their convenience.

June took off the coat, put it in the back room, and got to work on the arrangements for the big wedding order. Laine turned on the TV that was mounted above the front counter. The crawl beneath the local news announced the name of the murder victim. Franklin Lamont. The man who was a man no more. Forever an empty space in his family where his life had been.

When David left, it wasn't like he disappeared and left an empty space, it was more like he shattered, June thought. There was no void where he had been, she didn't wait around or sit around feeling lonely waiting for it to come and swallow her. She went out and lived. So it felt like David, or more like what had been their life, had shattered into parts, all of them lesser, each of them a distinct piece of what they had and what he had been to her; and each of the parts residing in the different men she kept around.

Franklin Lamont, or Frankie, as June called him, had been one of those men. He hungered for her where David had grown complacent. He was eager to please her. Pleasured her when fleeting moments of pleasure was the only respite she had. He was reluctant to leave her bed when she told him Ivy would be home soon, sad when she stole away so his wife wouldn't catch them in his. Along with these somewhat endearing things came his refusal to take no for an answer when she decided it was time for her to move on. He repeatedly called at all hours. Showed up at the 7-11 where she got her morning coffee. Sometimes even waited in the lot or came into the Flower Shop. On her bad days his twisted attention was the only indication anyone gave a damn she was still alive, that she still mattered in some way, to someone. Even if that someone was broken and embodied everything that was broken about her.

Frankie's stalking was what sparked her epiphany. It had dawned on her that these men she numbed herself with were mere pieces of what she'd once had, approximations of the things she missed, the things she feared she'd never have again. And she was drawn to them because they each filled her emptiness in a different way. But it took a while to realize they were poison. Poison that tasted good going down but never, ever filled the void, only fed its insatiable burning with fuel.

After what felt like countless days doing everything she could to make ends meet she decided she didn't need men to preserve herself.

So she resolved to stop seeing them. All except for two. Andrew, the accountant from town with whom she had a date tonight. And Randall, mister big shot, who was walking through the door of the Flower Shop right now.

Laine giggled as Randall approached the counter. He was a retired cop. Laine claimed his week-long absences to "consult with certain law enforcement agencies" as he put it, were really because he had another life and another family in a different state. June never asked. She didn't care.

"Nice coat," Randall said. "Fur? A bit warm for it, no?"

She hadn't realized she'd put it on.

"Yeah," she said.

"You got yourself a fur coat after I just spotted you another month's rent, plus…"

"Plus what?"

"Plus you don't strike me as the type."

"And what type is that?"

"I mean…you know how they make them, right?"

Not you look good in it. Not what do I think. All about himself. Just like David.

Yet she wanted him. Just like she had still wanted David. Even in the end.

Sex with David had been a lot of things. Transcendent at best, tender at times. Healing. And then a mediocre downward spiral to the way it was in the end. Dead. Just like their relationship apparently was, long before she knew it. She thought they would get better. Thought the sex would get better. If they would just stop fighting. What did he know about raising a daughter? Their headstrong daughter who failed in school. Took drugs but refused her prescription meds. All the time she had been hoping, hoping, hoping he had been methodically transferring their assets into his name alone. He had cleared out their bank accounts. A week before he left he had even told her he was taking her wedding ring to be cleaned and she had fallen for it.

Sex with Randall was nothing like it had been with David, even at its best. In the absence of the familiar she found rage. And pleasure. And a rage for that pleasure. For the depth of pleasure that could blot out all else. Where she could be lost in the heat and freedom of serving lust and only lust. No contemplation, no self. The rage only knew heat and skin and teeth and sweat and the pulsing from the inside, the rush of blood pushing faster and faster. That was being alive. That was being whole again, serving pleasure faster and harder until she disappeared and the sting and dullness of the world and remnants of the smoldering ashes of her life subsided for a few sweating, heart-pounding moments.

Laine and Randall were both standing there awkwardly. Had she missed something?

"Well, I just came in because I saw on the news about Franklin."

"Yeah, terrible," June said.

"Guess he's not going to give you trouble anymore."

"Really? You're sick. You came here to say *that*?"

Randall had been nowhere to be found on the nights she had needed him because Frankie had been waiting around.

"No, I came to tell you my wife is out holiday shopping tonight and is staying at her mother's in Jersey."

She decided just then that Laine was right. She deserved a nice guy.

"And why would that matter to me?" she said. "I'm done with you."

He slammed his hand down on the counter.

"You're not done with me, yet."

June decided she was going to jump over the counter, put her hands around his neck, and show him just how done with him she really was. But Laine interceded.

"Randall. I'm going to have to ask you to leave my establishment," she said.

When he didn't move, Laine picked up the telephone.

"Okay. I don't want any trouble," he said.

His tone sounded like he did want trouble and that he'd be back. But he left.

"You're sweating," Laine said. "I actually saw you gnash your teeth. I've never seen anyone do that."

"If he comes back I'm going to rip him a new asshole."

"If he comes back I'm calling the police. Alright? Calm down. Take the jacket off. Go out back and have a smoke and just calm down. Please."

She went out back. Lit up and called Ivy, who was sleeping and did not pick up.

"I *am* listening to you dear daughter. I'm not painting the town red but I am going out. Andrew's taking me to dinner and a movie. Don't wait up. Love you. Thanks for coming today."

Andrew picked her up at five. He brought flowers. Laine rolled her eyes at the sight but told them to have fun.

"Nice coat," Andrew said as he held his car door open for her. "You look lovely."

"Why thank you. This old thing? I just threw it on."

"Doesn't look like it. You look so, wow!"

"Okay, I lied. I wore it just for you, sailor."

JUNE WOKE TO a blinding light. The sun coming through windows? Morning already?

The bed was so warm. The man next to her, so warm. Still snoring, blissfully. Andrew?

No, Randall.

June sprung out of bed. Randall snored on.

How the fuck had that happened?

She got dressed and stole from the room, not bothering to wake him.

As she crossed the living room heading for the door, one of Randall's daughters, a teenaged girl whose name she didn't know, emerged from a doorway and crossed the hall to the bathroom, sleepy-eyed.

Oh shit, did she see me, June thought as she left the house.

"Fucking, whore," June heard the girl scream as she closed the front door behind her.

That settles that, June thought.

Thankfully her car was outside. On the short ride home she wondered what had happened. Had things gone that badly with Andrew? Had she had *that* much to drink and went to Randall's without remembering? She didn't feel hung over.

The door to her apartment was open when she arrived. Ivy had just gotten home too.

As June walked in Ivy gave a startled cry.

"It's just me, love," June said. "Just getting home too."

"Mom? You scared me. What the fuck? You're wearing the coat?"

"Indeed I am."

"Mom, where are your pants?"

June looked down at her bare legs and bare feet. She could have sworn she had gotten dressed. She felt the coat's silky lining on her breasts, the bare skin of her arms. She was naked except for the monkey coat.

"TAKE IT OFF," Ivy said. "I don't like it one bit."

June didn't hesitate to comply.

"It's going back into the trunk. I'm putting it there myself tonight on my way to work."

"Fine. Good riddance. I wanted to sell it anyway."

"Mom, take it off. Now."

"I could have sworn I just-"

Ivy stomped over and helped her take one arm out, then the other. It looked like a deflated, dead thing was draped over her daughter's arms.

"Suffering," June said.

"What?"

"I said I'm freezing," June said.

"Get dressed. You have to be at work. What's wrong with you? I told you to go out and hit the town. But I didn't expect you to listen."

June went to the bathroom. Showered, got dressed, and went to work.

Her day added insult to injury. It seemed like only blissfully married couples came into the shop.

Who were these people? Were they real? Didn't they have real problems like her? Like she and David had had? Ivy wasn't David's biological child. She was pregnant with her when she had met David. Ivy's real father, a man twice her age she had met while cocktail waitressing at the Limelight, had told her to get rid of it. She hadn't even been attracted to him. He was rich. And older. The glimmer of the fancy hotel he had taken her to didn't make him better in bed or keep her warm when he left at dawn. She had only wanted to try being someone's trophy on for size.

David told her to keep the child and to forget that guy. They put David's name on Ivy's birth certificate and raised her as if she were his own. But she wasn't his own. And what did he know about raising a daughter? What right did he think he had to try to force her to go to school or to take medication that dulled her down?

"How'd your night with Andrew, go?" Laine said. "You have that glow, darling."

"It's the glow of embarrassment. Not so good."

"No? What happened?"

"Don't know."

"What do you mean don't know?"

"I mean a got into a fight with him and went to Randall's."

"Oh, dear."

"I know. I like Andrew. How do I fix it?"

"Flowers fix everything. I'll make you a bouquet. And your job today is to go deliver it."

Laine made her a wonderful bouquet and sent her to Andrew's office. Andrew's secretary up front was delighted and let her into his office unannounced and without an appointment.

"For me?" Andrew asked.

"You like them? I'm sorry."

"Get out of here," Andrew said. "And take your flowers too."

"What? What'd I do?"

"Are you kidding me?"

June burst into tears and ran with the flowers back to her car. She returned home. Ivy was already out doing something before work. June put the flowers into a vase and turned on the TV. She changed into sweats and went to 7-11 to get fuck-the-world ice cream.

She was halfway through the pint when she started thinking of David saying, find a way or make one. She threw the ice cream away. Showered up and dolled up. She took the flowers out of the vase, wrapped them as best she could and headed for Andrew's. It was time to find a way or make one, fuck David and his phrase, it was her phrase too, her phrase now.

She rang Andrew's door and was pleasantly surprised that he answered even though she knew he had seen her through the peep hole.

"You're wearing that coat," he said.

June looked down to see the black monkey fur. Apparently she *was* wearing the coat. She hadn't given it a second thought and just assumed Ivy had taken it.

"Andrew, I don't know what I did. I honestly don't remember but I came here to tell you I'm sorry and I really like you-"

She noticed cat-sized shapes moving in the darkness of the tops of the tall oaks on Andrew's front lawn.

"June, you don't look so good," he said.

Andrew helping her inside was the last thing she remembered before blacking out.

A NAKED MAN laid face-down splayed on the bed. His arms and legs were tied, pillows under his mid-section propped his ass up. He struggled to get free.

Randall?

Randall mumbled muffled curses through a gag over a tinny sounding Suffragette City.

Bowie singing, *Wham-Bam-Thank-You-Ma'am*, played in a loop on her phone. It was on Randall's night stand. No, it wasn't Randall's night stand, it was the night stand of a fancy hotel. She realized it was the hotel where Ivy had been conceived. It had been redecorated but it was the same place all right, she recognized the layout and remembered bits and pieces of arriving with Randall.

Ivy was ringing again and again. June wondered what could be so important and contemplated the lamp from the night stand she held in her hand.

She wondered why she was holding it. Then she remembered, walked to the night stand, and silenced the phone.

She took the shade off the slender lamp and smashed it against the top of the night stand. The bulb shattered. The bound man on the bed screamed through his gag. She bashed the lamp on the table again and again until part of the metal cylinder broke away revealing twisted white and red wires. A lone spark arced from the jagged mess to the plush carpet, extinguishing as it fell.

June knew the way monkeys were farmed was with a stainless steel instrument much like a thermometer but with enough electric current to kill without marring precious fur. First they were restrained. That caused only a little discomfort but the whole process lacked dignity. When the juice flowed there was a blossom of pain, then it was over.

This she knew was going to be different. The broken lamp was not like the stainless steel instrument. It wasn't going to fit so smooth. She tried. Randall struggled. The stink of burnt hair and skin along with Randall's shit and piss and flatulence filled the room. He kept struggling, so she leapt onto his back and choked him until he was still enough so she could get it done right.

THE LOCAL NEWS broadcast an interview with Franklin Lamont's mourning family. They claimed he had died of electrocution and expressed concern why full details had not been released. The police spokesperson denied protecting one of their own. They did not want specific information about the manner of death released while awaiting forensic testing so as not to compromise their investigation. Both sides asked anyone with any information to come forward. Which always meant that they had nothing of value to go in.

EVEN FROM THE hostess stand just inside the Golden Stallion, Ivy knew it was her Mother's voice she heard in the lot arguing with the bouncers.

"I told you," June shouted. "I do not want her working here."

Ivy rushed outside.

"Mom? How'd you get the coat? You're not wearing pants again, aw Mom. Are you wearing anything at all under there?"

Two tall muscular bounces each held one of June's arms as she strained against them, struggling to reach the entrance of the club. Patrons on their way in watched from a distance.

"You think you're hot stuff walking around with dead things on you, bitch," one of the patrons called, a young girl Ivy recognized as one of the newer dancers. "Don't let her touch you. Lady's got a cloud of bad juju on her I can see a mile away."

Ivy ignored her and the crowd snapping cell phone photos.

"Guys. It's okay. I'll take it from here," she said. "Just help me get her to my car."

"I said I don't want you working here."

"You got it, Mom. I'm done. I quit," Ivy said and winked at the bouncers. "I'm taking you home, Mom. Just come."

Mother and daughter sat in silence for the short drive home. Ivy opened the car door for June and June walked with her to the front door and rattled off the list of chores she needed Ivy to do, the bills that needed to be paid, and things that needed taking care of as if nothing had happened.

"Mom. Cut the shit. Are you okay? What's going on? Is that blood on your hands? Did you hurt yourself?"

"No."

"Did you hurt someone?"

June didn't answer. They went inside.

"Okay Just take the coat off. We'll get you cleaned up."

"No."

Ivy tried to take the coat off but June wouldn't let her.

"Fine keep it on, let's get you into the shower."

"Fine," June said.

June let Ivy lead her into the shower. June went under the running water coat and all. Dirt and sweat and monkey hair and a little blood ran down her body and pooled at the slow drain.

"Mom, whatever happened I know it was the coat. Not you. You have to take it off. It will be okay."

"Why does everyone always think things are going to be okay? Things are not going to be okay. I didn't raise my daughter to be an idiot."

"I'm not an idiot, Mom. I'm just saying I can come up with something. Please just get out of that thing."

"Nobody tells me what to do. Nobody forced me to put it on. I chose to."

After an hour of trying to get her mother out of the shower, Ivy went to the couch to wait her out but fell asleep to the sound of the water running and her mother talking to herself.

Ivy woke sometime during the night and checked on her mother. She was met with curses and a command to close the door and let her shower. At one point Ivy went outside to check the bathroom window to make sure she hadn't stolen away but she was still in there, cursing and showering. Ivy woke again before dawn and this time she knew her mother was gone. Just like the day she knew her father was gone. She just knew.

The bathroom was all clean. Spotless and shiny. Not a speck of dirt or water to be seen. The coat was hanging from the hook for robes behind the door all clean and dry; its black sheen out of place among the dingy, old blue tile.

Her mom hadn't left a note or taken anything.

It was terrible each day she was gone. Worse was each day that passed where no one noticed or seemed to care.

Weeks later the police came calling. They asked questions about her mom and some of the guys she had slept with. They asked if she knew where her dad was and she told them last she knew of it was Paris. They asked if they could look around. They did and that was it.

Over the years Ivy resisted the temptation to sell the monkey coat. It reminded her of her mother. Ivy wore it to work now and then on those days she was feeling spite or the rage that sometimes came, but mostly she just wore it because she knew it would piss off her Mom. She still worked as a hostess only, never the other stuff. Eventually she became one of the managers of the place. She found she had a way with numbers. She listened to one of the regulars and enrolled in business school aware that it was what her mother always wanted. She told herself she didn't care at all what her mother, or father for that matter thought. She never saw or heard from her mother again.

She sometimes daydreamed that her Mother was working as a showgirl in Paris, like Great Grandma Estelle. She once woke from a nightmare that she had received a postcard, from Paris with the words, *sorry now you really will never see your father again*, scrawled in her Mother's handwriting along with bloody fingerprints.

Ivy took it that she imagined these things because some part of her wanted her mother to understand that she had left her the way Dad had left them both. Alone and with only the monkey coat to show for it. But eventually she even stopped caring about that and wondered if the coat would look good on her, on those times when she even thought about it at all.

TOMMY'S SHADOW

TOMMY RIPPED INTO the anthemic end chords of *Spirit of the Radio* and swung his cherry-apple red guitar high. Everyone in the gym, probably half the damn high school, roared with approval. I turned to Richie as he packed up our keyboards and stuck my finger in my throat. He laughed, but I couldn't deny it, Tommy was good. Our set had gone okay, but I knew we were going to come in second place this year. Again.

Tommy's brother, Don, jumped out from behind the drums, his bare chest coated in sweat. He gathered Tommy and Eric Nelson, their bass player and lacrosse teammate, to take a final bow. Their amps were professional gear from Sam Ash, stuff I could never afford even after a million summer's worth of washing cars and mowing lawns.

Tommy wiped his wavy blond hair out of his eyes. It was just long enough to be cool, but not wild enough to bother Coach Ritter. He thanked everyone and smiled that smile that drove the girls crazy. Alana stood at the foot of the opposite bleachers snapping pictures with her long-lensed Canon. Today her chunky combat boots were laced with hot-pink thread. She wore black and white striped tights beneath her black skirt. Her long legs seemed to have gained six inches over the school year and she'd blossomed into an elegant velvet pixie. So yeah, it was clear why Tommy dug her, but I couldn't figure out why she went for him.

Richie could sense the trouble brewing on my face. "So we gonna blow this taco stand?" he asked.

"Just gotta get something from the Death Star, I'll be right back."

I dashed out, grabbed the Evil Robots cassette from the front seat of the Death Star. I rubbed my Darth Vader pez-dispenser hood ornament for good luck, and ran back.

I realized I hated the designs I had drawn on my chuck T's. Dad's old black blazer that I had dug out of the basement hung loosely on me. Suddenly my idea of trying to devise a punky-retro look felt really stupid. And my long hair was probably all sweaty and messed up by now.

Some guy I'd never seen before was standing behind Alana, too close for comfort. Maybe one of her older cousins or something, yet another lemming transfixed by Tommy. He moved his head slightly and we found ourselves staring at each other for a second. I almost turned back, but he was gone, disappeared into the crowded bleachers, no doubt.

"Hey Alana," I said and thrust the tape at her. She smelled like strawberries. Silver skull and cross bones earrings hung against her porcelain cheeks. She turned the tape over, confused.

"It's got that song on it," I said. "The one I said that sounds like it was made by killer robots that had taken control of a recording studio."

She graced me with a mercy smile.

"That's so sweet of you, Marco."

"Don't play it around Tommy. I know he's not big on industrial."

"So, didn't you just love their set?" she asked.

"Everyone's seems to be digging it."

Richie had finished with the gear so I had to get to it.

"Listen, me and Richie are going over to Pilgrim State after this. You wanna come?"

She finally took her eyes off the stage for more than a second.

"No! Really?"

"Yup, might even grab some decorations for the Death Star."

"Very cool."

She clicked her camera lens a few notches then spun it back.

"I promised Tommy we'd all cele-, I mean hang after they announce the winner."

The band left the risers and Tommy bounded over to us. He slid his arm around Alana's waist.

"You were awesome!" Alana said.

"Thanks. I was so nervous," Tommy said, sheepishly. He pecked her on the cheek.

They stood so close her breast pressed against his side. Tommy looked down at me with his clear, blue eyes. No way I could ever take him in a fight.

"Dude," he said. "Loved your set. You guys should do soundtracks to vampire movies or something."

Bastard. It was the nicest thing anyone had ever said about our music and it had to come from him.

"Hey! Shhh, shhh!" Eric Nelson said. "They're about to announce the winner."

"See ya," I said and ran back to Richie.

I clapped him on the back, careful of his arm strap.

Alana wrapped her arms around Tommy as the judges awarded him first.

She used to tell me about the trippy books she read like *Count Zero* and *Still Life With Woodpecker*. We had gone to the Disintegration concert together in the 10th grade and she kissed me after they played *Just Like Heaven*. I went to sleep with her black lipstick on my face and didn't want to wash it the next morning. I'd known her since we were seven. Why did none of this matter anymore?

"I'M NOT ALLOWED," Richie said, trolling the index finger of his good arm along the rows of candy bars. "What am I going to tell my Mom?"

"Tell her you're with me, at my place."

He didn't like the idea. The smooth skin around his eyes and forehead bunched, the fluorescent lights tinting it yellow.

I filled two Big Gulps and clasped the plastic cover over them, eyeing the six packs of beer in the refrigerator case. Tommy had fake ID. He'd been to shows at L'Amoure East and the Bitter End. His parties had kegs. He was taking Alana to the senior prom and no doubt his limo would have beer and wine coolers and maybe even champagne.

The automatic doors slid open. I saw Brett Malone's flat top bob along over the end cap of Doritos and heard Darren Rothchild's loud mouth sounding off about getting wasted on the bleachers. In the circular security mirror in the corner I saw them at the counter pointing to cigarettes behind the register. Then Brett's ugly mug noticed the mirror. His expression went vacant and I could sense his feeble mind searching for words.

"No mongoloids allowed," he said, using the mirror to stare straight at us.

Darren laughed. Richie pretended not to hear. But he always did.

"So get the fuck out," I yelled.

I'm like rubber and you're like glue, words bounce of me and stick on you, Alana's Mom used to say in her sing-song voice when one of the kids playing ringelivio in her yard inevitably decided it was more fun to tease Richie. It just didn't work that way anymore.

The old lady behind counter gave Darren his change and Marlboro Reds then went back to minding her business of staring at the hot-dog broiler.

"Mongoloid freak," Brett said.

I saw them in the mirror and then Darren was right up in my face, breathing hard and stinking of cigarettes and too much Right Guard.

"What'd you say?" he asked.

"You heard me. Shut the fuck up."

"Why doesn't Domo-Arigoto-Mister-Roboto fight his own battles?"

"Cause if you say it again I'll kick your ass right here."

"Fuckin pip-squeak. Try it."

"You try it."

Maybe he remembered me saying the same thing to Christopher

Hamilton last January. Christopher had kicked my ass left, right, and sideways, but I went down swinging and made him regret it. He had to have his lower jaw wired and his Dad sent him to military school for the rest of the year.

He looked down at me and I didn't flinch. Just because they were monsters with no sense of right and wrong didn't mean Richie had to put up with their shit.

"Fucking freaks," he muttered.

They backed out of the aisle and tramped out the door, the word "retard" punctuating their mumble.

Richie never let on that shit like this bothered him, but it bothered the shit out of me. I expected people to look and all, but when people choose not to have a heart it makes me hate the world.

"Screw 'em," I said to Richie. "They're going to grow up and be garbage men and you're going to be a serious archeologist doing all sorts of cool stuff in Egypt and what not with a seriously a hot wife and shit, man."

Richie plunged a long red straw into his Big Gulp and brought it to the counter. In the security mirror was the guy from the bleachers. He was closer and I could see him better. He was all disheveled like he had just woken up. His boyish face looked familiar, definitely not one of Alana's cousins. But it was the shit-eating-grin on his face really bothered me, made me feel like I was in an elevator going down too fast. What was there to be so giddy about? I turned to steal a better look but he was gone.

"An anthropologist," Richie said. "I'm going to be an anthropologist, not an archeologist. It's different."

Alana's Mom had the rhyme all wrong. Words *were* like glue. Alana's were stuck all over me. Her voice telling Tommy he was awesome sang in my head. I wanted it to be me that she was saying it to. Just like it used to be.

A FAT MOON hung just above the horizon lighting the lamp-less Sagitkos parkway. I turned off the exit feeling more nervous upon seeing the weathered Pilgrim-State-Psychiatric-Asylum-ahead sign than I did before the battle of the bands.

"We have to bring something back for the Death Star, like from the kitchen, maybe," I said.

"Probably nothing left," Richie said.

We pulled into the complex, which consisted of a half dozen three and four story red brick buildings. The huge stained-glass window in the center building, the tallest one, made the cluster look like a cathedral.

The place was supposed to be deserted, but a lone car idled in front of the stairs leading to the center building. Tommy's black Trans-Am.

I pulled alongside then parked in front. Tommy and Alana were in the front seat. Don and Eric Nelson were in the back drinking beers. Smoke wafted around the interior light.

"What are they doing here?" Richie asked.

"I told Alana we were going."

We got out of the car and Alana and Tommy got out of theirs. I searched for a hint of strawberry beneath the reek of smoke and beer.

"Hey, Marco," Tommy said. "This was a totally cool idea. I figured we could all go in together."

"Screw you," I said. "Why the fuck do you have to be everywhere?"

Saying it felt awful. I wanted to take it back and ease the sinking sensation in my stomach but instead I glared at them and said, "Don't follow! Come on, Richie."

I darted up the curved steps, jumping over fallen sections of a rusty rail. Richie followed more slowly. I pushed the heavily tagged left door and it swung open, a cut chain clinking like a 7-11 chime. The main room was four stories high. Three levels of corridors, stacked like catwalks, overlooked it. Moonlight streamed through the windows, the stained glass sending warped streams of color into the dark. Old chairs and milk crates had been pushed in a circle around the charred remains of a campfire near the door. Beer cans, cigarette butts, condom wrappers, and empty bags of chips surrounded it.

"At least we're not the first," Richie said.

"But everyone else are wusses. They stay here. We're going in."

"Let's just find the kitchen then get out."

We wandered farther back but the light wasn't reaching in. I thought I might have a flashlight in the Death Star but I wasn't going back there now. We took the stairs to the first corridor. I tried the doors, each time turning back, half expecting Tommy to follow at any moment. The last two doors had long slots on the bottom.

I jiggled the handle of the first one and it swung open. Empty, except for heaps of garbage. The next one opened the same way. The moonlight shone on even more heaps of debris.

Richie followed me in and I really wished I had that flashlight and some nose-plugs. It stank of ammonia and rot.

"I bet this was solitary," Richie said.

"Much better than the kitchen," I said. I sifted through the junk, squinting to see. My hand found something square and cold. I held it up to the catch the moonlight.

"Hey, Richie. A buckle."

"From a straight jacket?"

"I dunno. But it's gonna look awesome on the Death Star.

Something rattled in the other room and Richie and I froze. Had they followed us?

We snuck to the other door expecting to surprise Eric Nelson or Don and give them a scare.

Some guy was over by the window messing with the bars. A night watchman? He was singing to himself, sounded like something by the Cure.

"Fuck," Richie said.

The guy stopped singing and turned. Just when the day couldn't get worse. It was the guy from the bleachers and 7-11. He looked surprised to see us. For a long second we both just stared at each other, like we had in the gym.

"Sorry, man," I said. "We're really sorry. We were just poking around."

When I spoke he looked confused, even a little relieved. Did he belong here? Did he think we were busting him?

"Um, yeah," he said. And then he smiled, as if coming across us was the best thing that ever happened to him. For some reason this was worse than as if he was all gung-ho on busting us.

"This isn't happening," Richie said.

"Can't you just not tell, please," I said. "We'll leave, right now."

"All right," the man said. "But don't go. You seem like good kids. Are you?"

What a weird question. I wanted to just run but I didn't want Alana to see us high-tailing it out of there like some scaredy cats or having this end with my Mom telling Alana's Mom how we got busted by some rent-a-cop so I said, "Uh, yeah. We're cool, right Richie?"

"It's been a bad day, let's quit while we are behind."

"Why such a bad day?" the man asked.

With that I knew we should leave. Maybe this guy was some weirdo or perv but I got the sense he genuinely wanted to know. I was burning to tell.

"We lost the battle. And people are fucking assholes," I said and launched into a rant about Tommy.

"How about you?" he asked Richie

"I want to get out of here," he whispered.

"Stay. Your face. I can take care of it."

"Fuck you!" Richie yelled and took off.

I'd never heard such anger from him, but I always knew it was there. The guy was only offering to help, he wasn't rousting him like Darren and Brett. I should have followed but I just stared at the man. My shadow filled the room but it seemed the moonlight just passed through him.

"He'll be alright. But you gotta stop protecting him. What's this

Tommy fella's name?"

"Tommy Mullen," I said.

"Tommy Mullen, huh. And he's been outshining you for too long, right?"

"Right."

"I'll take care of it."

"You can?"

"Of course. You don't have to do anything. Just say yes. I'll do the rest."

"Why?"

"I like you. Feels good to be around you. Maybe this will sound strange, maybe it won't but it's like you bring out the best in me. Know what I mean?"

I did. Being around him felt good even though I knew something was wrong and I should just bolt and follow Richie. He was definitely strange, but mixed up in all that strangeness was potency, like all I had to do was say the word, and my troubles with Tommy would be over.

"Hey, Marco, you okay up there?" Tommy yelled. I heard him bound up the stairs and down the hall. Even during this fucked up moment, this unexplainable, odd moment he was there.

"All right. Yes," I said to the man. "What the fuck."

He smiled like he had just sold me the Brooklyn Bridge. Suddenly there was something horribly familiar about his crew-cut hair, and blackened, sunken eyes, and mouth. Then he was gone and Tommy was in the doorway.

"What's going on?" Tommy said, looking around the small room. "Richie's all freaked out. Come on, let's get out of here."

I had no idea where the guy had gone or how he had disappeared. I didn't care.

"Everything's cool," I said. "What are you a scaredy cat?"

"I don't like it here," Tommy said. "Let's just split."

I slid the buckle into my pocket. Tommy was scared and I couldn't wait to tell Alana.

RICHIE CLOSED HIS locker and turned the corner. He hadn't returned my calls all weekend and Monday when the silent treatment began, I knew he was seriously pissed.

"Not talking to me?" I asked.

He turned the corner without a word.

So I hurried up the stairs to catch Alana as she left study hall. I twirled the buckle on my finger and said hello.

She made the same face she reserved for broccoli on old pizza.

"From the asylum," I said.

"Tommy said it was pretty creepy," she said.

"Nah, he was *scared*. I don't know why you are going to the prom with him."

She sighed and started to speak then stopped.

"Listen, Marco. I've been wanting to tell you something."

Her brown eyes fixed on me. It felt good.

"We were always such good friends. I want to know why can't we just go for pizza and talk about life and whatever. You know, just be my friend."

"It bothers me that you're the prettiest girl in school now and Tommy just wants to get in your pants."

"No, Marco, you do."

"What? What the hell?"

She stormed away. I watched her go. It all happened so fast, I couldn't believe what had been said.

"Just let the bitch go," a voice said. I looked around and saw the guy from the asylum reflected in the classroom door.

"You don't need her," he said.

"Yes, I do. And you'd said you'd take care of this."

"Well it takes a lot of effort, much more than just talking to you. I'm working on it."

"Yeah, but so far all's gone to shit for me."

"Don't worry. Not long now. I'm feeling stronger. Just remember. You don't need them."

Some tenth graders walked by, looked at me and laughed. I took off in the other direction.

"You only need me," I thought I heard the man say as I turned the corner.

THE AFTERNOON BEFORE the senior prom, Richie finally caved in and talked to me. He said his Mom forced him to, but I didn't care. I told him what had happened after he had left the asylum.

"And you said yes," he said.

"I know it was stupid, but nothing's happened."

"Doesn't matter, you're still an idiot," he said. "And you were a real dick to Alana. She was trying to be cool. So was Tommy."

"I know. I'm going to make it up to her."

"So you're going back there?"

"No."

"Then how? You should go."

"Why?"

"I dunno. To take it back."

It made some sort of odd sense so I got in the Death Star. The Sagitkos, bleak and empty without rush hour cars made me think of empty veins without lifeblood. Pilgrim State's decrepit buildings seemed inert crumbling husks in the setting sun. Inside, the orange light bathed all the litter in a warm glow. It was odd how it made all that trash looked almost nice. I walked up the stairs and to the room slower than I intended. Then I threw the buckle down with the rest of the junk.

"Fuck you. Deal's off," I said.

Nothing happened.

I stood there a long time all the while straining to know where I knew his face from. I was just about to leave when he said, "Don't do this."

"I'm through with you."

"Come on. I love you. I need you."

"I hate you."

"I didn't ask for this," he said. It reminded me of when I once yelled at my parents I never wanted to be born. And with that I knew his face. It looked like me. An all grown-up, fucked-up-me. I wanted to smash everything in the room. Start a fire and burn it all down, but instead I just ran and drove away, again.

I was freaked out but relieved I had listened to Richie and made things right.

On the way home I stopped at a flower shop, for Alana. I'd been imagining a spread of tropical flowers, the pointy ones. I considered going all out and buying as many books as I could carry to go with them, but I settled on a nice corsage. Then I figured Tommy would be doing that, so I bought roses instead. White ones. A dozen, with the long thorny stems. Cost me two weeks worth of mowing lawns. Alana always said the color of roses meant something. The girl at the store said white ones were for friends.

I wrote on the little card. "Sorry for being such a dick. Have a rocking time at the prom with Tommy!"

But when I got to Alana's house. I noticed there were too many cars in the driveway and parked haphazardly on the street. Something was wrong. Alana's mother was on her lawn, crying. Her father and brothers and a lot of people who looked like relatives surrounded her, hugging and consoling her.

Alana's big brother noticed me and took me aside. "Marco. Marco. Thanks for coming," he said.

"Okay, I'm leaving now," I heard the thing from the asylum say.

Alana's brother's face was sweating and red. "She was necking with Tommy by the abandoned Sears up on Route 106," he stammered. "That's when these guys grabbed them. Dragged them out of the car into their van. Took them to a storage locker. They hurt them pretty bad, and," His voice cracked. "Him first. Made her watch. We're going to find this monster and kill him. Fuck the cops."

I kept looking around, to see him. Hear his voice, but he didn't need to say anything. He kept our bargain and took care of Tommy for me.

I put the flowers on the ground.

I RIP INTO the end chords of *Just Like Heaven*, Richie's lush synthesizer line swirling beneath. We move to the front of the risers for our bow and I know this is our year to win. Everyone in the gym, probably half the damn school, roars with approval. But not Tommy. He moved to Texas with his Dad instead of going to college. They say he's in full time physical therapy.

Alana's watching in the bleachers, her camera just hanging around her neck, though there are a million pictures to be taken. She doesn't talk about books anymore. Or really anything at all. We're going to the prom. Her mother says that will be good for her.

I tell the eleventh graders to stay away from Pilgrim State but Richie says Pilgrim State had nothing to do with it. He's only in the band because his Mom makes him. He makes me listen to songs with messages like how you can't un-ring a bell and I think I understand what he's getting at now.

I bound from the risers to Alana and slide my arm around her waist.

"How were we? Awesome? Right?"

"Awesome," she says, no trace of the elegant pixie that I knew.

Yeah, Tommy's gone but I wish he wasn't. I'm still in his goddamned shadow, and it feels like I always will be.

REBBE YETSE'S SHADOW

THE FIVE-FIFTEEN TRAIN home to Brooklyn was full. No hope for a seat by myself, but the woman with the last open seat next to her looked pleasant enough. A plain, black skirt covered her thin frame to her ankles. She wore no make-up and her brown hair was cut straight and simple, like the Hassidic women I saw all the time on Queens Boulevard. She was pretty. Her blue, blue eyes stared through the passengers filing on; her lips parted in a slight smile, as if she was watching something the rest of us couldn't see and it humored her.

I sat down and remembered my nametag was still pinned to my gray polo shirt. Getting my life together made me feel like such a dork. The woman's closeness and faint floral smell was a painful reminder that I wouldn't be seeing Melissa tonight. She didn't see a future with a guy "like-me." If I wasn't walking the 'straight and narrow' I couldn't afford a nice car, weekends in the Hamptons, dinners in nice places, and all the other things Melissa said didn't matter but I knew really did.

I squirmed into the molded plastic trying to get comfortable. All I had to look forward to was another Friday night crashed out in my room in Uncle Saul's basement.

If I could gather the energy, maybe I would return what I had left of Melissa's things- a hair band, some contact lens fluid, two CDs, and her beach sunglasses.

"Lylah tov," said the woman next to me. Her Hebrew wish of good evening was thickly accented somewhere between Russian and Israeli.

I knew the accent well from all the Saturdays spent at Congregation *Bais Shalom* as a kid with Dad. I pictured him with the same white *kippa* he always wore on top of his square, rugged face. It matched his *talis*, the one his father brought him from Israel as a bar-mitzvah gift. I used to wonder if the gold trim on the prayer shawl was real gold. He never was able to take me to Israel to get mine. His heart stopped, just like that, right after my twelfth birthday.

The woman looked at me, patiently, waiting for an answer.

"Good evening to you," I said, despite myself.

"Going to temple?" she asked as if she knew the answer, those piercing eyes never leaving me. It creeped me out.

I was obviously on my way home from work.

"I don't want to get into it," I said. I doubted she would think I was a nice Jewish boy if she knew my previous "employer."

"How 'bout you?" I said to change the subject. "You on your way to temple?"

Her smile widened with the question. "Not tonight. I'm going to see Rebbe Yetse."

"Isn't he dead?" I blurted, then hoped I wasn't wrong. I knew he had been head of the congregation when Dad was still around.

"You knew him?"

"I haven't been to Temple in years."

"A shame," she said.

It had been almost six years. I remembered the rabbi only as a black robed figure leading the prayers on the pulpit. I would have known him better had I completed my Torah studies for my bar-mitzvah. I vaguely recalled a big stink when the rabbi's brother-in-law had replaced him.

"Did you mean to say you going to see Rebbe Tankel?"

Uncle Saul talked about him all the time.

"No. No. Never mention that name. Rebbe Yetse," she said, sternly.

"Sorry, sorry," I said. "Going to pay your respects," I said more to myself than to her. She reminded me I was remiss in paying such a visit to Dad.

"I pay my respects by walking in the light," she said, her blue eyes accusing me. "I am in need of the rabbi's wisdom on a family matter. My brother is…" she paused, "not well."

I had prayed for some sign that Dad was watching over me. I soon realized he wasn't listening and neither was god, so I stopped going to temple, and not long after that I stopped praying.

"Tell me, is praying at his gravestone really going to do anything?" I didn't mean it as an accusation. I really wanted to know. Her face was so confident, her eyes so focused and free of doubt. She looked at me as if *I* were crazy.

"Do not sell prayer short," she said. "You should be old enough to know this by now. I didn't come to pray. I came to see the Rebbe himself for assistance with my brother."

"The Rebbe is dead."

"I'm sorry you don't believe," she said with a sigh.

I believed in what I could do for myself. Like going to work and then at the end of the week collecting a paycheck, as shitty as it might be. Dad always told me to have faith that things could be better. After he was gone it was easier to have faith in people like Fydor Yetvenshenko and his "enterprises" than in the slim hopes of someday saving enough money for college and the empty messianic promises Uncle Saul believed in.

I started by delivering packages. By the time I was fifteen I was officially part of a 'crew' and on my first job; a safe in some rich guy's house out on Long Island. It went so smooth and my cut had been more than my entire salary all summer. The next one didn't go well. At all. I was lucky to have landed in Juvenile Hall and not state prison. Giving straight and narrow a try was a lot simpler and I liked the prospect of feeling in control again. But the lack of resources that went along with it had cost me Melissa.

The woman looked at me intently. She squinted, as if trying to read fine print on my forehead. After a few seconds, her face went sour.

"Poor boy. You need the Rebbe just as much as my brother." She looked concerned. "This is not my responsibility, but I'll see what I can do."

"Yeah right," I muttered as the train whined to a halt.

"My stop," she said. "Come to Parkland Cemetery anytime after sundown. He is very busy, but maybe he will help you."

"Thanks," I said and smiled politely.

The woman rose and filed out with the rest without another word.

Part of me fantasized that I'd go to Melissa's tonight and that we'd talk and maybe even work things out. She was a good girl and when I was with her I felt like the person I wanted to be, and not some lost, washed up excuse for a life.

If there was a chance of what the strange woman was saying was true, I had to know. If she really could talk to this Rebbe, then maybe I'd been doing something wrong and could... It was crazy but her eyes were full of conviction. You get to be a good judge of character in Juvi. I believed that at least *she believed* what she was saying was true.

At my stop I exited with the flood of people, walked up the stairs, and out of the station. For a moment I thought I saw Melissa and started toward her, but I was wrong and I walked to Uncle Saul's alone.

THE THREE FAMILY walkup had been Uncle Saul's since the seventies. He had gotten out of Russia a generation before my Dad and had made his way in construction- mostly putting up paneling and carpets and the occasional deck for rich people. The red bricks were weathered and stained. The door had a fresh coat of brown paint.

Uncle Saul was in his worn blue suit readying himself to go to worship. He stood in the dim hallway in front of the rectangular mirror with the gilded frame, his old fingers tying his tie.

"Who's the head rabbi over at Temple?" I asked.

He continued with his tie.

"The head rabbi?" I repeated.

"I heard. I heard," Uncle Saul said. "I was just checking that the sound was really coming from you. Why do you ask?"

My mother had died back when we lived in Saint Petersburg, before I could remember. Uncle Saul and Dad were the only real family I ever knew.

"Can't I ask a simple question?" I snapped at him. He didn't deserve it. I was lucky he had taken me in after everything I had done.

"Sure, sure," he said. "Rebbe Tankel. The head of the congregation…"

"…since his brother-in-law died, right?"

"Who knew you remembered these things? You're a strange boy." He looked at his watch. "Do I dare ask if hell has frozen over and that you'll be coming?"

"No, I was just wondering."

He went back to the mirror and started over with his tie. I took a step toward the basement door.

"Do you think about my Dad?" I asked.

"Now what brought that up? Of course I do," he said into the mirror. "I say the mourner's prayer for him, every time."

"Do you ever want to see him? To talk to him?"

He frowned and turned to me.

"Why would someone believe they could talk to the dead?" I asked. "Something in the Kaballah?"

"How old are you?"

"Eighteen."

"Did I hear you say forty?"

"You know how old I am."

"And so do you. We can have this conversation again, in twenty two years, when you are old enough." Uncle Saul frowned. He could tell his answer had not satisfied me. "Mitzvot, prayer, family, going to worship, things you have been noticeably absent from, are the ways of light. Everything else…"

"I was just asking why someone would think something like that could be true."

"No more talk of this. Not in my house," he said and went back to his tie.

I tramped down the steps, took off my name badge and tie, and looked at the box of Melissa's stuff on my dresser.

Earlier in the week, I ran into Natan, from my old crew in the city after work. There was a job going down, as always, and they needed an extra pair of hands, which meant there was a chance things could get rough, though he said it would be easy money. I turned him down, but all week I had been thinking with my cut I could be taking Melissa to the Hamptons instead of giving her stuff back.

I heard the front door bang shut. I grabbed a flashlight and keys to my rusted Dodge Dart, and tramped upstairs.

I had no problem finding Parkland. It was huge, its own city within a city. Thousands of stone markers were packed together like buildings. As I walked I realized not an inch of unclaimed ground remained. In death as in life, I thought. The masses packed together, not much to distinguish one from the next. Looking at all these final markers of unremarkable lives, I didn't blame Melissa for wanting more than me.

About a mile away on a raised slope, mausoleums loomed. A ring of large plots with tall ornate statutes and hulking family headstones surrounded the ultra-elite 'neighborhood'. Though the woman hadn't told me, I figured I'd find the Rebbe's resting place there.

As I trudged along the sounds of cars buzzing past on the Brooklyn-Queens Express way faded to a distant, droning hum. There were no night sounds. Only the silence of the stone.

I reached the larger plots and had a clear view of the first mausoleum about a hundred yards away. I shined my light and saw no Friday night service. No gathered congregation, that was for sure. The lady on the plane was nuts-o, and I was nuts-o for even coming here. Still, I figured I'd take a quick look at the old Rebbe's resting place, see what kind of luxurious box the old man found himself in and put a stone or two on it, for my Dad.

A low-pitched chuckle sounded from somewhere up ahead, resonating in the near silence. I froze at the sound. The wind rustled through the shrubs, for an instant masking the barely audible buzz of cars.

The deep, male laughter rang out again.

I stepped forward, my foot crunching on something dry and crackly. I shined the light and saw hundreds of beetles crawling past me. I recognized the Japanese kind that ate roses and black ones with red heads, fireflies or lightning bugs as I used to call them. They parted around my shoes, and kept moving like a miniature stampede fleeing a fire.

All at once, the insects took flight with an awful buzz and chitter of wings. I swatted and spit as they brushed my mouth and face. Then all was quiet. The last of them had risen above me. A yellow-green flickering cloud of them floated into the sky. They flashed and answered, their glow illuminating the old stones. I'd never seen so many together in my life.

I rubbed my shoe on a gravestone, to clean it of crushed beetles and was surprised to see a young man sitting on a concrete bench a few plots away. He wore typical Hassidic garb, a long white shirt, black slacks, and shoes. A stiff, black hat and heavy overcoat lay on the ground near him. He fiddled with a small bag like a shaving kit. Three lit cigarettes were stuffed into his mouth.

"Hello," I said, hesitantly.

The man laughed, confirming it was he who I had heard a moment ago, but he paid me no mind. Smoke curled from his mouth. He lifted a straight razor from the bag and held it to his long curly sideburns.

Muttering in Hebrew in between his laughter, he scratched off the long curls. He dropped the razor and took a cigarette from his mouth and brought it to his forehead, as if burning off ticks. I winced and smelled the reek of burnt hair.

He smiled ecstatically and touched the cigarette to his forehead again and again.

It was time to leave, but I had to watch, like it was an accident on the road. I felt itchy and patted myself, checking for beetles. There were none. I squirmed in my clothes, suddenly aware of the humidity of the night like I was too close to too many people on the subway.

The man began unbuttoning his shirt. I could see his eyes were unfocused, each unnaturally staring out in a different direction. That was it. I ran back through the tall section and didn't stop till the crowded low markers.

What the hell was he doing? And what was he burning off himself?

I slowed so I wouldn't trip over the stones and found myself walking straight toward a crowd of people. Two-dozen men, and half as many women to their right, were standing silently among the graves as if in configuration for a temple service. Everyone's eyes were open, though they were trance-like, somewhere far away. I noted an old man who could have easily been one of Uncle Saul's pasty, old friends. His mouth moved as if muttering a silent prayer. Across from him was the woman from the train.

I watched for a moment. When no one turned around or spoke I walked as close as I dared. A cluster of candles and small rocks was amassed around a single, unremarkable headstone. I couldn't read it but I knew it had to be Rebbe Yetse's.

I don't know what I was looking for. For the ghostly Rebbe to rise from the ground and jump around? For a disembodied voice to ring down from the heavens Old Testament style? I hadn't expected anyone to be here. Who the hell gathered in a cemetery on a Friday night? I didn't get the sense of danger from them though, something in me screamed to run, over-riding my curiosity.

The woman from the train turned and for a second her clear, focused eyes looked directly into me, beckoning me to join them. I felt a renewed tug to go over and stand with them but that voice inside ordered me to leave those freaks where they were and pretend this hadn't happened. I turned and headed back to my car, looking over my shoulder, flinching at every small sound and at the sight of my shadow.

W‌HEN I RETURNED home, Uncle Saul was snoring away. I made myself a sandwich of leftover turkey and brought it downstairs. I kept glancing at the box of Melissa's stuff while I watched the late show and picked at the sandwich.

I kept seeing Melissa's disappointed, quietly angry face as we walked past Christopher's lounge in the city. I hadn't wanted to even stop because I knew I could afford to take her.

I picked up the phone and thought about calling her. What was I going to say? Nothing had changed except that I had just spent Friday night watching a junkie and bunch of nut jobs in the graveyard.

I lay in bed and tossed and turned, the fan doing nothing for the musty heat. Just as my eyes grew heavy, I felt the itch of an insect crawling on my foot. I whipped off the sheet and turned on the light but saw nothing.

I adjusted the fan, turned off the light, again, lay back and fell asleep.

At some point in the night I drifted awake to the smell of stale earth and smoked salmon left out too long. I moved to turn the fan up and felt the distinct pressure on the mattress of someone sitting down at the edge of the bed.

"Uncle Saul?" I asked, still half asleep.

"No, I'm not your Uncle Saul," a familiar voice said.

"Dad?"

The voice laughed. "You flatter me boy. Your Dad is not here. He wishes he could be."

"Uncle Saul, this is not funny," I said and flicked on the lights.

An old man with a long, black beard sat at the foot of the bed.

I scooted to the headboard, drawing my feet in.

The man regarded me kindly. He wore a heavy black overcoat and strings of wispy black hair crept from beneath his wide black hat. His face was familiar.

He had Dad's strong Russian features. Our distinct mouth and thin lips.

"Who the hell are you?" I yelled. I couldn't believe someone would have the nerve to come down here and even worse, that I had slept through it. I eyed the edge of my bed where underneath I kept a baseball bat in case of this kind of emergency.

The man took off his hat and placed it on the bed. He was balding. Brown liver spots marked the top of his head.

"I am Rebbe Yetse, young man," he said. For a flash, the flesh appeared tightly pulled tight over his gaunt face, his hands thin and skeletal, his nails overgrown and curled. Then, he was just a wizened, old man again.

"I don't know what kind of a sick joke this is, but you have three seconds to get the hell out of my room."

He looked like an older version of the rabbi I remembered, but he couldn't be. I tried to roll and reach for the bat but found I couldn't move.

"I saw you tonight at the service; you didn't stay," he said.

I struggled but every muscle was frozen. This can't be real, I thought. I'm dreaming.

"Oh, this is very real," he said. "As real as the forty-five Yetvenshenko gave you for the Long Island job and the unmarked bills you were paid in.

So he knew things. That didn't explain why the hell I couldn't move. I strained. All that resulted was sweat dripping from my forehead.

"A good thing one of my congregation ran into you. The Lord works in strange ways."

"The woman from the train?"

"One of the loyal ones."

His insinuation touched an old pang of pride. "Uncle Saul goes to Worship every Friday and Saturday and on all the holidays. He's loyal."

"Not to me, my boy, but to my brother-in-law. This may be hard for you to hear, but he was responsible for my death. Not in cold blood, but it was he who killed me all the same. I know these things don't mean much to someone like you, they are of great concern to your father."

"My Dad? My Dad is gone," I said and struggled.

"Your Dad is one of the loyal ones. He's here. With me."

This is crazy, I thought. I willed myself to wake. I pictured sitting up with a start, telling myself it was all a dream. I strained to reach the bat. All I managed was more of a sweat, the salty drips in my mouth as real as the stale, earthy smell.

"Are you finished now?" he asked.

I wasn't waking up. Whatever was happening, dream or haunting or bad joke, I had no choice but to go with it.

"So, what do you want me to do?" I asked. "Pray more? Start going to worship?

"Normally a good start, but no. I want your help."

The Rebbe looked at me intently reminding me of how Dad used to look before dishing out some of his stern, but wise advice from the old country. If he was real, then maybe what he said about Dad was true.

"My boy," said the Rebbe, "I need you to kill my brother in law."

"You're freakin' nuts!" I ordered my body to thrash, to break free of what invisible bonds were holding me. I pictured myself grabbing the bat and smashing it into him. With each imagined blow the Rebbe appeared for a flash as a skeleton surrounded by a murky, black penumbra. But I was still frozen and my tired muscles burned.

"If you're the great Rebbe Yetse back from beyond the grave, why don't you use your followers or your mystical powers or something."

The Rebbe smiled. "You can get close to him, my boy. Something my followers and I can not do. You are just a wayward, troubled son returning to the flock. My brother-in-law is well protected and trained in ways you do not understand. But he will not suspect, nor detect you. It is too much to explain for tonight."

"Like what? Crazy Kabballah shit? Are you going to give me some magic words?"

"I could, but no, teaching them would take too long. And you could never best him that way. I'm going to give you a gun."

I sensed where this was going. He had laid out his plan, like they all do. Like Yetveshenko had done. He would offer a reward next and he knew the one I wanted.

"Your Dad wants you to do this. He told me so."

"No," I said, with less force than expected. But he knew things about me. He knew I had been willing to kill before. But I was different now, on the 'straight and narrow'.

"I wouldn't ask this of you if I didn't think you had it in you. Straight and narrow, where has it gotten you?"

"Why should I get involved in your petty shit?"

The glass of water on my night table rose into the air. The TV snapped on and the wires snaked into the air. Uncle Saul's old books flew from the bookcase one by one.

"Because if you do this, I will see to it that your Father will thank you, personally."

I watched the water float from the glass and separate into droplets. The books thumped against each other and the ceiling and walls like pool balls.

"You will go to the graveyard," he said. "In section thirteen, on the headstone marked Moskowitz, you will find a pistol. Tomorrow you will go to Shabbat services and you will kill my brother in law."

Footsteps thumped above. Uncle Saul knocked on the basement door. "What's going on down there?" he called.

The lights snapped off. Everything fell to the ground. The Rebbe was gone; in his place a faint yellow-green glow, that lingered for a second like an after image from the sun. I could move again.

"Nothing, Uncle Saul," I yelled.

I heard muttering and his footsteps tramping back to bed.

"He told me he wanted to take you to Israel," the Rebbe's voice whispered, "but the lord had other plans for him. Lylah Tov."

Then I was alone in the dark.

IN THE MORNING with the hazy daylight reaching through the trees warming the rows of gravestones it was easy to tell myself nothing had happened. The mess in my room was real, as was the memory of the Rebbe's weight on my bed and the stale earthy smell.

If the gun was where he said, then I couldn't explain it away. How much more of a sign could I ask for? Maybe Dad never answered my prayers because he wasn't able.

I walked through the jumble of thousands of grave markers and came to the correct section. Hirsch. Goldstein. Moskowitz. This was it. I breathed a sigh of relief. There was no gun.

I heard rustling and I turned to see the woman from the train a few stones away. Next to her stood the crazy junkie-guy from last night. His clothing was soiled and rumpled. Bloody scratch marks adorned the now bare flesh where his sideburns once were and his face was marked with raw cigarette burns.

Their eyes looked down, at my feet I thought. I looked to the ground and saw a squat, black-gripped pistol resting in front of the tombstone a few feet away.

My shoulders clenched as if someone was gripping me. A cold radiated through my body, steeling me for what I was going to have to do.

"I know what is happening," the woman said, "and we beg you not to do it."

When this was over the first thing I would ask Dad, if he had heard me all those times.

"Last night the Rebbe helped my brother Eli," she continued. "He was in the grip of a ghost like the one that is now steering you."

"Funny, the Rebbe came to me, last night. He didn't mention a ghost. Don't you think he would have? He told me to come here and find this gun, and here it is."

"Rebbe Yetse would never say or do such a thing," she said.

She squinted and stepped closer to me. "But the ghost would. I see it above you right now. An opportunity has come for you to rid yourself of it so it seeks to steer you away."

"What opportunity? The Rebbe? You?"

"No. The path of your life. Choices."

"I'm going to help the Rebbe take back the congregation. That's my choice."

"Justice will be done," the woman said. "But not with guns. The ghost misleads you. Don't listen. Stay strong just for a little while. Come sundown, the Rebbe will set you right."

"So, where is this ghost? Hello, evil spirit. Hello, Rebbe. Come out. Where are you? Tell him to come out. Tell him to tell me himself."

I picked up the pistol. It was loaded. "The Rebbe told me to set things right. And if I do, he's going to bring my Dad to me."

"My brother, don't do it," Eli said. "The ghost did the whispering but I chose to listen. They whisper lies. Don't you see your choice only strengthens its hold on you?"

"This gun was here, like the Rebbe said. This was all meant to be."

"The pistol is mine," Eli said. "I brought it here… in case the Rebbe could not help me."

"Bullshit! You had a knife last night."

I turned to leave and they scooted around the stones to block my way.

I held up the gun. "Out of my way. I don't want to hurt you."

They calmly walked toward me. I un-clicked the safety.

"You have gone to the path of shadow," she said, and took a backwards step.

CONGREGATION BAIS SHALOM was almost as I remembered. The gray concrete was worn and the metal Hebrew letters and Star of David on the wooden doors had lost their silvery shine. The pine tree in the fenced in lawn by the parking lot had been replaced by a small, purple leaved maple.

Services were going on and I walked in without seeing a soul. Inside the scale seemed smaller than I remembered but the smell was the same- musty, old books, fresh paint somewhere, and cheap disinfectant that reminded me of Juvi-Hall.

Down the long, linoleum-tiled hallway was the entrance to the sanctuary. I could hear the murmur of the congregation praying. I took the pistol out from where it was tucked in my pants, under my shirt.

Looking at the doors I realized I had no plan. Would I just bust through the doors and fire? I walked halfway down the hall and ducked into one of the vacant Hebrew school classrooms to collect myself.

I flicked on the lights. Sitting at the edge of the desk were two identical, bearded old men. Two Rebbe Yetses.

"Welcome, my boy," they said in unison.

I laughed. This was too much. I wished I could just shoot them both and have it be over. Was one an imposter, the ghost the woman spoke of? Maybe they both were. Maybe I had just gone out of my mind.

"So," I said. "Which one of you is here to stop me?"

"We're both powerless to stop you," said the first Rebbe. "The choice is yours; put down the gun or go fire away and ruin your life."

"Wonderful," I said. "Since you are both wise old rabbis, advise me. What do I do?"

"That's easy," the second Rebbe said. "Do what I told you to do last night. Set things right. Kill my brother-in-law and I will bring you your Dad. Your proof."

Besides the fact they were here before me, what proof did I have?

"Okay," I said to the first Rebbe. "Can you bring proof? Is my Dad happily floating somewhere in the afterlife?"

"I wouldn't be so sure there is an afterlife, if I were you," he said.

"Then who are you?"

"A good point. But I am not proof of an afterlife. What does our encounter prove? I'm just a shadow, a fragment of Rebbe Yetse left behind. *He* is just a fragment of you. The worst of you."

The other Rebbe laughed. For a flash he appeared withered and gaunt with those long overgrown fingernails.

"Only the here and now is real," the first Rebbe continued. "The Torah tells us that is where only real spiritual journeys are. If you learn only one thing, let it be that. Do you think God wants you to spend your life in prison? Do you think your father does? What would be the spiritual purpose in that?"

"What do *you* think my Dad wants?" I asked the second Rebbe.

He was angered by the question. His face looked like mine, only much older as if I were my Dad's age. Why hadn't I noticed this before?

"Just this morning he told me to remind you about the time you went tubing in the Delaware," the second Rebbe said, "and about Ralph your pet turtle from the third grade. He's sorry about the time he hit you when you broke your Mother's last plate."

My hand was shaking. He knew so much about me.

"And you?" I said to the first.

"I'm sorry, boy. Your Dad is gone. When you die it is over."

"Then what's going on here?"

"You decide. Either you've come to set yourself free or to put your life in chains. I'm still here because a great wrong has gone unfixed. I died violently at the hands of my sister's husband. When this is set straight, then I too will be gone."

"So you want me to kill him."

"That would be the way of shadow. That is what *he* wants. But he is just a shadow of you. Every moment is new. A new choice. A new grand rabbi will be elected, in due time. I ask nothing of you. But if it is in your heart, then walk the path of light. You know how. It takes faith. There will be hardship. But no matter what, put down the gun."

Suddenly it felt very heavy. I could see myself marching upstairs. Firing. My body was cold and strong as the steel. I could do it. But then what? I'd be on the run. In real jail this time. What would I tell Dad then?

I heard a thud as the gun hit the floor. My open hand had stopped shaking. I felt lighter and I noticed I was breathing deeply.

The second Rebbe rose and looked at me, his sad almost loving expression asking me to reconsider. His face was younger now, almost identical to mine, then the skin stretched so horribly thin I could see the shape of his skull. My skull. His black robes were breaking apart and dissolving like ink in thinner. Beneath, he was gray bones.

Rebbe Yetse's Shadow stood. With amazing speed he had his hand around the ghost's neck. It struggled like a bird about to be slaughtered but the Rebbe did not falter. With his other hand he touched my forehead, my throat, my chest, my lower back. My skin burned in each place.

There was a flutter of wings and I thought I saw a cloud of beetles. Books, and crayons, and sheets of colored paper flew into the air. Then where the ghost was, there was only a cloud of dust, and a yellow-green afterglow lingering among the mess of falling school supplies.

A single book rose and moved back to the shelf, then halted and fell to the floor.

"No. Better yet, clean this up yourself," the Rebbe said.

As his last word resonated, he began to fade. He walked to the door, becoming more transparent with each step.

"Wait! Wait," I yelled. "Tell me. Tell me all the secrets. How do I get my life on track? I want Melissa back, and a good job!"

He stopped and looked over his shoulder. "You don't deserve it," he said. "Wisdom and reward is earned. Do not ask for such things for free."

"Please, tell me."

I collapsed to the floor. He was right. I didn't deserve anything.

"You did make the right choice today," the Rebbe said. "Even in the most wretched, there is hope, so I tell you this. The answers you seek are before you. The only good that can be done is in the here and now."

With a blink Rebbe Yetse's shadow was gone and I hoped the worst of me with him.

I RANG THE doorbell hoping Melissa was home. I was glad it was she, not her parents who opened the door. She wore a nice white sweater and brown slacks that hugged her lean frame. Her olive cheeks were flushed as if she had darted to answer the door. Her face was made up for going out. Her dark brown eyes looked straight at mine then at my work outfit and name tag then to the box of stuff in my hands. "I didn't expect you," she said.

"I can go."

I held out the box.

"It's okay, I have a minute," she said, taking the box. "How've you been?"

"Good," I said. "Things are alright. I may be promoted to sales soon."

She looked me up and down, as if checking my clothes before an evening out. "You look good," she said in a perplexed tone. "Something's different about you."

I wanted to tell her about Rebbe Yetse, but standing here I had my doubts about what really happened.

I shifted my weight nervously from foot to foot. "Thanks."

"Thanks for bringing this," she said, then paused. "I think you should go now, though."

I smiled and probably wished her well or something. I had fantasized about it going different but maybe we were never meant to be. Maybe I didn't deserve a girl like her. At least not yet.

Walking to work I wished I could have told her that everything was going to be okay for me. I wished that I could come home from work and tell Uncle Saul that I was going to read the Torah and go to temple and all that. But it wouldn't be true.

I straightened my nametag before going into the store. A familiar looking woman walked by and I couldn't help but stare. Was she the woman from the subway who had told me about the Rebbe? I thought I saw a hint of a smile before she looked away.

CLOUDLAND EARTHBOUND

BRISBANE, AUSTRALIA. 1982

"You can tell the Premier I'll never sell," Ben Meyerson said.

The perspiration beading on his forehead wasn't from the humid Brissy afternoon; he was used to that. Premier Johannes Bjelke-Peterson, "Sir" Joh, had dared to send his man in person just as Ben was preparing for one of Cloudland's midnight to dawn dances.

Ben and the man he knew to be Erwin Baak stood under the big arch of the domed entrance to the Cloudland Dance Hall, the same place generations of partygoers and ballroom dancers had stood before them. Ben's long sideburns, graying like his five o'clock shadow, suited his square face well. The darkness under his eyes was not from ten years of fatherhood- that suited him well too- it was from the mounting stresses of running the landmark dance hall. His lanky build and height could be construed as formidable if he would ever un-hunch his shoulders and stand up straight. Baak was a decade older than Ben but his crew cut and round baby face gave the short, stocky developer the appearance of youth. Broad shouldered, Baak carried himself as if he already owned the place. Ben took him more for a scrapper and thug than for the contractor and businessman he was known to be.

From where they stood the two men could see Cloudland's decorative columns flanking the main entrance doors and the ornate ballroom inside but they were too focused on each other's faces. Inside, musicians were setting up in the bandstand oblivious to the standoff. The antique mirror ball above them reflected the late afternoon sun from the skylights. Squares of shimmering white light slowly moved across the hardwood dance floor and the two levels of tiered seating framing it.

Baak stepped closer and Ben thought the man was actually going to push him. He hoped Baak didn't see him flinch. His father had taught him how to fight- and how to maneuver his way out of one. He'd settle for either in this case. He just wanted this man and all the men who wanted to level Cloudland to go away. For good.

"This place is a piece of history," Ben said with all the vitriol of a terrible insult.

"I'll tell Sir Joh. For sure. Just like you want, mate," Baak said. If Ben's words bothered him he showed no sign. "You can calm down. I'm not here to tussle. I'm telling you I think you should do this easy while you can. Brisbane's a city where things go bump in the night. Things go bump. Our Premier gets what he wants. You wake up and everything is gone and your pockets are empty when they could have been full."

"Thanks for the advice," Ben said. "You've done what you came for so now you can please leave."

Pop wouldn't have asked so nicely, Ben thought. His father was gone and the ease with which he dispatched Cloudland's troubles gone with him. Ben's son, Aaron would soon be the same age when Ben had started working with his father.

"Oh, Mr. Baak," Ben said. "While you're at it tell Sir Joh he doesn't scare me."

Baak said nothing. He didn't have to. Meyerson knew historical landmarks like the Cloudland Ballroom disappeared in Brisbane all the time because of Sir-Joh. The Premier's corrupt administration bought, demolished, and developed properties seemingly overnight. Just a few months ago the beloved Bellevue Hotel was razed and a grocery store and car park built in its place.

"There a problem here?" a gravelly voice called.

Angus Clayton, Cloudland's Maître' d' had just turned the corner and was walking the last bit of uphill road, his battered saxophone case in hand. The old timer, one of Ben's Dad's close friends, sometimes sat in with the band during the midnight to dawn parties after all the patrons had been shown in. He liked to walk from the bottom of the hill and often reminded everyone he'd been doing so since the old rail car had gone defunct back in '67. For the decade since Ben's Dad had passed the big guy practically ran the place. His help was a blessing that had enabled Ben to spend real time with his wife and be there as his son grew up.

"No problem here at all," Baak said to Clayton. There was something about the way Baak took pause after sizing him up that triggered a pang of jealousy in Ben.

"Don't I know you from somewhere, son?" Clayton said.

Baak ignored him and turned back to Ben.

"You have three days," Baak said. "Don't make this hard."

Baak strutted to his red pickup truck and drove away, down the hill, the way Clayton had just come from.

"You got nothing to worry about, Ben," Clayton said. "He's all hot air. Cloudland is a National Trust site. Let Sir Joh try and fight that."

"Yeah, he don't scare me," Ben said.

He had lied. Just like he had lied to Baak. Sir Joh did scare him. He scared him very much. It seemed to Meyerson that reality conformed to Sir Joh's will with an uncanniness that was otherworldly. Sir Joh was changing Brisbane from the world's biggest sleepy old town to a modern, turn of the century city seemingly overnight. And Cloudland was next in his sights. Ben remembered dirt roads and houses built by hand. Now Brisbane was a city on its way to becoming like Sydney. He didn't know what to do.

"Go on home," Clayton said. "I'll finish getting everything ready. Melaina and Aaron are waiting for you."

"And miss one of your pre-dawn recitals? Never," Ben said.

"I jam, I don't *recite*," Clayton said. "They'll be plenty more times to hear me play. Go to your family tonight."

The sun had dipped below the hill Cloudland was built upon. A trio of fruit bats glided on the air currents high above, their shapes small black etches against the orange-grey sky, uncaring of what was below them. For a second Ben wished he could be so carefree. It's not their place to care or even know, he thought.

Clayton left Ben to his thoughts and the view of the city. Brisbane had begun to glow with lights. Ben heard the blare of horns tuning up as the old man opened the door to go inside. In a few hours there would be grand music, fancily dressed people, and dancing.

MOCKINGBIRDS SWOOPED BETWEEN the Jacaranda trees lining the footpath across the road from Ben's house. Soon their calls would halt for the day and there would only be the sound of the Brisbane River flowing alongside the road. Ben bounded up the front steps of his old Queenslander. Dinnertime smells of curry and roasting fish from the neighboring houses greeted him. A thumb-size, green garden spider hung in its web that stretched from the top step into the darkness under the house.

Ben greeted Melaina in the family room where she stood behind her easel and canvas. Her glossy black hair was tied in a ponytail, like it always was, while she painted. Her jeans and button up work shirt bore old stains of paint and grease from working on the car and repairing their house, but she didn't care. Nor did Ben. He thought her porcelain skin and facial features were classically beautiful worthy of the Old Masters she studied and he often told her so. He yelled hello through the open door to Aaron who was sitting on his bed reading. Then he quietly told his wife about what had happened at Cloudland.

"You really told them to go to hell?" Melaina said.

"I did," Ben said. "I told him I'd fight."

"Thousands of protesters didn't stop them from tearing down the Bellevue. What are you going to do when they don't roll over and go away? You're not a fighter like Angus, you could get hurt."

"I'm gonna do what my Dad would do."

"You ever think maybe it's time," Melaina said.

"No," Ben said. "I'm not going to just give in. It's my job to protect the place."

Melaina calmly walked to Aaron's room and closed the door.

"Ben, I'm leaving," she said.

"Leaving? Melaina, now?"

"Now, Ben. There's never a good time to tell you."

"But you said you'd think about it."

"You *asked* me to think about it. And I did. I don't want my son growing up in a battle zone."

"He's our son!"

"Yes, Ben. Our son. Not just yours. You're about to try and stop an unstoppable tide. I know the toll that's going to have on you. Brissy's changing whether you fight or not. Whether you like it or not."

"If Brissy's changing then stay. Change is what you want, right? Aaron doesn't have to be involved with Cloudland. I never had to. I chose to. I wanted it. We can at least let him choose."

"You know that's not true, Ben."

She was right. He was the protector of Cloudland just like his father before him and like Aaron was destined to be. Up until recently it had been relatively easy. Clayton did so much. The hardest part was dealing with the music promoters and getting used to the names and sounds of the new rock bands that played the hall, like Madness and Midnight Oil. Protecting Cloudland and places like it had cost his father his life. How could any mother want that for her son? He felt lightheaded and let himself sink onto the couch.

"Where are you going? When?" he said in a lowered tone. Aaron's door was closed but he knew his son could still hear.

"Bondi. During school break," she said. "It's still nice down there but close enough to everything we need."

"Please don't," Ben said. "Things will never be the same if you do."

"I know," she said. "Things will never be the same anyway."

"What are you going to do?"

"Keep painting," she said. "There's a gallery I know that's already interested."

"You can do all that from here," Ben said.

"But I'm not going to. If you would only just let it go. Let Brissy be what it's becoming."

"You go on and on about what Brissy is becoming," Ben said. "Did you really ever know me?"

"I do, Ben. Better than you know yourself. Which is why I have to do this. I know you won't ever leave and I can't stand to see what staying's going to do to you. And I won't let you hurt Aaron."

Melaina went back to painting without any fanfare. This painting was a photo realistic scene of surfers on a beach. The boards and swim trunks were delightfully vintage. She used no reference. The image was in her mind. Ben found it beautiful and even though they'd been fighting so much he found her- her way, right down to her habits and everyday motions, beautiful. He didn't believe beauty was something that had to be a memory or in a frame on canvas. Beauty was and could be everywhere. Beauty was having a place like Cloudland or the Bellevue to go to. Beauty was the look in the kids' eyes when a rock band shouted, "Welcome! Enjoy the concert in the sky!" Cloudland was part of the magic that made the moments special. Only it wasn't magic, it was something real. Intangible. Elusive. But real as the good feeling you got on a perfect sunny day.

Ben sat and watched Melaina and replayed their conversation in his head. She wanted to paint. She wanted a normal life for Aaron. They had talked about these things when they married and again when Aaron was born. She knew everything that would be involved in protecting Cloudland, but now that Aaron was coming of age things were different for her.

He thought back to when he was ten. His father often returned home so late Ben was already getting ready for the next day of school. One night he was determined he would find out more about his father so he had followed him when he left the house.

At the time Ben wasn't sure exactly what he saw. There were bulldozers. And workmen. His father had stopped at the old blue house a couple of blocks away that was for sale. The dozers weren't running. The men weren't working. But the house was disappearing like a ship fading into morning mist. Then his father was fighting with the men. Some of them ran away. Some of them fell to the ground and didn't get up. Somehow Pop had taken them all on. Pop moved in front of the house and slowly outstretched his arms. The old house stopped disappearing. It came back, right before Ben's eyes, the blue colors returning like a Polaroid picture emerging from washed out grey. Somehow Pop was doing this. Then he realized he was there.

Is this what you do, Pop, Ben said. Is this what I'm going to do too when I grow up?

You're not strong enough, Ben.

Not strong enough, yet, you mean, right Pop?

No. Not strong enough ever. But someday you may have sons and daughters that might be. Which is why you must learn what I do.

Melaina knew all of this. She knew everything about him. He went to her.

"Look at Grand Central Station for example, Mel," he said. "In New York they work wonders with how they handle historical sites."

"Really Ben, New York? You can't have your cake and eat it too."

"It's a protected place, for Pete's sake!"

"Even if by some miracle you win, you lose," she said. "You're one man. How much of Brisbane can you protect?"

"I'm not alone," Ben said.

Pop had been right. Aaron was strong. He'd been teaching him.

He knew Melaina did not want to hear that. She stood there painting trying to pretend it was just another night.

Ben went to Aaron's room. Aaron lay on the bed with his book draped over his face.

"I know you were listening, son. You don't have to pretend to be sleeping."

"Sorry, Pop."

Aaron's bowl cut mop of unruly brown hair was even more unruly from his pillow. He had his mother's thin crescent shaped lips and porcelain skin. His eyes and square jaw always made Ben think of his Pop.

"Nothing to be sorry about. What do you think? Do you want to go to Bondi?"

"I don't want you to ever get hurt, Pop."

Ben said nothing. He didn't know how to tell the boy that in life, there are never any guarantees. He guessed he'd have to, someday.

"So, you want to go?"

"I don't want to leave Mom. Or you."

They sat in silence. Ben moved the book; something with Samurai and Ronin and an impossible stand off and put his arm around Aaron.

"I also don't want to be around any fighting," Aaron said after a while.

"You remember the things we've been talking about," Ben said. "About me. And Grand Pop. And things you'll someday have to do."

"Yeah," Aaron said.

The genuine delight in the boy's voice gave Ben hope.

"All the places in Brisbane you showed me, right?" Aaron said. "Especially Cloudland."

Aaron closed his eyes.

"I can see it in my mind like you showed," Aaron said. "The mirror ball, the shiny floor, the big archway-"

"Good," Ben said.

Melaina barged into the room. "Ben enough of this!"

Aaron cried as they argued. It lasted only a moment but it was enough to leave Ben drained. Melaina told him to leave and he obeyed.

"I won't forget," Aaron called from the window as Ben tramped down the stairs with his hastily packed bag.

He hoped the words were true.

BEN DROVE TO the abandoned church at the bottom of Bowen hill. It had been one of his Pop's favorite buildings. He parked his car and fell asleep looking up at Cloudland's lights. He woke many hours later. It was nearing morning. Fruit bats were returning to roost inside the church tower. He pictured them, hanging upside down from the rafters, huddled together, leathery wings wrapped around their dark, furry bodies.

When returning from the blue house with his Pop, Ben had stumbled across an injured fruit bat on one of the neighborhood lawns. Wings spread and writhing on the ground the creature was almost as large as he was. It regarded him with dark, sentient eyes. He had never seen one up close before and its strange but familiar face touched him. He ran over and tried to lift it to help it fly again.

"No, Ben. Stay away," Pop had said. "It's hurt. And we have to go."

Ben lifted the creature anyway. The bat flapped its wings then fell and disappeared into the shadows of the trees on the lawn. He heard it struggling to fly. Pop pulled him along. He was never sure if the bat made it into the air or wound up on the ground again.

Ben watched a bat crawl into the tower. It wasn't sun up yet. If he hurried he figured he could make it to Cloudland and maybe catch Clayton play before the party ended.

Brisbane's lights dotted the darkness below as Ben drove up the hill. Though the sky was pregnant with dawn Cloudland was still illuminated with the glow of strings of white faerie lights wrapped around the columns and the bright lights adorning the great arch. Inside, a few couples remained on the floor, men in their black and white finery, women in their bright colorful gowns. They spun round and round as the band played a slow, dreamy number. Squares of white light reflected from the mirror ball circled with them unifying the moment into a perfect vision. It was like one of Melaina's nostalgic paintings come to life. There had to always be a place where moments like this could happen, Ben thought. Clayton placed his hand on Ben's shoulder from behind, breaking the spell of the moment. Ben was glad to see him.

"Missed me play," Clayton said.

"Melaina's leaving me," Ben blurted.

Clayton pressed his hand harder against Ben in sympathy.

"Meet me at the bar," he said. "I just have to get my sax."

Ben went to the bar opposite the bandstand and sat in the dim light of votive candles burning low. Patrons sat in the alcoves surrounding the dance floor watching the remaining dancers slow dance.

"Hey boss, got a second?" Richard the bartender asked.

"Sure," Ben said.

Richard was one of the old timers like Clayton. Ben noticed the line of numbers tattooed on his forearm beneath his rolled-up sleeve. He'd seen it before but had never given it much thought. Where was Richard from? What horrors had he lived through? There was so much about Cloudland he didn't know. So much more he could have done if he hadn't let Clayton carry the burden. Night after night the old man ran the place and went out into Brisbane like his father had done.

"I just wanted to take this opportunity to shake your hand and thank you, boss," Richard said.

"Cheers, mate," Ben said. "But for what?"

"For not selling out. Angus told me you're going to fight. I wasn't sure you had it in you."

Richard gripped Ben's hand and didn't let go.

"Everyone's welcome here," Richard said. "Here it doesn't matter that

I don't celebrate Christmas like our dear Premier. It doesn't matter who I love. Or the color of my skin."

"Of course," Ben said. He'd never given these things a second thought. Cloudland was a place for everyone. It always was.

"Well, with Sir Joh in Brisbane I have to worry about who sees me with my partner," Richard said. "I'm glad that you're not selling out when it gets rough, boss."

Clayton sat down on the stool next to Ben.

"You missed him play, again," Richard said, changing the subject. "The man's enlightening. When he plays, nothing else matters."

"With the band behind me and with your cocktails in me nothing else does," Clayton said.

Ben grunted in agreement. He was lost in his thoughts about what Richard had just said. Soon he found himself telling Clayton about what had happened with Aaron and Melaina.

"Melaina's right," Clayton said. "You have to let things be what they are. You have to let her be. She has to do what is right for her. If that road leads her away, then so be it."

"Let her go?" Ben asked.

"What she does is not your choice," Clayton said. "But don't let her choices get in the way of what you believe. If you believe in her, tell her so. If you believe in Brisbane and Cloudland do what you have to do."

"Why? Angus," Ben said. "Tell me why. I know what this place means to me. But when I try to say it, it never seems enough. What do I tell Aaron? Now he won't be here for me to show him."

Richard finished shaking the cocktail he had made and poured it into two highball glasses for them. Ben smelled the alcoholic bite of Bundaberg rum. Clayton and Richard nodded to each other, a mutual acknowledgement of something Ben didn't catch or understand. He felt as if he were in his father's shoes. Here he was sitting at Cloudland before dawn, drinking and contemplating such things with his father's friends. Why had it taken all these years for this to happen? Why had he waited until things felt so grim?

"Times change, Melaina's right, Ben," Richard said. "People change. Places change. No man can ever go into the same river twice."

"Because they are never the same man and never the same river. Pop always said that."

Richard poured himself a shot of Bundy and held it up.

They all said cheers and drank to Ben's father. Ben wished he were here. Pop had continued running Cloudland and going out late at night protecting Brisbane's places until one night ten years ago he did not come home. Mel was right in that there was only so much one man could do. He was not his father. Ben had seen him do miraculous things. He'd bested groups of men half his age. Even dodged bullets fired right at him. One day a bullet had found him. At least he had lived to see Aaron born. At least they had that.

"Cities are like that saying too," Clayton said. "Always different yet still the same somehow. Our bodies' cells are always replacing themselves but you're still you." He sipped his drink. "Change is the natural way. It doesn't have to be bad."

"I still can't believe the Bellevue is gone," Ben said.

"Isn't the new place where Melaina gets that fresh vanilla and spices to make her special cake?" Clayton said.

"Good prices there too," Richard said.

"How can you be talking about cake? That place was special-"

"Some places it's just their time to go," Clayton said.

"You can't be telling me to give up on Cloudland," Ben said.

"Quite the contrary. Some places are never meant to go. You're right. There are special places. Places that are sort of a key log holding the whole damn thing together."

"The whole damn thing?" Ben asked.

"You know. The status quo. The block. The neighborhood. The city. Places that if they go the whole thing comes undone. Cloudland is one of those places."

"A place like Cloudland goes. Other places go like dominos," Richard said. "It changes things. In the wrong way."

"Magic?" Ben asked.

"In its own way, I guess," Richard said. "I'd say it's more like, power. The power of the beliefs and habits of people."

Pop had mentioned things like this. He had called them lynch pin sites. They had something to do with the big picture Ben never understood. He wished he had spent more time with Pop and had tried harder to comprehend his teachings instead of retreating to his role as husband and then father. A pang of loss hit him when he thought of Melaina and Aaron.

"My family. How can I just let them go?" Ben asked.

"Maybe you have to. Maybe you don't," Clayton said. "But it doesn't mean you give up on your son. You can't. You have to teach him. And be his father. No matter where he is or what he chooses."

Morning light found its way in from the skylights. The band had stopped their song and was breaking down their gear. One couple remained on the floor, slowly circling, holding each other. With the dream like quality of the night dispelled, the dancers looked sad and Cloudland looked old. Ben didn't know whether to smile or cry. He realized he was doing both.

"Sleep it off," Clayton said. "It's a new day."

Clayton walked him to the back office. Ben lay down to sleep on the couch. He went in and out of a dream of the Brisbane River and the jacaranda trees on its banks. In the dream he wasn't sure if it was day or night or if the black shapes gliding between the trees were bats or birds. He saw the injured fruit bat. It's soulful face. The line of blood that trickled from its mouth. The sky went dark and he thought it might be choked with bats and not really night at all. Clayton's words had inspired him. Later he would go home and fix everything. He'd make everything all right. He'd compromise with Melaina, somehow. He'd get her to stay. Even if it meant not fighting over Cloudland. He'd work it out. He knew he'd find a way.

BEN SLEPT INTO the afternoon. It was a beautiful day. The view of the city from Cloudland was clear and unobstructed as he drove down the hill. Sleep and talking to the guys had done him a world of good and he still had some time to talk to Melaina before Aaron came home from school.

He felt something was different about his house as soon as he arrived. The image of the couple on Cloudland's dance floor sprung into his mind as he climbed the steps and opened the door. Melaina's canvas and easel were gone. Aaron's bedroom door was open. His son's drawers were open and his clothes were gone. Melaina had left. She hadn't waited.

He slammed the door and raged down the front stairs and into his car. He sped downtown to the government office buildings. Ben didn't allow himself to feel the sadness, or loneliness, or the helplessness he would come to feel. He'd find Sir Joh and end this once and for all. Clayton wasn't the only one who could fight, he thought. Cloudland would be safe. Brisbane would be safe. There'd be no more fighting. No battle zone. And then Melaina would see the light and come back. His family would be together. Pop had been wrong. He was strong enough. He could protect Brisbane as well as anyone else could. He knew it now. Pop had only been trying to protect him like Melaina was trying to protect Aaron. It was all clear.

Ben bolted though the lobby and up the stairs to the officials' offices. A flabbergasted secretary shrieked as he burst into Sir Joh's waiting area. He didn't notice how quickly the secretary regained her composure nor did he see her lift the phone and said "he's here" into it. He had already charged through the door into Sir Joh's chambers.

The first thing Ben noticed was that Sir Joh was not there. Big sheets of paper and blueprints were draped over the mahogany desk facing the door. Sunlight filled the room from the two big windows behind the desk making the framed photographs that covered the walls hard to see from the glare. Most of the photos were of buildings and places in Brisbane. Some of the old ones were black and white. Many were of Sir Joh standing outside Brisbane's new buildings. In all of them he was in a white suit and wide

DANIEL BRAUM

brimmed white hat. Shaking hands with officials from cities across Australia and the Pacific Rim.

He moved to Sir Joh's desk. The top sheets were blueprints. Designs for a building. He flipped past the structurals. Past the mechanicals and site map then pushed them aside. The next sheet was a map of Brisbane. He recognized many of the locations marked on it. As he studied the map strange lines appeared on it connecting these points. Ben blinked and rubbed his eyes but the lines remained. Blue. Pencil thin. When he looked closely he saw they were comprised of thousands of words and characters. Hebrew? Greek? Pictograms? He wasn't sure. They were so intricate. So detailed. So precise. He found himself unable to focus on one individual character for long. Were they moving? The strings of characters were vibrating, he realized and swapping places with each other while still keeping the form of a solid line connecting the dots and X's on the map. Recognition chimed inside him. The places marked with an X were places Sir Joh had already demolished. Dozens of places. Dozens more were marked with green dots. Seeing a big red dot covering Cloudland he felt the unease he experienced that night he had followed his father to the blue house. He deduced the rest of the dots were places Sir Joh wanted. The lines didn't follow any roads or topography. But they all connected with each other and all converged on Cloudland.

Ben glanced around the room and realized many of the photos were of places marked on the map. Were they trophies? Maybe the map was a chessboard. Or a log marking all Sir Joh's moves and plans. He didn't know what the map was but someplace inside him recognized it and what he was seeing leaving him only with a sense of frustration.

"I knew you'd find your way here," a voice called from outside the office. Erwin Baak stepped into the room.

The lines disappeared from the map with the hiss of a match touching water.

"Now that you've seen what the boss is doing, what do you think?" Baak said.

Ben steeled himself to fight. He had just forced his way into the office and was caught going through Sir Joh's stuff. Baak was going to have him arrested. Might as well make this count, he thought. He darted from behind the desk and took a swing at Baak as he approached. Baak pivoted with a grace Ben didn't think the man possessed. His punch went wide and he lost his balance and fell.

He braced himself for the kick he knew was coming but Baak only bent down and extended his hand.

"Let me help you up," Baak said.

Ben gripped Baak's hand and let himself be helped. He thought about trying to hit the man again but face to face with Baak his courage faltered.

"The map," Ben said. It was all he could say.

"Yes, the map," Baak said. "Our plans. They're not a secret."

"Where's Sir Joh?" Ben said attempting to control the situation with the demand.

"The Premier is busy," Baak said. "Working. Somewhere safe."

Somewhere safe. It pleased Ben that they viewed him as a threat and that they had taken precautions.

Ben stumbled out of the office. Baak followed.

"If you're going to have me arrested let's get this over with," Ben said.

Baak helped steady him. "This is between us. You don't look too good. You hung over, mate? I'm not calling the police"

He hated that Baak had just helped him.

"You're not?" Ben said. "But Cloudland?"

"What about it?" Baak said. "You see the light and decide to sell?"

"No way in hell."

Baak sighed.

"Didn't think so," he said. "I thought if you saw things our way, if you sold, maybe things could be different."

"What?" Ben said. "You think asking nicely changes anything?"

"No. I only thought things don't have to happen the way you might think. But I guess you're right this doesn't change anything. We're still coming. Tomorrow night it is. Sometime before the dawn. It will be easier for you if you aren't there."

Ben ran to his car. As he drove to Cloudland he thought how Baak could have easily beaten him up or had him arrested. Why the compassion? He hated that Baak was everything he could have been. Strong. Trained. And terribly confident.

Clayton was on the dance floor with a broom helping the cleanup crew.

"I always knew that they'd be coming, someday," Clayton said after Ben had told him what had happened. "I always thought we'd have Aaron with us when they did."

Ben recognized the way Clayton looked at him. It was the way his Pop had so many times. There was love in his eyes, yes. But also a disappointment, that Ben didn't think was intended, that the old man could not hide.

THE FIRST BULLDOZER chugged up the hill just past four AM the next night as Baak had promised. More bulldozers and a few cars full of men followed. The men filed out of the cars one by one. Ben didn't like how precisely they moved. Most of the men wore caps or glasses that hid their faces. A few of them wore ski masks like American bank robbers.

Erwin Baak was the last man to get out of the final car. He and his men were all lined up facing Cloudland's entrance. Ben and Clayton watched through the door then came outside and stood beneath the archway.

They're here. At our castle in the sky, Ben thought as he looked at Cloudland's silhouette against the night.

Baak's men broke their formation and were surrounding Cloudland.

The lights went out.

"There goes the power," Clayton said. "Probably the phones are gone too."

Ben heard the crackle of a walkie-talkie. There were more men, somewhere. Probably blocking the road at the bottom of the hill.

"This is it," Clayton said. "No police or firemen coming to help tonight."

"It's okay to leave now," Baak called. "Last chance. No need to do this hard."

"No," Ben answered. He wished he had something more defiant to say.

Baak took a few steps back. Ben had the impression of an actor finding his mark on stage.

A figure clad in white appeared at the final turn in the road down the hill a hundred yards away. Ben recognized Sir Joh's white wide brimmed hat, though he could not see the man's face. He had seen Sir Joh's photos in the office and in the newspaper but now with the man so near he found it odd he could not recall the man's face and features. The Premier stood there, a general on the outskirts of the battlefield, his white hat and suit strangely visible in the starlight and ambient glow from the city.

Sir Joh raised his hand then flicked his wrist. It was a small movement. The kind to signal a waiter or a servant.

For an instant the night sounds were gone. From somewhere far away Ben heard the bop of a big band playing and the din of a ballroom full of bustling people. Then the night sounds returned, whatever Sir Joh had done was over, but the air felt different. A light wind blew at Ben's back. He turned. Cloudland was there behind him but it was fading as if it were a ship that had receded into mist, same as what had happened to the blue house he had seen with his Pop all those years ago.

The night exploded into motion. Baak's men were running at them from everywhere. Straight on. From the sides. Clayton rocked back and forth on the balls of his feet; his hands open. He grabbed the first man that came at him then pivoted and used the man's momentum and weight to send him crashing into the man charging from the side. Clayton dodged blows from the next attacker with small, efficient movements and a much younger man's speed. Ben's stomach turned over when he realized despite the chaos of brawling men it was un-naturally quiet.

Pain exploded on the back of his head. Someone had hit him from behind. He turned and the sight of his attacker sent him into a rage. He threw blow after wild blow at the man and somehow they both wound up on the ground. Ben didn't know the man's name but recognized him from around town. He was just an ordinary man yet there was no recognition of Ben in his eyes, only a cold, impersonal stare that struck Ben as wrong and scared him more of the prospect of being overwhelmed and beaten.

The man muttered strange words in language Ben didn't recognize. Were the words prayers? Spells? Or just a manifestation of the man's fanaticism? He told himself to stop thinking and willed himself to punch the man in the face. Blood trickled from the man's mouth. Ben saw the injured fruit bat in his mind's eye.

Two attackers broke away from the chaos, grabbed Ben's arms and threw him down. As he tried to roll away and evade their blows, he saw Cloudland had become transparent.

Clayton ran over and knocked into Ben's attackers pushing them away. The old man hit them with solid body blows and they stayed down. Ben had given everything he had against his first attacker and it hadn't been enough. Seeing Clayton fight, everything about the man finally made sense. He fought with the same focus with which he played his instrument. He had only seen the man's peaceful side. His passion for beauty. For music. For family. Now, he realized he hadn't really known Clayton at all. He was a warrior like Richard had said. A warrior like his Pop must have been.

Clayton helped Ben to his feet. Dozens of Baak's men were sprawled on the ground, motionless. Down the road, Sir Joh waved his hand again then turned and disappeared down the turn and into the night.

Baak emerged from the darkness a few feet away and approached with a gun in his hand pointed toward the sky. The pistol looked as if it were made of the blackness of night.

"Put that down young man," Clayton said. "Now I know where I know you from. You used to come dancing here when you were a boy."

Ben thought he saw recognition on Baak's face. Maybe it was terror or the result of the heat of the fight but Baak had finally lost his composure. Ben thought Baak was going to speak but he only lowered the gun and fired.

Clayton swung his arm out and away from his chest. Ben heard a ding as the bullet hit a tree. Baak fired again. And again. Somehow Clayton was deflecting the bullets. One whooshed past Ben. Baak stepped closer. Too close to miss. Ben screamed and dove at Baak. The gun fired. Clayton fell; blood welled from his side.

Ben wrestled Baak to the ground but the man was strong and quickly turned the tables and pinned Ben.

"It didn't have to be this way," Baak said, his face pressed against Ben's. "I tried everything in my power not to do this. If you had just done this the easy way we could have worked something out. We didn't need all the land for the Cloudland Apartments. Maybe the hall could have stayed."

"Why?" Ben said.

He had to know. They were so close. And the fight had bound them, brought them closer with the logic of its violence. Surely Baak would not refuse him now.

"It's only business," Baak said.

He broke Ben's hold, rolled off him, and headed for one of the cars.

Ben wanted to go after him but he crawled to Clayton instead. Baak's men were dragging their fallen and helping them into the cars. Ben grabbed Clayton under the arms and dragged him into Cloudland.

The entrance door felt soft as if it were made of compressed dust that might dissipate at any moment. He laid Clayton on the dance floor and put pressure on the old man's wound.

The columns, the bandstand, the fancy railing and tiers of seats. Ben could see through them, through everything to outside. A pair of Baak's men were at Cloudland's entrance with a metal can. The mirror ball came to life with orange light. The smell of smoke and petrol filled the air.

Bandstand music from far away wafted over the crackle of fire. In the flames Ben thought he saw ballroom dancers. Barely visible, transparent wisps of people made of smoke and flame circling the ballroom floor. Clayton opened his eyes. He and Ben watched the dancers step. One two. One two. The dancers rose off the floor. They stepped into the air, continuing the revolutions of their dance into an upward spiral. They rose and rose as Cloudland disappeared. Then Ben could see them no more. Everything was gone. Ben and Clayton were on the bare ground surrounded by smoldering brush and rubble. Morning had come and Cloudland, every last bit of it, had vanished.

Ben couldn't process the fact it was gone. Sir Joh had won. The Premiere controlled the cops and fire department but had made what had just happened look like a fire anyway.

Clayton was crying.

"It's alright, man," Ben said. "You're all right. You're gonna make it."

"I know," Clayton said. "I know everything goes sometime. But…"

The wind blew sparks onto Ben's face. He held Clayton on the hilltop as the fires burned. Smoke billowed into the sky. Ben watched it rise, listening for the sound of music, for anything that might hint that this had not happened. There was only the sunrise and the unimpeded wind feeding the crackling fires.

CLAYTON RECOVERED FROM his injuries after a few weeks in the hospital. Ben bought him a new saxophone, the best money could buy, for the day he was to leave the hospital. Clayton died the night before he was set to leave, peacefully in his sleep. Richard the bartender told Ben it was from a broken heart.

Melaina didn't come to Clayton's funeral. Some of Cloudland's regulars were there but not enough for Ben. Where was the groundswell of outrage? Ben hated how life went on. He hated how it seemed that no one remembered or cared Melaina and Aaron came to visit. The silver lining was that Aaron wanted to start spending every other weekend and most of school end break with him.

Their first weekend together Ben and Aaron watched a lot of television. They went to a cricket match and flew a kite by the river. Two weeks later, minutes after Melaina drove away, Aaron asked Ben to take him to Cloudland.

After dinner they drove up the hill and parked outside the chain link ringing the construction site. The entire top of the hill, an area the size of several cricket fields, had been cleared of trees, made level, and paved. A sign outside a work trailer showed an artist's rendition of the apartments that were to be built there.

Because of the insurance, Aaron would grow up with money. And choices. Enough of both to do anything he wanted with his life.

Aaron took his father's hand.

"Come on, Pop," he said. "Let's go. I'm ready."

They stepped over the chain.

After a few minutes of walking around and a lot of doubling back and forth they stopped.

"Here?" Ben asked.

"Yeah," Aaron said. "I think the mirror ball was right here."

Aaron let go of Ben's hand. They both closed their eyes.

Ben saw Cloudland's mirror ball and archway. He remembered the feel of the carved wood railings beneath his hands. He knew Aaron was thinking of these things too. He tried to keep the image of the dance floor full of dancers in his mind but he kept picturing the last couple spinning in their embrace.

Ben opened his eyes. Aaron's hands were outstretched. Ben heard the tones of horns tuning up beneath the whispering wind. Aaron was concentrating. He was trying. Too hard, maybe.

A square of light appeared on the ground. White and shimmering. It lit the area like a firework. It circled round he and Aaron then was joined by another. Ben looked up and thought he saw the lights of Cloudland's great archway appear in the dusk sky.

Aaron sighed and coughed and fell to his knees. The light and the arch disappeared. Ben hugged his son.

"I'm sorry, Dad," Aaron said.

"Nothing to be sorry about. Never be sorry," Ben said through tears. "You did good. No, you did great. Let's go home. For now. We'll get it next time. Next time, alright?"

A fruit bat sailed high above as they returned to their car. Ben listened for music. The evening wind blew dust across the hilltop unobstructed.

BETWEEN OUR EARTH AND THEIR MOON

I WAS JUST getting to the best part of the story of the man who met himself and Claudia was indulging me when the guy with the hard hat interrupts us.

"I got a special kind of problem," he says. "I hear you're the one who can help."

Claudia's eyes light up the way they do when she spies a mark. I know I should turn on the charm and hustle up some work but all I can think about is finding a way to feel okay again. I'd been pouring my heart out to Claudia all afternoon, telling her that if I could do it all over, live my life differently, I would. I'd do anything. I thought finally getting some recognition around here would make me happy. But I'm the same old me. Maybe stronger and smarter, yeah. And with a few more tricks up my sleeve but I still feel alone in a world that feels colder every day.

The guy keeps his poise even though I don't answer him. The din from the tables full of hipsters and posers and even a few real practitioners fills the silence between us. Claudia clears her throat and stands there fanning her order pad. She's wearing the black apron, black slacks, and black shirt the wait-staff wear even though she's not one of them.

The conversation at the next table over lulls as the wannabes take a break from sipping expensive coffees and cooing over their old books and posing and showing off to try and listen in. I've had enough with the attention but this guy isn't one of the ordinary gawkers. With his clipboard and bright orange work vest I thought he was just another workman when

I spied him leaving Maria Elena's chambers. I should have known better.

"The man's talking to you, Nate," Claudia says. "Looks like he might be a paying customer."

This is Maria Elena's place. Maria Elena's town. Everyone knows all jobs must go through her or there's trouble. I don't want any trouble. Claudia's fondness for me has made her reckless.

"Who's asking?" I finally say and look up to face him.

His thinning hair only has a hint of brown left in it. The dim light makes the lines in his middle-aged face look even deeper than they probably are.

"Grant Donovan," he says. "Union Chief. National Six Twenty Five. The Sandhogs."

We shake hands.

"National? You've come a long way," I say.

"It's all relative," he says.

Claudia blows a strand of her blond-dyed bangs out of her face and goes back to waiting tables. It's the shit part of the otherwise sweet position she has. Donavan sits without asking.

"Hard day in the tunnels?" I say. "Maybe one of these days you guys are gonna finish that crosstown line?"

"I'll let you ask again once you've taken a shift drilling solid bedrock."

There's an uncomfortable silence. I hope I haven't run him off. Claudia's right. I do need money.

He unclips papers from his clipboard.

"Uh, uh," I say. "Around here all jobs go through Maria Elena."

"Of course," he says. "I only want to show you that my Union has a contract but it hasn't been honored. In my book that's a green light."

"A green light for trouble," I say. "The city's full of practitioners who'll do any work for a buck."

"This is a sensitive matter. I don't just want anyone," he says. "You *are* as good as they say, right?"

Claudia returns and slaps two menus on the table. "Of course he is.

How much does it pay?"

"A lot," Donovan says.

"I appreciate the offer," I say. "But no."

"No reason to waste any more time then. There are...things, things in my tunnels stopping my machines from running. I thought that would interest you."

He stands and places a business card on the table.

"There's that," he says. "If you wise up and change your mind."

I watch him walk out the door.

"Don't let him go," Claudia says. "He offered you a real job."

"He's nothing but trouble," I say. "I can spot it."

She looks at me like I'm an idiot. The world of the arcane is more than status and position in this fancy place Maria Elena has set up. Claudia hasn't learned this yet. On the last real job I took everything burned and a young girl, not terribly unlike her, got killed. So I'm not an idiot no matter what she thinks. I'm learning. I'm finally learning.

"YOU'RE REALLY GOING to sit here and whine to me instead of trying to land a job?" Claudia says. "He's still outside, smoking."

"There's nothing at all you'd do over if you could?" I say. "No advice you'd want to give your younger self?"

"Yeah, I'd tell myself to smack you hard enough to make you listen when I said go out there and get that work a second ago."

"Guess you're too young to know regret," I say.

"You don't know the first thing about what I regret," she says. "Want to know what I regret? I regret knowing that you're good, but you only take shit work and con jobs. You have the rep and the skill to back it up but you just mope and obsess about second chances. I've heard about the man who met himself and all the same stories as you. I might actually even believe that there *are* other worlds where things are different. But at some point you have to just decide to get off your ass and live..."

She's right. She's never tasted loss but she's right. Someone's gonna part that fat cat from his money. It might as well be me. Claudia smiles as I go outside.

The Christmas lights flashing on and off in the big plate window do little to fight the gray November afternoon. I pull my coat closed and walk to where Donavan is smoking a few feet away.

"My lad. I had a feeling you'd come around."

"I came to tell you can smoke inside," I say.

He flicks his cigarette butt toward the window.

"Maria Elena picks and chooses which rules she follows. Yet I see she has all of you following hers. You want to take my job to spite the one who holds your leash."

"I'm done with spite. I came to my senses and remembered I need the money. How much?"

"I think what the Union was going to pay Maria Elena you'll find fair."

He shows me the contract. The sum is enough to keep me going for a while. A long while. More than enough to do everything I need to do to make amends for those who got killed because of me.

"Come," he says. "I need you to begin right away."

He walks toward the corner, his hand trailing on the building's dirty brick wall. A door I've never seen before appears and opens. Hot subterranean air spills into the street carrying the reek of burnt hair and plastic.

There is no subway station for blocks yet I hear the distinct screech of a subway car braking to a stop.

"Coming?" he says.

A secret subway line. Here under Maria Elena's nose. That's strong stuff. Beneath his showboating I can tell he's a nasty piece of work. But I follow anyway. Guess I was wrong. I never learn.

I DON'T BOTHER asking about the subway. Those like Donavan and Maria Elena and my old boss, they never give guys like me a straight answer.

"So, about my payment?"

"It's done," Donovan says.

I check my account with my phone. The money is in there. I'd love to learn the trick of how he got my number and signal down here.

The money's gonna do me good. I would have settled for a trade. Knowledge. Or information. Even Claudia admits that the stories of those who started over could be true. Cheating time and space and fate with enough power and force of will. I know it can be done. For me. For Alexandra. Alexandra was her name. She died on my watch. I should use her name when I think of her instead of trying to forget.

"Focus lad," Donovan says, "We're here."

The train stops and the door hisses open. The trip was too fast. Not a portal moving us instantly between places like my old boss could create, but a level of power and knowledge above my pay grade for sure. The platform is much too clean and leads into a cavern the size of several football fields; it's rough, stone walls scarred with the marks of heavy machinery.

"The hub," Donovan says as we walk. "This is where we're building the crosstown line… and more."

At least a dozen tunnels, each with a diameter larger than a train car, are spaced throughout the cavern. Who knows where the hell they all lead to? Could be anywhere. The one thing I am certain of is that this is not an ordinary construction site.

A few dozen Sandhogs in khaki work clothes, orange vests, and hard hats like Donovan are going about their business. A crew of six are soldering a rail line that disappears into the tunnel behind them. Hot orange sparks burn bright but are quickly swallowed by the dark. We pass another crew tinkering with the treads of a construction vehicle the size of a subway car with a giant drill for its front. Its sharp, spiral nose cone sparkles in the work lights strung along the ceiling.

"Hey! You the one here about the gremlins?" one of the men working on the machine calls to us. The name 'Sandoval' is embroidered on his shirt. He's young and can't hide he's excited to see us. I recognize the fire in his eyes as akin to something that once filled me.

Donovan deliberately ignores him and steers me away toward another of the drilling machines.

"This is one of the borers I need to keep running. The drill is diamond tipped. Only eight of these beauties exist," he says. "Six are here."

He's showboating again. It's his "tell." If I could only figure out what he's hiding.

"Some of the men say there are demons in the tunnels," he says.

He leads me by the arm to a steel job box and retrieves a hard hat. He puts his finger to his mouth making the sign for silence. "Don't want to spook the men any more than they are. Here, put this on."

He strides into the tunnel nearest the borer. The beam of light from his hard hat lamp cuts the darkness.

"And what do you think?" I ask him.

"I don't think. I know. These demons keep shutting the borers down faster than we can repair them."

"And you want me to figure out why."

"I don't care why. I'm paying you to put a stop to it."

His beam illuminates plastic sheathing draped across the tunnel fifty yards ahead. Two armed men stand outside. They're dressed like sandhogs but I can tell they're pros. Killers. Much too alert and comfortable with their guns. Behind the plastic I see the silhouette of a borer and the mess of debris and rock of the aborted tunnel surrounding it.

"Where does it go?" I say. "If you want results from me you have to tell me what I'm getting into. And don't feed me the line that this is the crosstown project or anything like that."

He's silent for a few seconds then says, "Alright, lad. Since you need to know, the tunnel leads to the moon."

A dozen smart-ass responses run through my mind. He doesn't respect me enough to tell me the truth. So that's how this is going to go.

"The moon?"

"You heard right," he says.

He's a stranger bird than I thought.

"Problem?" he asks.

I'm used to not asking questions. But he just ensured that this job is nothing more than paycheck to me.

"No problem," I say. "Let's go to the moon."

He looks at me like I'm the crazy one. I don't like that I don't have a read on him or the situation.

The guards hold open a slit in the plastic and we walk through. Donovan runs his hand along the borer as if it were a muscle car.

"See anything?" he asks.

The tunnel ends in a pile of rubble and stones.

"Nothing," I say.

He opens the door of the borer and steps up into the cab. He pulls a control lever that brings the engine roaring to life. The big corkscrew drill rotates. Changes direction, then spins into a blur.

Pieces of debris on the floor move and hop, more than can be attributed to vibration. A pebble flies into the air. The big stones against the wall shake. Fist-sized chunks of rock rise and spin forming a ten-foot-high vortex of stone. I jump out of the way. The whirling mass sails past and slams into the borer. Donovan pushes the lever, cutting the engine. The vortex spins a few paces more then stops. Rock rains to the floor.

Donovan jumps out of the cab and walks to me uncaring of the still-vibrating rocks.

"Heads up," he says, exhilarated. "See, there's your demon problem. Time to get to work."

I have no idea what I'm going to say or do. As usual I'm in over my head. I have a few guesses but they don't involve demons. Plus I don't have any of my tools. Thankfully Donovan's phone rings.

"What?" he answers. "Now? I'm with the... exterminator."

He turns to me. "Damn emergency at the Hub. Everyone's incompetent I tell you. Stay here and get started."

He exits through the plastic sheathing. The quiet after that rock storm is unsettling so I pace the perimeter trying to get a sense of things. I circle the borer and decide to climb inside.

As I touch the door something hits my back. I open the door and a stone chip flies through the air and pelts me. The debris and rubble rises again.

"Alright," I say. "I won't go in."

The debris hovers but does not lift higher. I stand next to the machine watching the shaking stones and something slams me and knocks me to the floor.

Everything goes black, but I know haven't passed out. The blackness fills with points of light. Stars. The night sky? Something is connecting with me. Giving me this vision of space. The earth and the moon appear in the star-dotted black. A furry, clawed hand passes across my field of vision. A comet sails across the sky towards the moon. I think it is going to hit it but it passes between it and the earth. The moon is different. It has atmosphere; green and white and blue, like Earth. The clawed hand passes in front of me again then a furry face appears blocking the view. Its mouth is full of sharp teeth. Dark, deep-set eyes peer at me for a few seconds then the face is gone. I'm on my back looking up at the cavern ceiling.

The Sandhog, Sandoval, is standing over me hand extended.

"Hey, we don't have much time," he says and helps me to my feet. "I sent Donovan and the guards on a wild goose chase but he'll be back."

"What's going on?" I say. "What do you know about the demons?"

"Demons? I told you they're gremlins. But I call them moonlings."

"The moon? I just saw the moon."

"Oh, oh," he says. "This is good. They know you're going to side with us so they showed you. That's where they're from."

I want to tell him I'm not on anyone's side but I hear Donovan barking orders.

"Out of time. Listen," Sandoval says. "You can't trust Donovan. He isn't who he says he is."

He pulls an envelope out of his work coveralls. "This will explain a lot. I brought it when I heard he got an exterminator."

Donovan storms through the plastic. I slide the envelope into my pocket.

"Don't let him hurt the moonlings," Sandoval whispers.

"Sandoval," Donovan says. "This is a restricted area. Why in god's good name aren't you on your assignment?"

"He was consulting with me," I say. "I have reason to believe your problem isn't demonic. Sandoval's observations have been… helpful."

"Is that so?" Donovan says.

"Yes," says Sandoval.

"Back to work," Donovan says. "I need those borers up and running."

"Yes boss," he says. He mouths 'thank you' to me as he exits.

"So what do you think, lad?"

"I got another reaction by touching the borer. I think we may be dealing with a poltergeist."

"Sabotage. Gremlins. Now ghosts? Can you handle this?"

"Absolutely," I say. "Ghosts are my specialty. I'll need my tools though."

It's true. Ghosts I can deal with. Except for Alexandra. Things didn't end well for her because of me. But ghosts I know. I only want out of here. I'll decide later if I'm ever coming back.

"I'd rather you take care of this now," Donovan says. "We have tools here."

"You have snake venom, syringes, and adrenaline?"

"What the hell kind of tools are that?"

"The city doesn't tell you how to drill a tunnel," I say. "They just care if you get the job done, right?"

"Yeah, right," he says. "But you better come right back, lad."

He escorts me out of the tunnel, back to the hub and into another tunnel that slopes up and ends in winding stairs that lead to another subway platform. Instead of waiting for a train he leads me into an elevator. The elevator takes us up and opens into the back room of an old bar.

"Where are we?"

"Sullivan's Pub," he says.

I know the place. It's a few blocks away from Maria Elena's.

"You sure you got this?" Donovan asks.

"Absolutely," I say. "I'll be back this time tomorrow."

"Don't let me down, lad. Great reward awaits you when you finish. You know I can give you what I want."

"You've already paid me generously," I say. "What more could I want?"

"To go to the moon, of course. Could be that everything you want is waiting for you there."

How does he have any idea what I want?

He pats me on the shoulder patronizingly.

"Don't make me sorry," he says.

I watch the elevator doors close and I exhale. Maybe that tunnel really does lead to the moon. Could it be a portal he's hiding? Maybe he's just crazy. I know he's dangerous. Question is how dangerous. The only thing I'm sure of is that I'm in way over my head.

"Didn't expect to see you back so soon," Claudia says

"I forgot my bag. Have you seen it?"

"Yeah. And Maria Elena wants to see you."

"Really? Am I in trouble?"

"Don't know. Couldn't tell you if you were."

She escorts me to the door to Maria Elena's chambers and to the front of the line of people waiting for an audience. She opens the door, nudges me in, and whispers, "Good luck."

The space feels larger than I remembered. Last time I was here was right before my old boss disappeared. He had just given me the job that went to hell and got Alexandra killed. When all the dust settled Maria Elena was running things.

Thick curtains of purple and red and shades of brown cover most of the brick walls. Maria Elena sits behind a huge wooden desk in the center of the room. The desk is the only furniture and has nothing on it except my bag of arcane tools. Not good.

"Come," she says.

She's tall and her body fits snugly in the big antique upholstered chair. She sits confidently and has every reason to; she could kick my ass without even touching the arcane. The thin lines that radiate from the sides of her eyes and her lips don't diminish her beauty. Her smooth brown skin gives no other clue of her age. I want to take this opportunity to ask her take on stories like the man who met himself but I'm in a boatload of trouble.

"You know anything about a portal to the moon underneath Midtown?" I ask.

She smiles warmly.

"Nate, I like your style," she says. "Hiding your fear with bluster. But you don't have to be afraid of me."

I want to trust her but I know I shouldn't. I hate that she's read me so accurately and so fast.

"I know you've improved," she says, "But portals?"

"Making a portal is big. Nothing like that goes without you knowing."

"Correct. And correct again," she says. "I should turn you into a frog for being so arrogant. But Claudia likes you. And you know what? Despite myself I think I might like you too. So I'll give you this small lesson, free. Sometimes big undertakings go wrong. Sometimes things don't go right the first time. And even when they do go right there are consequences. Prices. Costs. And consequences. Consequences are the heart of the nature of arcane practice."

So I was right. There really is a portal behind all of that rubble. Could it really be to the moon? I hope my amazement doesn't show.

"I took Donovan's job because he told me you turned him down. I'm sorry," I say.

"I turned Donovan down because he's not who he says he is."

"Then who is he?"

"All you need to know is he's someone I choose not to do business with," she says.

"I needed the money so I said I'd help him."

"I said don't be afraid. I've already decided to let you leave."

"Really? Just like that?"

"No. If you come back you report to me about Donovan's operation."

"If I say no?"

"Do what you think is right. But if I see you again. I expect you to report to me."

I take my bag from her desk and just like that I'm railroaded into working for her or never showing my face again. So much for keeping out of trouble.

AFTER A FITFUL sleep I change clothes and ask myself if I'm going to head back to the Hub or run for the hills. Then I remember the envelope Sandoval gave me. Inside there's an old black and white photograph. A half dozen arcane big-wigs are gathered behind two men shaking hands. I realize the men are the same. Donovan. *Both* are a much younger Donovan. Maria Elena is one of the people standing behind them.

I return to where Donovan was smoking yesterday and I run my hand along the wall like I saw him do. The door to the hidden subway platform opens. I've become a fast learner. Instead of satisfaction from figuring out Donovan's secret I feel alone. I have people I could brag to but no one who would really listen. Alexandra would have. The life we dreamed of having together might have even turned out good had I brought her to safety like I was supposed to.

I ride to the hub thinking about the two Donovan's but the face of the creature I saw in the tunnel won't leave my mind. The moon. The earth. The comet. It was trying to tell me something.

I expect Donovan to be waiting for me at the platform when I enter the hub but I see only Sandhogs at work. I grip my bag, tell myself I can do what needs to be done, and head for the collapsed tunnel. In my bag is enough poison to kill me. And enough antidote to bring me back. A few paces in someone claps me on the shoulder from behind. Sandoval.

"You're back," he says. "I knew once you knew about Donovan you wouldn't help him."

I walk with him trying to appear casual.

"What exactly is it you think I know," I whisper. "All I know is he's dangerous."

"It's okay," Sandoval says. "He's off on another wild goose chase I sent him on."

"Tell me about that photograph," I say.

"Go ahead, tell him," Donovan's voice answers.

He and six guards emerge from the nearest tunnel. The guards surround Sandoval. There is nowhere to run. They lead him away back to the hub and leave me with Donovan.

"Don't hurt him, he was trying to help," I say.

"Help who," Donovan says.

"You," I say. "But who are you, really?"

"My name is indeed Grant Donovan. This is true. Only I'm not the Grant Donovan of *this* world. I'm from the other side of that tunnel, lad."

"You said the other side is the moon."

"I spoke the truth. Yes on the other side is the moon. Just not your moon. It is the moon of another world. One not very different from this one."

"You opened a portal?"

"Wish I could do that, lad. I found it. Came through it. Now if I could only get back through just think of the possibilities…"

"So where's the real Donovan?" I ask.

"I'm the real Donovan. At least I am now. This distinction hardly matters. You're here to finish the job."

"What if I don't?"

"Let's focus on when you do instead," he says. "Finish the job and I'll let you go through to the other side. You'll find the moon to be very different than ours. But the Earth, it's the same as here in many ways but not all. Perfect for someone who's looking for a second chance."

"A second chance?"

"I know that's what you want. Yes, you can meet yourself. Like I did when I came here. Kill the "you" over there and take his place. Start new. Whatever you want."

"How do you know what I want?" I say.

"You're a man of opportunity like me. I know you. I see myself in you. Which is precisely why I chose you. Maybe the other you, in the world beyond the tunnel is different."

I hate him because he's right. A second chance *is* what I want. A chance to live in a world where Alexandra and I are together and happy. Or at least a world where I haven't failed everyone. That isn't so much to ask.

"So you're ready to finish the job?"

"I brought my tools," I say. "Just bring a couple of big guys willing to move some rock. I think I have your problem all figured out."

I open my bag and hand Donovan a syringe.

"The antidote," I say. "To what I'm about to take."

"What the hell are you doing?" he asks.

"Solving your problem. You don't have demons, you have ghosts. I'm going to stop my heart long enough to cross over and reach them."

"Finally, action," he says.

Bastard doesn't even tell me to be careful.

"You have to help. Your job is to stick me with that. Once I go down if

I don't get up in ten minutes then you stick it right in my heart."

"I hope you know what you're doing," he says.

I hope I do too, I think as I push through the plastic into the tunnel.

"WHERE ARE YOU, where are you?" I whisper.

I go straight to the borer hoping to get a reaction from the ghosts. I need to cross over just long enough to reach them. I open my bag and take out the syringe full of snake venom. My elbows go weak. My body is instinctively trying to stop me. I tap the vein on my inside elbow and inject the poison. Pain shoots up my arm. I gag and fall to the floor. The poison reaches my heart quickly. My field of vision narrows. Everything blurs and becomes transparent in places. My body is dying. I'm crossing over.

There is movement near the borer. One, two, three forms the size of ten-year-old boys are there; but they are not boys they are covered in fur. One a light colored silver. The other two a gray-white. The silver-furred one approaches me. His face is the one I saw before. Cat-like. Human-like. Something more and less than both. Long ropy braids that might be hair frame his round face. His dark eyes show concern as he pokes me with one finger of his clawed hand.

With each touch an image fills my head. The earth. The moon. A comet. He is communicating with me.

"I hear you, I hear you," I say and realize I am poking him back and not moving my mouth.

The other moonlings come. One's fur is marred with dozens of raised pink scars. All three poke me. Bump up against me. Rub their faces against mine.

"You are ghosts," I say. "But ghosts of what?"

The scarred one points to the collapsed tunnel. He grasps his claw around my wrist and then I'm seeing a double image of everything. An understanding of their language blooms in my mind. It is a combination of physical contact and shared visions. He's showing me the past. I see a shining sphere of light. It melts rock like butter and forms this tunnel. The portal. It is as Maria Elena hinted; this tunnel was created by some great arcane undertaking gone awry. The vision changes to the view of a cavern on the other side. Hundreds of moonlings are there, coming and going from the cavern's mouth which opens into a lush meadow. The trees and plants are somewhat familiar but the shades of green and bright flowers I have never seen before.

The scarred one points up. I see the earth and the moon in a field of black. A comet passes between them and tumbles away into space trailing dust and gas and ice.

"Bring our bodies," the moonling says. "Bring our bodies to the other side of the tunnel so we may go home."

I don't comprehend individual words yet I understand. I have traveled deep. I'm close to death and have to hurry.

The silver one touches me, telling me about their world. Their moon never lost its atmosphere. It never suffered the cataclysm of impacts ours did and developed into a green world side by side with this earth. They know of us. They know of other worlds. Their society is advanced, more advance than ours.

When the portal opened these three came through because it was their job to investigate. Donovan captured them. Tortured them. Experimented on them. The moonlings collapsed the tunnel to prevent Donovan from using it. But they want to go home.

The third moonling touches me and I understand what is binding them. Their bodies. Their dead bodies are here. If I bring their bodies to the other side then they will be at peace and can go. So all I have to do is get their remains through the portal and I will have…earned my reward.

I wonder if there is really a me on their world. A me who didn't make my mistakes? A me who doesn't hustle for a living? A me who is doesn't deal in the arcane?

"Yes," the silver one tells me.

"I can find your bodies. I can get you through," I say.

My body spasms. I'm out of time. I have to return.

"Help us and we will help you. We can help you find yourself on this side. If this is your desire."

"But what about Donovan?"

"Once we are through our kin will seal the tunnel. One of we three will stay behind and make sure he can never use it."

My body shudders on the cavern floor. I try to return to it but I can't. The moonlings are communicating something about destroying the hub but I'm consumed with watching my body sweating, shaking, and turning blue.

"I tried," I say to the moonlings. "I stayed too long but I tried-"

A jolt of pain rips through my chest. I cough out fluid and taste bile as I gulp stale cavern air. The moonlings fade then disappear. I hear Donovan's voice. I'm back.

"Holy hell, lad," Donovan says. "You *are* the real deal. Is it done?"

I pull the syringe out of my heart. Pain radiates from the little bloody hole.

"It's not done and it will never be done until you do exactly as I say," I say hiding the pain best I can.

"Bring the bodies here."

"What bodies?"

"Don't lie to me. Not if you ever want your project complete. The bodies of the things from the other side. Bring them to me."

"Why do you need them?"

"Why do you?" I say. "Bring them now. I've cut a deal with your 'demons'. Once I return their bodies to their home they'll go away. You'll be free to finish your tunnel."

I lie to him. It comes easy. I like how quickly he believes. Once I get the bodies through, I think it's going to be the end of his project, whatever the hell it really is he's doing here.

THE MOONLINGS ALLOW Donovan's men to clear a hole just wide enough for me to crawl through and reach the tunnel behind it. I've placed two child-sized body bags inside. Donovan hands me the third. It's covered in labels and bar codes. Inside is what remains of the scarred moonling. There is almost nothing. Only bones.

I crawl through into the hole, alternating pushing and dragging the three body bags until I reach where it opens into a perfectly round cavern with perfectly smooth walls. This space wasn't created by a borer or drill. This was where the arcane portal was. This place is nowhere. The nowhere between our earth and their moon.

Across from me is another hole. The mouth of the tunnel coming from the other side.

A clawed hand reaches from the dark. A moonling leans through the hole. Its fur is golden brown, silver on the face and hands and the ropy things that might be hair. Its build is more muscular than the three ghosts who must have died emaciated. Before me is what the three should have looked like in life. Its dark eyes do not leave me. It doesn't make a sound. No dance. No words of language. It leaps out and approaches, cautiously then grabs the body bag and bounds back to the tunnel.

"There, it's done," I say.

I've done my part. What do I do? The moonlings said they'd help. Am I going to find my way to their earth? Find myself? What is back home for me? Nothing.

A sound fills the tunnel. Some kind of horn I've never heard before blowing a long single tone. The lone, mournful note resonates in my chest.

A dim glow illuminates the narrow crawl space but I see no light source. Beyond is a cavern as large as the hub. An asymmetrical vehicle of metal and what looks like resin moves on treads into the cavern. A red point of light appears on its pointed front tip. A beam shoots from the vehicle into the tunnel from which I came. Smoke and steam from heating rock fills the cavern. Through the haze I see a mass of arms and legs; a dozen moonlings are walking away into the mouth of the tunnel holding the body bags above them. The horn-like tone sounds again. Another single mournful note.

One of the moonlings at the end of the procession halts and turn to me. I hear no words but I understand. He is asking if I am coming.

"I'm sorry," I call out.

It's not my fault. I've done nothing wrong. Certainly not to them. But I'm still sorry. It's all I can think to say. Speaking the words, I realize I tried to help Alexandra. I tried to protect her. I tried to love her. As best I could but failed on all counts. Is there a me in this world who succeeded where I did not? Maybe another world out there somewhere? Donovan said I wanted a second chance. This chance. I hate that he knew what I yearn for.

The moonling returns to the formation. The procession does not stop. No other turns to look as they walk away disappearing one by one into the smoke and mist filling the cavern.

Two of the treaded machines roll to a stop. Their turrets whir to life and rotate toward the entry tunnel. The red beams that erupt from them turn the rock around the hole white hot, illuminating the smoke. I run and dive through before my only exit is melted closed. Heat scorches me. I scramble on my hands and knees for a few paces before I dare to look back. All I see is a cascade of glowing, molten rock. Heat washes over me. I crawl away from their world, away from a place where another me might be sitting with the love of my life in a bougainvillea-covered patio by the sea without a care in the world. An ache awakens in my gut. The gnawing emptiness expands through my body, hollowing me. I search for something to tell myself to allow me to feel okay. I know I shouldn't and that this is what I need to feel. In the dark, on my hands and knees I am alone with my tears.

"Is IT DONE?" Donovan asks.

"Yeah. *Now* it's done," I say. "Your demons are gone. You can go fix the rest of your machines."

He claps me on the back.

"You did it. You really did it. But lad, you don't look so good."

I want to go home. Or somewhere, anywhere but here where I can hide away and sleep. The only bridge left to cross is to see if he really intends to let me leave now that my part is done.

"There's going to be a celebration," he says. "I've been saving a case of whiskey for this day."

"I'm going to be sick," I say. "I'm going to go."

He looks at me skeptically and I hope I don't have a fight ahead of me.

"You have my thanks, lad," Donovan says. "Remember what I said. When I open that tunnel you can come back and pass through."

Then he barks orders into his radio to bring the borers.

A gentle stab of pinpricks erupts on my shoulder. I cannot see, but I know the hand of the moonling ghost who stayed behind is touching me.

I walk as fast as I can through the hub. I should be as far from here as I can when Donovan realizes the moonling won't let his borer run. And did they say something about destroying the Hub? I stagger to the platform and onto the train. The doors close. I speed away into the darkness under the city. Clutching my knees and rocking back and forth is a small comfort but it doesn't close the hole inside me. I'm not sure what will.

AFTER A WEEK of sleep and eating chicken soup and turkey sandwiches from my corner deli I go out and buy myself a new suit and a pair of strong boots. Maria Elena is expecting me.

Claudia smiles as she escorts me ahead of the line and into Maria Elena's chambers.

"Your report?" Maria Elena asks.

She says nothing of how clean and groomed I am or how exhausted I still must look.

"I know about Donovan," I say. "I wish you would have told me."

"I wanted to see if could figure it out yourself. And if you could, what you'd choose," she says. "I asked you for your report."

The pain flares in my gut. I could have easily stayed there. On their moon. I could have reached for my second chance.

"My report, right. The tunnel. The portal. It's gone. You probably know that. Donovan's machines and the hub- I don't think they'll be causing trouble anymore."

"You did this?" she says.

"I crossed over and made a deal with the things from the other side if that's what you mean."

"I'm impressed."

"Don't be."

"Don't sell yourself short. Good help is hard to find. But there's the matter of you taking Donovan's job in the first place."

"I didn't mean to break your rule."

"Yes you did," she says. "You knew exactly what you were doing."

"What do you expect? You never give me work."

"Never? Did you ever ask yourself if you were working for me all along?"

"I'm not so sure I believe that."

"Doesn't matter if you believe," she says.

"What's that supposed to mean?"

"There's no meaning other than what we assign to things to makes us feel better. Choices. Actions. That's another story. Sit down. I'll have Claudia bring you a drink. Then we'll talk. I have another job for you."

"I'll take that drink," I say. "Not sure about the rest."

I wonder about the "me" in that other world. Is he a good man? I hope it was all worth it. I made a powerful enemy getting the two moonlings home. And here I am. Same old me. Another job in my face before me. That other me, I hope he's happy. And I hope he's nothing like I am. No matter what I do, it seems I never learn.

PALANKAR

I ASK MY brother if he is afraid, and like most people would, Steven says no. But I can tell that he is. Out of sight of land, with only the endless blue water and sky, I know he no longer wants to go down. The early morning sun is starting to get hot and I wish I wasn't in this thick wet suit. Sitting against him on the little boat's cross beam bench I think I can his feel his heart beating. His leg nervously shakes up and down, absently, like it does when he is thinking about hammering two-by-fours together and figuring out fitting joints. Our oxygen tanks clank against each other. The little motorboat speeds across the calm surface to the Palankar reef.

I tap Steven's thigh to still his leg. He's not thinking about building a house. He's seen my phone. He's thinking about Becca and Avi. They miss him desperately. He knows they are why I'm here and that I want him to call. And he has to be thinking about Dad. How could he not be?

Dad took us here, to the Palankar Reef, to Mexico, thirty years ago. I was fifteen and Steven was seventeen. It was our first family vacation, our first really fancy one, in winter like all the rich people did. Dad always took us places. He made our trips to the pet store and the beach and my whole childhood a thing of wonder. But that first trip to Mexico was something new. It was a time in our lives where the world was opening up before us and all there was ahead was possibility. I came to equate the trip with that feeling and with the time when all we knew was comfort and stability.

Dad had just landed his first big job, renovating a house for some rich family in Cedarhurst. I remember seeing a stack of cash for the first time. Mom went to the grocery store more often. Dad bought a new TV for the family room and didn't work as many jobs at night. Steven and I were told we would be going to college and that the family was going on a vacation Christmas week. Dad's customer had bartered with him so part of Dad's payment was a prime week in this guy's time-share in Cancun. Life was charmed after that. For a while. For a long while. I hoped that coming back here would be good for Steven now that he thought his life had gone to pieces. This was the only idea I had left. And the only one he would agree to.

The boat banks. The wind carries clean ocean air. It is the smell of perfect. The smell of nothing at all. Miguelito, the guy not driving the boat, doesn't look up from texting on his cell phone. Even here the world intrudes. I guess he doesn't see it that way. He's seen all *this* before. I can't imagine ever getting numb to it. The vastness. Sea and sky stretching as far as I can see. The sun sparkling on the most perfect blue. And beneath us, the great reef and the continental shelf. The giant coral wall and chasm waiting silent at the bottom.

"Beer?" Mara says from the bench behind us. She thrusts a Dos Equis at Steven.

"Really? It's seven a.m.," I say. "Don't drink that. We're going down a hundred feet, maybe more. You wanna die?"

"Gotta die sometime," she says.

Steven makes that condescending funny face at me that says he thinks she's right. I don't want to fight with him. Not here.

He has Dad's sandy brown hair and kind round face. With his receding hairline and gray stubble he could pass for Dad.

He takes the beer and swigs. "I think I'm still a little drunk and high from last night anyway."

"Come on," I say. "Don't fuck around. Lose buoyancy down there and...you're gone."

I scoot around on the bench and check Mara's buoyancy vest. I shift it into place and tighten the buckle.

"Stop, I got it," she says and puts her hand on mine. A few sun freckles spot her forehead just beneath her unruly mop of short black hair that has grown in wild.

"Your hands," she says. "You have your brother's hands."

Her breath smells of the tang of beer and last night's alcohol. A bit of pink lipstick clings to her thin lips. They purse, as she looks me in the eye. I haven't taken my hand away.

"It's fine," Steven says. "You can fuck her. I'm moving on after this anyway."

"No, you're not," she says and slaps him playfully. I can tell she's hurt.

"Not sure *the Girl* is gonna like it though," Steven says to me.

He knows I can't stand that he still calls Elle "the Girl" even after I've been living with her for six years.

He was already in Cancun, for Spring Break of all things, when I told him we were doing this. Cancun used to be so different. Now it's where a guy like him could find a girl like Mara, half his age. We had a hell of a fight on the phone and he flat out admitted that he just couldn't be a Dad anymore. His divorce had been raging on for five years. Last year, when it became clear that he was actually going to win custody of Becca and Avi, Melissa tried to kill herself and the kids. She only half succeeded. Becca and Avi bailed out of the backseat and watched as their Mother went to sleep with the motor running. I never guessed that after all that Steven would just give up on them, and on everything. But he did.

It couldn't have been easy for Dad but the life he made for us was the most precious of gifts; the true magnitude of it I didn't comprehend until I began to grow up. His arrival home from work was a daily cause for excitement. Sometimes there were tangible things too, like flares and smoke bombs from jobs around Fourth of July time. Bows and arrows made out of fishing wire and saplings from our yard. The composition book he'd draw pictures in, made up fish and underwater houses, instead of bedtime stories.

All we knew of the world was that it was full of wonder and possibility. Because of him we grew up without fear, without want, without believing in limits, and we flourished. It is something I know I am not capable of giving to Steven's children.

The boat slows. We all lurch forward. Antonio, our driver and dive master, is circling. Zeroing in on a place.

"Alright," I say.

I take the beer from Steven and hold it up.

"To Dad," I say. "And our trip, all those years ago."

"Yeah, and to how he chickened out at the last second when it was time to dive," Steven says.

I'm not sure if he means to but he cracks a smile.

"To sending his kids, yours truly and my fine brother here, down on one hell of a first dive, a decompression dive without any training," I say.

Mara swigs her beer. She looks horrified.

"Another one of his well-meant disasters," Steven says and actually laughs.

"We were lucky as hell," I say.

Steven looks relaxed as he checks his gear. I think my plan might be working. I see the brother I used to know shining through.

I hope he sees the light, that he still does have it all.

I can't just let him go. I hope that returning here, to this high point in our history, will have some significance and that I can find the key to making everything okay for him again. He doesn't think so. But he said he'd do it. Because he's moving on and wants to say goodbye. I know that doesn't mean going back to his life and back to Becca and Avi like he needs to.

The boat stops. For a second there is only the sound of lapping waves.

"Everybody get ready," Antonio says.

My phone rings.

"Check your weight belts. Double check your buoyancy vests," he continues, ignoring the ring. "And remember to watch me for signals on the way down and up for our safety stops."

I touch the phone to silence it. The call is from home. Its Becca and Avi. Steven makes a face but it's not the funny one.

"Uncle Jake? Did you find Daddy yet?" Becca asks. Her young voice sounds like its right here, not a thousand miles away.

"No, not yet, sweetie," I say. "Soon. Real soon now."

"I really hope so," she says. I hear the sounds of home and four-year-old Avi saying Daddy, Daddy and something about fireflies in the background.

Since Steven left, the kids live part of the time with me and Elle and part of the time with Mom.

"I'll call you tomorrow, Sweetness," I say. "Hopefully with good news."

"Jacob, the kids really want you to come home."

It's Elle.

"And I don't have to tell you I do too," she says.

"Soon," I say. "I just want to try one more thing-"

"It's always one more thing," she says. "It's time to stop. How long are you going to chase him for? I'm sorry, if he doesn't want to come home, he's not going to. Nothing you can do will change that."

"Listen I gotta go. We're about to dive."

"No. The accountant called again. And we have to decide what we're doing about the roof at your Mom's house-"

"I can't talk now," I say. "I love you. You'll see, I'll bring him home."

"No. You won't," Steven says. Loud enough for her to hear.

Elle hangs up. Mara sticks her finger in her mouth to mock me.

"You. Stop," Steven says to her.

"That's great," I say. "Your kids are at home crying for their father. I bring you here to honor *your* father and you bring this worthless smart-ass along."

"You can shut up, too," he says. "She's a better diver than both of us. I said I'd go on your little adventure but I didn't say I wanted to die."

"What are you doing?" I say. "Why are you doing this? Why don't you just come home?"

"You really don't know anything, do you?" he says. "Can we just dive?"

I should have never picked up the phone. The whole situation is impossible. But like Dad always said, life is dealing with impossible situations and finding our way through them.

Somewhere along the line Steven forgot this.

I DIVE FIRST. Antonio, Mara, and Steven circle above me as we descend. Their air bubbles distort in the sunlight as they float to the surface.

We sink, letting air out of our vests to control our descent, inching down, down, down. The water grows colder and then chilly as we hit the thermocline. By the time we reach our first safety stop at sixty feet the sun is another world away. Stopping on the way down is to get acclimated, but going up it is a matter of life or death. Go up too fast and nitrogen bubbles can form in the blood. Which will kill you. Antonio looks at his big dive watch, monitoring the time before we can proceed. On our trip with Dad, Steven and I did this but we didn't understand. We had no training. We went through the motions of decompression dive safety and made it through by sheer blind luck. It wasn't until years later when I took my first dive course did I realize what we had done and the risks we had taken.

I see the top of the reef twenty feet beneath us; it's teeming with life. A sea turtle rises from the coral and glides past on its way to the surface. Visibility is perfect in all directions. In the distance, a giant ray sails through the water like a bat through air. We float, motionless. Everyone's buoyancy looks good. Mara points at the ray for Steven.

Antonio signals. We let air out of our vests and sink. And we descend into a giant school of fish. Tens of thousands of silver bodies surround us, silver scales glinting in the sunlight that has managed to reach here. We emerge from the school at the side of a wall of coral taller than a skyscraper.

The Palankar reef. A living megalith that goes on as far as I can see. To my right there is only coral. To my left, the abyss. The continental shelf. A few long rays of light struggle down the slope through water every gradient of blue. They fail to penetrate to the dark violet layer, the last color before the black. The chasm is unfathomable. Losing buoyancy here means being swallowed and lost forever. I realize I'm sucking air too fast and try to calm myself.

I breathe deep and slow and let myself drift. The current is strong. It carries us along the wall, immersing us in the activity going on all around us. A pink and blue and green parrotfish nips at a coral head then disappears into a small cave. It emerges a second later chased by a green moray snapping its jaws. All the caves are occupied. Lobster. Scorpion fish. Damsels and angels and butterfly fish of every color.

Mara points up. A reef shark noses around the coral above us. I'm not afraid- of it. It is the abyss that worries me. I don't look. I focus on the wall. It is everything I remembered. Coral. Fish. Big robust morays half out of their caves floating in the current like ribbons. It is magic.

The current has carried Mara further away than I'd like. I can still see Antonio but he is also too far away for comfort. I kick with my fins and swim toward them.

Out of the corner of my eye I see Steven below me. It looks like he is messing with his vest. I kick against the current to halt myself and look. He unbuckles the snap securing his tank. It floats above his head, tethered to him by only his airline. A tendril of blood unfurls from his hand. Why the hell is he taking off his gear? A green moray snakes out of a cave in front of him. It is giant. Ten feet long. Maybe more. Is it growing? It snaps its jaws and I see its face is all wrong. It's not a fish. It is something horrible. It loses its eel shape and becomes a mess of intestines and limbs undulating in the current before Steven. I roll and kick towards him. I see two mirror images of my brother. One with gear and a wet suit. One naked. Whatever *it* is it has taken Steven's shape. Naked-Steven unhooks Wetsuit-Steven's gear and puts it on. He kicks and rises out of view.

My Steven, my brother is floating there without gear, without air. I kick harder to reach him. He sinks.

I swim as hard as I can. I realize I'm not thinking about an emergency ascent and buddy breathing like I know I should be. My mind drifts to thoughts of taking off my gear and joining him. He is a perfect form framed in dark blue. I envision myself next to him. Sinking with him. Nearing the black until we are surrounded by it. Until we are one with it. I pull off my mask. The purples and blues blur with the darkness. Everything Steven has done makes sense now. I get it. I reach for him. I want to feel his hand in mine.

I take my left glove off. My right one sticks as I try to peel it. I let air out of my buoyancy vest and slowly sink. I slip my feet out of my fins.

"I'm coming," I yell. My regulator is out. My mouth fills with water.

Something grabs me around my waist. I feel my weight belt drop. My buoyancy vest fills with air. Instead of sinking, I am rising. My ears pop. I hear hissing air. All the colors fade to gray then there is only quiet and darkness.

THE CLINIC'S TREATMENT room is large, larger than I imagined. Everything appears state-of-the-art and is very new and clean. Equipment on carts and rollers are up against every inch of wall space. In the center of the room is the hyperbolic chamber. It is oval like an aspirin capsule but twenty feet long and metal and painted pale green. Wires and tubes run to and from the pumps and machines surrounding it.

Elle is doing the paper work to sign me out. I walk over and touch the chamber that saved my life before I go.

"Good luck to you," the doctor says. "Rest. Stay out of the water and-"

He goes on about safety. And I thank him, but I'm not really listening. I was unconscious for two days. Mara came but Steven wasn't with her. Steven didn't come.

In my mind's eye I see him, receding into the depths and becoming insubstantial like a ghost.

Elle pushes through the swinging doors and collects me, a tote bag full of stuff and paperwork in her hands.

There's more gray in her long, auburn hair. I know taking care of the kids and the business with me are the reasons for the lines around her mouth and her eyes but there is no way to tell her that these things only make her more beautiful.

I ask the doctor about Steven again but he has no information.

Elle ushers me inside a shiny rental car and we head off.

At the first traffic light she kisses my face and takes my hand and squeezes it.

"I was so worried about you," she says.

"I'm worried about Steven," I say.

She didn't want to hear that.

"You need to rest," she says. "Let's get you back and ready to go home."

Our hotel is off the main strip and near the airport. We eat dinner in the room. An American crime drama is on the TV as we eat.

"The clinic didn't treat my brother," I say. "I don't get it. If he was okay, why didn't he come to check on me?"

"His flavor-of-the week brought you in," Elle says. "She reported the accident. Sounds like she saved your life. Saved both of your lives."

"The accident report says when we got back to shore, he took off. That's not like him."

"Don't you get it? Nothing he's done for the last year is like him. Maybe now you'll see why you've been wasting your time chasing after him."

"He's my brother. I have to know he's okay."

"Jake, he's okay. The question is, are you? Are you going to let him drag you down with him? He's doing what he wants to do. What he thinks he has to do, or whatever. You don't like it. I don't like it. But we can't change it. You can't kill yourself trying to rescue him, or whatever it is you're doing. We're lucky that girl of his had a good head on her shoulders and took care of you."

"Two days," I say. "I can't believe I was out for two days."

"You took in a lot of water. And you had nitrogen bubbles in your blood. You're lucky to be alive. Thank god you were in Cancun and not the middle of nowhere."

"It's not right, Elle. Steven was in trouble. I saw-"

"You saw a grown man- correction, two grown men get their reckless asses saved by a young girl. That's what you saw."

"Something's wrong," I say.

"You'll feel better when you are home, in your own bed," she says. "Our flight to Kennedy is first thing in the morning."

I get into bed. Elle organizes her carry-on bag.

"The kids?" I ask.

"Don't worry about them right now. They're going to be all right. You know we have our work cut out for us but everything's going to be all right."

"My Dad used to say that a lot," I say.

"I know."

"He used to say we make lessons out of things. Out of past relationships and past situations even if they aren't actually there."

"There?" she asks. "There, where?"

"You know. Out there, in the world. Reality. We make meaning out of things even if it isn't reality."

"I like that. Your Dad knew there's only what we choose."

"Life is choices. He said that a lot, too."

"Because it's true," she says.

She turns out the light and we say goodnight. I can't sleep. I think of Mara inspecting my hands. The flecks of pink on her lips.

Letting Steven go is Elle's choice. Not mine. When I am sure she is sleeping I take the car keys.

THE ACCIDENT REPORT contained Mara's address, a low-rise apartment building just off the tourist drag. She isn't there when I arrive. My gringo Spanish skills and some cash get me the location of where she tends bar. One of Steven's haunts, I presume.

The bar is on the bay side of downtown on the shore. The covered space is open air, with side tarps for when it rains. Inane pop music from the disco across the street bleeds into the old school reggae playing. A few kids and people my age are moving on the dance floor. Not bad for this time on a Monday night considering it isn't a Spring Break kind of place. It reminds me of one of the bars of the Cancun I used to know.

Mara is behind the bar, wearing a tight, white tube-top and shorts. Her arms are inked, partially completed sleeves that I couldn't see when she was in her wet suit.

"Really, you?" Mara says when she sees me approaching.

I sit on the barstool in front of her. She laughs and pours two shots of tequila.

"So, where is he?" I say.

"Where is who?" she says.

"Come on," I say.

"Oh, you mean your idiot brother," she says. "I thought you heard on the boat. He's moved on."

"Please don't mess with me," I say. "This is important. You saw what I saw. Something happened to him."

She downs her shot.

"You know, you're an asshole. A reckless asshole," she says.

"I saw him sink," I say. "It was like I saw his soul. His soul was sinking into the abyss and then this thing... this monster did something to him. I saw it. You did too, right? He needs us. He needs our help."

"Uh, right! Wow...you know what I saw? I saw you nitro narc out on me. I saw your precious Steven get bit by a fucking massive eel that almost sliced his finger off. He needed to do an emergency ascent and you narced out on him. I had to rescue both of you. Then the selfish prick took off, leaving me to drag your sorry fat ass to the clinic. Actually, it's a good thing you're here because you owe me for the taxi ride."

I drink my shot. I can't keep it down and spray half of it on the bar.

"Look at you," she says. "I should kick your ass but you're already such a mess. So where is he? Good fucking question."

"I think you know," I say.

"Yeah, I do know. It's a place called Gonesville. He's gone."

"Gone where?"

"You're a piece of work. You can't help him. You can't follow."

She pours another pair of shots and pushes one to me. I take her hand in mine.

Her ink is Japanese stuff, waves and fish on one arm, tropical fish and sea stars on the other. Nice, but incomplete. Only outlines. The centerpiece of each sleeve is a heart. Each with a name. Kids. They have to be her kids. And then I understand what Steven saw in her. She's running away from something too. I don't know what but she's running just like him.

"How old?" I ask. "The names. Your kids, right?"

Her hands are shaking. I don't let go.

"I know you care about him," I say. "You know he has two kids also. You have to. Come on, tell me. Follow where?"

"You really want to know?" she says. "You really fucking want to know? You asked for it. Come on, then."

I do want to know. Is that thing inside him? Controlling him?

She wipes her eyes, smearing mascara all over her face.

"I've been looking for him too," she says.

I follow her behind the bar, through the kitchen to the lot in the back. She leads me to a small motorcycle, an old 125.

"Get on, let's go," she says.

I get on the back and put my arms around her. She smells of the bar and something that reminds me of the sea. We speed off. The hotels and restaurants and clubs of the strip are a blur. After a few minutes we are on the open road. Going south. Down the coast. Miles and miles of nothing but tiny beach towns and luxury resorts where thirty years ago there was nothing. After twenty minutes the lights of Playa Del Carmen break the dark. When I knew it, Playa was just a ferry stop. Now it is this bustling tourist city.

Mara turns onto one of the long private roads. After a mile the road ends at the lobby of a fancy resort. Mara stops next to a granite sculpture, a huge rectangular slab, lit by spotlights. It reminds me of the reef.

The din of music and people grows as we walk through the lobby and out the other side to the beach, to the outdoor bar. Hundreds of well-dressed adults are mingling on a wooden deck above the sand. The bouncer stops us, then recognizes Mara.

"Antoli," she says. They exchange kisses on the cheek and he lets us pass. Black-clad wait staff maneuver through the crowd with drinks that are yellow and glowing. At the far end of the platform is a small bar five bar stools across. Only one is occupied. A woman sits facing the crowd watching us approach. Her side-slit black palazzo pants reveal one of her long legs. Her skin has that uniform sun kissed bronze only achieved by those with nothing but time to lounge. She belongs in a big city fashion show not at a beach bar. Yet no one is pestering her with attention. There are no barriers or velvet ropes enforcing the square of vacant space surrounding her No one is even looking at her. She is a clown fish but I don't see the anemone, yet I know one is present.

Mara stops five feet away from her just outside the vacant zone.

"Really, you?" the woman says, with the same cadence as Mara said to me earlier.

Her hair is short like Mara's only immaculately styled. I can tell Mara hates her. Hates her yet still wants to be her.

"Katerina, I- we need to see Steven," Mara says.

"You may come," Katerina says and motions us over with a curl of her hand.

She runs her hand along Mara's cheek, down to her chin, like an aunt would do to a child, while eyes like a perverted uncle size her up.

"Didn't expect to see you back so soon," Katerina says. "Change your mind?"

"Where is he?" Mara asks.

"You miss him," Katerina says.

There are guards in the crowd, black-clad men standing motionless, rifles slung around their shoulders. The partygoers flow around them. Leave it to Steven to graduate from a bartender to a drug dealer's girl. He really does want to die.

"Please. Katerina, where is he?" Mara asks.

She needs him. I don't know what tragedies befell her or what her story is, but she still thinks Steven is her answer.

"He's moved on already," Katerina says.

"No-" Mara gasps.

"Oh, no, no, no sweet girl. Not like that," Katerina says. "He's alive and well. But life is short. He's already left me for…other affections. He's free to do as he pleases. That's what love is, no? But he hasn't gone far. Not yet. I see you have a new friend too."

"I'm Steven's brother."

"I thought so," she says.

She pushes her black bangs out of her eye; their tips are parrot fish pink, like her lips, like her fingernails.

"I like the way you look at me, Steven's brother," she says.

"Please. I think he is sick," I say. "Will you please just take us to him?"

"I will…" she says. "For a price."

Mara and I look at each other. I don't have much money with me.

"Don't look so worried, brother. The price is only a kiss."

She reaches for Mara's face again. Mara jerks away.

"No? Still no?" Katerina says. "Tell me when then. Antoli knows you are always welcome. But you misunderstand. I meant you, Steven's brother."

She touches my face with her slender hand. I haven't been touched like that since the old days. I lean in to her. She pushes me away.

"Oh, no," she says. "You look like your brother but you're much too... soft. The kiss is for you two."

"Enough," Mara says. "We're out of here."

I grab her hands. "Wait," I say. "Please."

"Really?" she says.

"Please. For his kids," I say.

"How dare you?" she says. "You're a monster. Just like him."

She grabs my head. And suddenly her lips are on mine. Kissing her is knowing the abyss. Knowing what Steven knows. I feel myself sinking. I see how easy it is to get lost-

She pulls away. Only the briefest of seconds has passed.

"There. Hope you're happy now," she says and storms into the crowd.

I know I will never see her again. I'll never see how her tattoos get completed. I'll never know how she got so broken. And it is okay. I don't want Avi or Becca to grow up incomplete like her.

"Don't you just adore her?" Katerina says. "Your kiss was... not what I expected. But-"

"But a deal's a deal," I say.

"Yes, it is," she says. "About your brother. Come. He hasn't gone far."

She stands and takes me by the hand. She is taller than I thought. Her pants reveal her legs; on her left thigh is an arc of raised pink flesh, the scar of a terrible shark-bite. The guards in the crowd are looking to her. She signals with a curl of her hand. She is not the clownfish. She is the anemone. I was wrong about her. Like I was wrong about Mara. What else have I been wrong about?

She leads me along the beach. One of the gunmen follows. There is a hundred yards of nothing until the next property, where the skeletal frame of a hotel looms in the dark. Partially constructed cabanas dot the beach. Steven's work. I'd know it anywhere.

A dock extends into the water, a lone speedboat tethered to its wooden poles. Steven is standing there, at the far edge, a perfect form framed by the black of the sky and the sea.

"See, I said he hasn't gone far, darling," Katerina says. "And no, he's not sick but oh, what a strange creature he is. He's free to go. Yet here he is. I don't know why he doesn't just go. I think he's been waiting…for you."

"JACOB? WHAT THE hell are you doing here?" Steven says.

"You're okay," I say. "Why didn't you come?"

"Let's not fight again. I told you on the phone. I'm not coming home."

"You don't remember? We had an accident. We were diving."

"Oh shit. You're here for that dive thing I said I'd do for Dad."

Steven twitches and coughs. His right arm flails like he is having a seizure.

I grab him and stop him from falling into the water.

He thrusts his face close to mine, and says something incomprehensible. His words sound like gargles.

"I told you, he is so wonderfully strange," Katerina says.

Steven trips on a fishing pole and falls sending fishing gear everywhere. I help him sit on the edge of the dock. He stops twitching. He looks surprised to see Katerina and I fawning over him.

"Katerina, this is my brother Jacob," he says.

"I know, darling," she says.

"You do? Wait. How?"

"I will get drinks. You explain," Katerina says.

I sit next to him.

"What's going on here," he says

His leg is shaking. No way he is thinking about building houses now.

I'm worried he might convulse again.

I take his hand. It is the same hand I've always known. The same scars. Why would Mara think it was like mine?

His other hand is carving something on the dock with a fishhook.

Get me drunk, he has carved.

"Am I speaking to the monster?" I ask.

"Easy," Steven says. "I told you I don't want to fight."

As he speaks, he is carving something with his hand.

"If you came to lecture me, you might as well leave," he says.

Yes, he has carved. *Steven can't know.*

Katerina returns with a carton from the boat and sits in between us.

"I'm so sick of tequila, aren't you?" she says.

She opens the carton with a fishing knife. Inside are bottles of European alcohol I have never seen before. Their labels are in languages I do not recognize.

"Drink," she says and gives each of us a bottle.

The stuff in mine is green and tastes like licorice and dirt. They don't seem to mind.

"This dive you have planned," Steven says. "It isn't going to go like before. Like one of Dad's disasters."

"Hey! To Dad," I say.

"To Dad," he says. "I miss that big chicken."

We laugh. Katerina takes a deep slug from her bottle and I think she is going to wind up sick.

"It was worth it. The wall. The colors. The rift," I say.

"I hated the way the current just took us. The way my tank clanked against the wall."

"Yeah. I remember you holding on to my fins," I say.

"You ran out of air first. I was so scared when they sent you up."

"You?" I say. "I was treading water at the surface all alone. I know it couldn't have been more than ten minutes until the boat spotted me, but it felt like forever."

We drink with no more mention of the dive. Katerina has fallen asleep against the boat. One of the gunmen comes, rolls her on her side, removes the bottle from her hand, then leaves us be.

When Steven has made a solid dent in his bottle I gather the courage and ask, "Am I talking to the monster?"

"I'm not the monster, you are," he says.

I think for a few seconds.

"Why would you say that," I say. "I'm trying to help him."

"And I'm helping him with what he wants," he says.

"You don't know what he wants," I say. "He has a job. A home. Children to take care of."

"That's what you want for him. He wants to feel again. He wants to be free."

"He is free," I say. "He has people who love him."

"A cage isn't love. Love him. Love him like he loves you. He wants you to be free. With him. He knows you want to."

"I don't want any of this."

I am slow to say the words. They were heavier than I expected.

He makes that smug face I can't stand and walks to the boat.

"I'm leaving soon," he says. "I want you to come."

"Where, to the reef? To drown?"

"No," he says. "I want Steven to live. He is alive now. We belong together."

"How can I believe you?"

"I guess you can't."

He passes me his bottle.

"He's right," Katerina says in a stupor, eyes closed. "No cages. Just drink."

I lean on the boat next to Steven. We watch color return to the sky and listen to Katerina snore. A few partygoers from next door wander past and are turned around by the guard. The edge of the sun lifts above the horizon. Fish breach the water. Something beneath is chasing them.

I take out my phone. There is an endless amount of missed calls. Elle. Home.

I put it on speaker and call the kids.

"Shhhh don't wake Grandma," I say.

"Uncle Jake, where are you? Are you home yet?"

The tinny sound of Becca's voice carries in the quiet. Katerina stirs. The gunman looks for the source of the sound.

"Not yet, sweetie," I say.

"Are you with Dad? Can I talk to him?"

I hold up the phone to Steven for his answer. He shakes his head, no.

"No, sweetie, but everything is going to be alright," I say.

I hang up.

"I'm sick of letting them down," I say.

"You're not," Steven says.

Elle's face appears on the screen. I want to throw the phone. In my mind's eye I see it floating at the surface before disappearing.

Not now, Elle, I think. I can do this. I can make this right for all of us.

The fish have stopped jumping. Everything is too still. Too quiet. Any second now I expect something huge to rise from the deep.

Steven starts the boat.

"Coming?" he asks.

"Where," I say.

"South, somewhere south, I guess."

"To the reef? To the abyss?"

"No. I want to live," he says.

I believe him. I have to. I want to live too, so this is where our paths must part. Where he's heading, I don't know. It no longer matters.

SOGNI DEL MUNDO SOTTERANEO
(UNDERWORLD DREAMS)

ONDE

Waves

KIM, JULIANA, AND Theron James linger at the edge of the dance floor, the spot of beach under the wall-less thatched roof just outside the tree-line the surfers call the disco. A too-chipper, too-bouncy pop song from back home is playing but I don't care- the surfers are already dancing- the stars are out, the humidity has lessened a bit and the tropical night, cooled by the waves, is just right. Antonia is half a world away in New York, almost through her summer internship as a Federal Defender, but we'll be together again soon enough. And soon enough we'll get to enjoy nights like this, here, back home, or anywhere in the world we please. Life is long and ours together is only starting. There were so many paths our life could have taken, I thank my lucky stars that ours came together the way they did.

Juliana twirls a strand of her long, dark hair and unknowingly sways with the beat along with Theron James. Kim's a foot or two behind them stealing looks, as usual; all three of them hesitant to jump on in. She's a full head taller than Julianna and maybe has an inch on Theron James when she stands up straight. Even in cut off shorts and old tees we all stand out as definitely-not-surfers, but no one cares. They're as glad as I am to be free of Panama City's sweltering classrooms and here outside in the salt-air, despite the 6AM departure time for tomorrow's mandatory excursion.

A barefoot guy with a guitar slung over his back angles through my field of vision. I step over to him and gently reach for his shoulder.

"Hey. Excuse me, man," I say. "Was wondering if you have a sec. Can you show me where we are on this map?"

He's older than I thought. His boyish face a landscape of healed-over scars.

"Where you coming from," he says, a bit too slowly. "Where do you think you are?"

I feel like I anchored him out of a daydream.

"We walked from where the bus let us off," I say. "My friend was aiming for a place called *Il Pesce Danzante* but I don't think we're there, are we?"

"No, you're not. Never heard of it. But you could have found worse places."

He takes my map. The lines representing the small roads all end in unlabeled nooks and contours of the shoreline.

"Okay, I think we're about here," the guy says.

He folds the map. Then folds it again.

"So that gets you here," he mutters to himself.

He turns the map around and folds it once more.

"Then to here," he says, pleased with himself. "Okay here, just go here."

He points to a spot on the map and hands it back as I look.

"You sure," I ask. "We gotta head back real early I don't want to get us lost."

"Nothing's lost if you have the waves. And you do have waves."

"At least tonight we do."

"Why you gotta get back so fast?"

"School waits for no one."

"You're here for school? Sorry for you dude. I wouldn't give up this for anything."

A hundred yards off shore six-foot waves roll in- neat orderly sets, breaking before a good fifty yards of shallows. The beach is larger, exponentially wider than any back home, tons of open space stretching to the edge of the jungle; a tangle of tall, crowded palms, their hundreds of shapes a unified wall looming in the almost dark.

Before he wanders off I ask him if I can see his guitar. He hands it over. I crouch with it on my knee and strum out the chunky, opening power-chords of Van Halen's Panama.

Juliana turns around and throws one of her disapproving looks my way.

No one else reacts. I've had the song in my head all summer. Is everyone too young or just blissfully far away from TV and radio? The guy doesn't even say anything. He's just kind of Zen, not even indifferent. Did I really expect him to take back saying "sorry for you?" because I can play guitar?

I pass his guitar back with thanks then shuffle through the sand to join Kim standing behind Theron James and Juliana.

A blond girl in a bikini mindlessly pushes past us to the dance floor. She drapes her arms around a shirtless guy in board shorts who is sort of dancing. Lips on lips, they slowly spin- out of sync with the peppy reggae of the syrupy tune. Theron James watches the public display of affection awe-struck with a hint of what I read as I-shouldn't-have-come-along-we-have-school-tomorrow nerves on his face. He has no clue that Kim's sizing him up like he's one of her boy-toys from her modeling days. Despite his romance novel cover good-looks he's a preacher's son and I bet staying out late with us on this little jaunt is likely up there as one of the most rebellious things he's ever done. There's something in the sea and moss and smoke-tinged air I can't put my finger on giving me the feeling it's a hell of a night to be alive and with these young Americans far away from home with nothing but time on their hands.

Kim's left her little make-up bag behind but I can sense her thinking about it self-consciously even though any girl would kill to have her looks. On the plane down, both of us straight from work still in our conservative-cut dark blue suits, she was messing with that bag so much I figured minding her appearance was the only thing keeping herself together. Pegged her as a law and order type even before we introduced ourselves and started talking. Never found out what had her so undone- above and beyond the one-two punch of law school and her internship with the District Attorney's office in Hartford, but when we went out for 'just one drink' after landing I sensed the weight of it in the way she raged hard, way too hard for after a flight and long day. *Way* too hard for conservative Panama City. We finally called it quits around 2 AM only to find her room arrangements at the *Casita Libelula,* where the class had been instructed to meet Professor Armstrong in the morning, were all fucked up. Too late to do anything about it I gave her my room. I slept outside slouched up against the door. She didn't need protecting, she needed the sleep only a night in a safe space, alone, could bring and I was able to give her that much. Ever since I've been the go-to "safe guy" escort for extra-curricular jaunts.

Kim turns to me and with just a look I know she's asking "what's up where were you?" Julianna's noticed and is looking at me for my answer. Theron James is situationally clueless, as usual. He doesn't even hear me say "everything's cool."

Our common desire to drink in every second of our summer in Panama sent us scrambling when Kim rallied us to hurry from our last class of the week to make it onto the final bus out of the city for the night. We trusted that she would come through on her promise to have us back, on-time. A few weeks of kept promises, hard travel in the heat and rain and mud with the bugs and strange faces built an unexpected closeness. And with everyone hooking up like high schoolers she's the only one who acknowledges my commitment to Antonia.

Two surfer girls sidle up to Theron James and me. The tall one beckons us to join them on the dance floor with a come-hither curl of her finger.

"Sorry, ladies," Kim says throwing her arm around Theron James. "This one's mine."

She wants his virginity so badly even I can taste it. His alter-boy upbringing hasn't faltered but that doesn't stop her from trying and trying.

DANIEL BRAUM

Unfazed by Kim's rebuff the two girls each take one of my hands in theirs.

I pull away harder than I mean to. Julianna scoffs. The girls amble on to the dance floor without me, their alcohol-buzzed gait and sun-kissed smiles not betraying a care.

"What's the matter two's not your thing?" Kim says.

"Being happily engaged's my thing. But if I wasn't, for the record, no."

Theron James stands stiff despite Kim's hand migrating to his bicep.

"You must really love her," she says.

"I do."

"Look around, we're in fucking paradise. She'll never find out. Do you actually think she'd ever find out?"

"Doesn't matter," I say.

"Doesn't matter?" Juliana says, mocking me. "Enough with the judging already. Some of us just want to have fun."

She grabs Theron James' hand and leads him into the dancing.

"Don't mind her," Kim says. "If she were engaged like you she wouldn't be fun enough to be out here. So, cheers to you."

Waves crash. The smell of grilled sea food from one of the cooking fires illuminating the beach carries on the air.

"Cheers are to you," I say. "After four consecutive days of nothing but the finer points of the gold currency standard and filling in for Professor A, this beats just flopping down and passing out."

"That's what you think?"

I tilt my head inquisitively.

"You're not stupid, so don't be stupid," she says.

"What?"

"You're missing it."

"Missing what?"

"Everything," she says.

A young guy walks by balancing a tray loaded with sea food. Kim deftly snags a piece of blackened fish and bites a small corner.

"I like you. You know that I like you so I'm going to spell it out."

The air is saturated with the sound of waves on sand, animated voices, and in the spaces between- the ever-present whir and hum and buzz of the jungle reaching into the night.

"People like us, people our age, we go to school, meet someone, get married and a whole lot of steps down the line, we get divorced or worse," she says. "Don't wake up twenty years later to find yourself regretting what you could have done."

"Hey, but you're twenty-fi-"

"Don't interrupt me. Listen for a second."

"Okay. Listening."

"Good. You remember that thing you used to ask your friends when you were young, what would you do if you were on a desert island and could do something your spouse would never find out?"

"Sort of. We boys didn't-"

"Of course you did. Cut the shit. What would you do if you were on a desert island, without your wife or girlfriend or *what*-ever. *And* the most *beautiful* woman, wants to sleep with you and you are guaranteed not to get caught, would you?"

"There's no such thing. Never going to happen."

"Not the point. Just answer. What if there was? Remember you're guaranteed not to get caught."

"Honestly, I wouldn't want to."

"You. Are. Such. A *liar*." She pinches my arm. "You really wouldn't?"

"I love Antonia."

"Not the point. In this scenario she'd never, ever know."

"But I'd know. We have our whole life ahead of us."

"Look. Around. You. This isn't *exactly* the desert island scenario but might be as close as we ever get."

I've given up on trying to convince her that loving someone is more than just something you decide.

"Hey, I'm not judging," I say. "And don't worry I won't tell your fiancé."

She doesn't respond but I can tell her thoughts are spinning. She nibbles her piece of fish and stares off at the surfers gauging the swell at the shore. Then she turns and looks me in the eye.

"Listen, I want one thing to be clear. You're never going to meet my fiancé. And I'm never going to meet yours. When this trip is done no matter what we say or how much we promise we're going to stay in touch the reality is we're never going to see each other again. No offense, right?"

"Uh, yeah, of course not, no offense."

The words sting.

"Good," she says. "We're good, right? Let's go."

She takes me by the hand and leads me the few steps to under the thatch roof- her gait mocking the two surfer girls.

She taps Juliana on the shoulder and says "I'm dancing with your date."

She gets between them and moves right up against Theron James.

"Hel-lo Tee Jay, dah-ling," she says.

He turns to me, a deer in headlights expression on his face.

"It's just dancing," I say.

Juliana sneers but before she can say something snarky the two surfer girls shuffle over and match step with us. For a second I think Juliana's furious but then she breaks out in laughter. Kim has her eyes closed and is grinding against Theron James; instead of looking away I'm staring past them full of thoughts about what it was that had her so undone on the flight down. I know how law offices are, women out-numbered twenty to one. I wonder what Antonia is doing right now and how it's going for her and tell myself not to worry. I'm aware of the motion of the girl dancing with me but my attention is on the beach. The sets aren't as neat and easy as I first thought. Past the shore, in the surf someone yells. People are out there. In the dark. Riding waves. On their boards, half-blind trying to time the break.

☩

Buio

Darkness

We hit the road out of town before dawn. Turns out there's no bus departing early enough to get us back on time, only a deserted sign on the side of the road that says "bus stop." I wave down the only vehicle that passes, an old pick up, and get us a ride to Panama City in the back along with the dozens of caged chickens, much to Julianna's dismay.

There's no time to shower, no time to steal a moment to call Antonia, barely enough time to grab our things and run to *Casa Libelia.*

MONDAY, AFTER CLASS the Professor took me aside and asked me to cover the class because he had to "take off for a day or two."

"Just review the gold standard and the International Monetary Fund, you can do it with your eyes closed. It's going to be big on the final," he said.

"What's so important that you have to bail on a class?"

"They're going to try and blow up a coral reef to make another deep-water port for cruise ships. There's a protest and a court case. I can help. I'll be back and at the bus at 6 am Friday."

Julianna interrupted us to say she just had to tell us he was three times the size and three times as muscular as any other professor. What's important is that I've got a hundred times the heart, he replied without missing a beat. We helped him carry his bag to the old, gray Russian made Fiat he used to travel around. Not because he needed our help but because we wanted to hang around him. Being so far away from home being around the Professor made me feel safe. The conversation didn't feel safe at all.

KIM AND I are the last to arrive at the hotel. The entire class, all nineteen of them, are already lined up outside the mini-bus with their packs. Professor Armstrong is on the bus steps, his body blocking the egress as he talks to our driver with uncharacteristic seriousness. I notice a cast on his wrist but he's back, just like he said he would be.

Theron James is standing out of his line of sight, just off the back bumper feeding bread from a paper bag to a family of grey-furred raccoon-like creatures.

"Looks like you're making friends with the coati," I say as I come up to him.

One of the young coati rears on its hind legs and paws at Theron James' leg.

"Can I ask you something," he asks sullenly, ignoring the animal's cute attempts for the food.

"Sure," I say.

"What do you think of the name, TJ?"

"Um, its good. But I think what matters though is that *you* like it."

"It makes me think of my Uncle Constantine. We all called him Tino, *he* used to call me TJ. My Dad hated when he did. He was a weird, grown up I barely ever saw but Uncle Tino always seemed to... know me. Even though he's from Mom's side of the family. From somewhere out in Italy. When I was a kid I used to have these fits sometimes. On his visits Uncle Tino always found a way to take me aside to let me know he knew what I was going through."

The little coati secures a hold on the bag and rips the bottom, spilling crusts and breadcrumbs. All the others rush over.

"Dad told me I wasn't praying hard enough and if I only would pray, all would be fine," Theron James says without reacting to the frenzy. "I can still hear Uncle Tino's scratchy, accented voice saying don't worry they're only underworld dreams, TJ they can't hurt you."

I'm about to ask him about the fits when Professor Armstrong leans off the bus and announces it is time to board. Theron James and I stand there watching the coati tear into the bread.

"You know what, just call me TJ," he says. "Let's go."

We watch the animals a few seconds longer then walk together to the end of the line and join the class.

"Figures, you're here last," Julianna says, projecting to ensure Professor Armstrong hears.

If he's heard he doesn't show it. I follow Julianna and Kim on, wish Professor Armstrong a good morning as I pass, and sit next to Kim in the front seat.

"Nuh, uh," she says and gestures to Julianna sitting across the aisle. "Saving it. Sit with her."

"That's a no," Juliana says.

She gets up and walks to the back.

"Wow," Kim says. "I can't believe I didn't see it till now."

Professor Armstrong is pretending he isn't listening but his grin betrays him.

"Does she ever have a crush on you."

"No. *Stop*," I say. "She has a problem with everything I do."

"Exactly," Kim says. "*Aaand*, everyone is hooking up with everyone."

"That doesn't mean you're right."

"Right or wrong I think you should shut her up the way she wants you to. I fail to see the harm."

I let our classmates file past before speaking.

"Holy shit that's harsh. I know we got no sleep but come on, really?"

"Yeah, we're running on no sleep. Sorry," she says. "That doesn't change anything though."

"Change what?"

She leans into me.

"That somewhere out there, there's another you," she whispers.

"Another me? As in, you're not going to believe it, but I met this guy that looked just like you? I used to get that all the time."

"No, not like that. More like…"

I think she's going to tell me about what had her so undone on the plane.

"…It's like, I know out there, there's another me; a me but not me.

Instead of being here, having this summer, she's back home sitting on her hands. Maybe after everything she's been through one day she's decided not to live. No. Worse Maybe that's the way she's decided to live…"

"Hey. You can talk to me-"

"Nothing to talk about. I'm not her. I'm here. I'm right here. I'm not her because I know everything ends, which might be the only thing I know for sure. So I think about all the things I missed out on. Do you? Do you ever think about all the wrong choices you're stuck with?"

"I think it's a hell of a thing to think of in the morning. You might need some coffee more than I do."

"Might? Coffee, yes please. You're right I need coffee, but I'm not wrong. There's one way to make sure *you're not that guy…*"

She looks at me as if some understanding has passed. That she's just benevolently conveyed great wisdom.

Theron James clomps up the metal steps. Kim's face lights up.

"Hey, Tee Jay! This seats' saved for you. Get up, you."

I hop over into the seat across the aisle. Outside there's a guttural squeal, a sound I didn't think the coati capable of. Professor Armstrong closes the door behind TJ and sits next to me.

"Late night studying the gold standard," he asks with a hint of humor in his voice. "I heard the class loved you."

I answer him by rolling my eyes with a grunt of a laugh.

I tap my wrist. "How's that feeling? You know, I didn't hear anything about a deep-water port."

The professor winks. "You lose some, but you win others."

He stands, stretches, wishes everyone a good morning and launches into an overview of our day.

"…we'll pick up Mister Luis Rivera resident of the El Chorillo neighborhood who has agreed to be our guide through the area today. He lived through the 1989 Invasion…"

The bus comes to life with vibration.

I'm wondering where I'll be able to find a phone next.

"...we'll see the damage to the neighborhood first-hand. In the afternoon we'll split into small groups and official guides courtesy of the government will show us places of interest downtown. Tonight we'll meet the Kuna people and travel to their homes out on the islands. The Kuna defeated the nation of Panama in 1925 and the treaty they had drawn up found its way to the United Nations..."

We drive a few miles while he talks about treaties and history and war. After a while we near the water. An almost-naked man is scavenging on the huge heaps of trash choking the shore. Across the road are two and three-story buildings without windows and doors. We roll onto a street where everything is crumbling and collapsed. The bus slows and halts in front of a gated, well-kept house, its lush green plants and flowers and fresh bright paint out of place with the piles of concrete and blackened rebar. Next to the pristine house is a crater. A neat, deep hole the length of several houses.

There's a knock on the bus door. The Professor opens it and a stoic-faced man climbs aboard. He's wearing pressed gray slacks, old wing-tipped black shoes polished to a shine, and a pink dress shirt. Despite the morning's growing heat, he seems comfortable, not a bead of sweat on him. The Professor introduces him and they're off, talking all about the US Invasion but I'm far away thinking about Antonia and the night we heard about the Invasion on the news. I'm hearing her steady voice explaining to me the meaning of the phrase impressment of American sailors, and why it was a lie though I'm trying to focus on the lecture.

"...the house you are looking at belongs to a Panamanian-American musician. The crater, is all that remains of a Panamanian Defense Forces barracks that once stood right next door..."

Kim practically climbs over TJ to get a better look out the window.

I know I should be paying attention and taking notes but I'm playing back Antonia gently telling me that everything in the world is not as it appears. In that moment I knew my world was opening up, that I was crossing over a line with no going back, but I could only think about the soft cool skin where her neck met the curve of her shoulder.

Back then surrendering to the rush of comfort could still make the world disappear.

"Can we go outside," Kim asks.

Professor Armstrong turns to Luis.

"It is not safe," he says. "Not for Americans. Most here are still… resentful. Even though Noriega's gone. "El Toro" is not much better."

"Would you explain for the class what happened," the Professor says.

I can't point to a single feature that's changed but emotion has transformed Luis' face.

"On the night of the 20th of December. Great bats raced through the sky," he says softly, so softly I'm not certain those in the back of the bus can hear. "They moved too fast to see for very long but they were real. My mother was with me. She lives there."

He points out the front window.

"I was walking home from work and almost at our house when I looked up. My mother saw them too. She called them demons, but they were bats. I saw them. Purple beams shot from their eyes. Whatever the beams touched turned to rubble."

TJ and Kim and everyone are looking out the windows. I'm amazed at the crater. How the undamaged building is so close.

"I do not believe in demons," Luis says. "But you see, the destruction is real."

Professor Armstrong signals our driver to move again. We drive through the bombed-out neighborhood for a few moments and stop at another crater. And then another. And another. Next to each are undamaged buildings. At each stop Luis recounts a tale of a Panamanian Defense Force asset, each next to an undamaged building with an American connection.

I'm aware of time passing. I'm aware of the craters. Of the untouched buildings next to them. I hear my classmates whispering and the Professor and Luis speaking but I'm so tired and it is so hard to focus. And then I realize we're back at the first crater.

The bus halts. Everyone is uncharacteristically silent.

Luis and the Professor exchange a handshake; the Professor awkwardly using his left hand. In a few seconds Luis is going to walk off our bus and back into this bombed out place and we're going to just drive away.

Luis steps down the built-in metal steps, walks in front of the bus, crosses the road to one of the buildings I didn't think fit for living, and disappears inside.

"Did everyone put it together what our friend Luis was talking about," Professor Armstrong asks, breaking the uncomfortable quiet.

No one answers.

"American planes," he says after a few seconds. "Stealth planes. Made with classified technology. Their existence is widely known but for now they do not officially exist."

"The bats?" a guy named Phillipe asks.

He's one of the students from L.A. I pegged as being on the trip for easy credits. His hair magically always manages to stay perfectly coiffed and his shirts perfectly pressed in the Central American heat. I didn't think he had a thought in his head other than indiscriminately making out with as many people in the class as he could. I would have sworn he hadn't been listening to a word anyone said all summer until now.

"The accounts Luis gave are dramatic but I believe they are accurate," the Professor says. "It's easy to see how one could perceive the experience as he reports."

The bus mercifully grinds to life, putting a break in the moment, and we are moving again, rolling out of the neighborhood gaining speed.

"This week we've been talking about how international standards of money are determined and managed," the Professor says. "I hope you've paid attention. It will be on the exam. Give some thought as to how today fits in. We will review everything again this weekend."

He settles into his seat.

"Why do people do things like this," TJ asks Kim.

"Because they can?" Kim says.

"Is that an answer or a question," Professor Armstrong says.

I worry the notion reflects some natural order I cannot comprehend, something inherent about the world. Something undetectable and ever-present that I'm constantly missing. When the last of the ruined buildings are behind us. I scan the streets hoping for a pay phone.

"You okay," Kim asks me.

"Great, never better," I say.

But I have the sense I've accidentally touched something hidden; brushed up against a vast unknown. Something dangerous, uncaring, and maybe even incomprehensible.

And I feel a long, long way from home.

A GOVERNMENT GUIDE is waiting for us outside the Balboa Theatre, a pre-invasion landmark. To the left of the Marquis and entrance doors are a bunch of workmen sitting against the patched-up wall eating lunch.

"Is this all of you," the guide asks.

I don't give the Professor the satisfaction of protesting when he wryly smiles and whistles in response. The group is just him, Julianna, and myself.

The whole thing smacks of some propaganda but I can't figure out for what gain.

This guy doesn't seem so different than Luis. What twist of fate put Luis in El Chorillo and this guy in the employ of "the Bull" or whatever they call the new President? I have no reason for animosity but I find myself refusing to listen or acknowledge his name.

"So the Kuna were able to retain their sovereignty, even during Noriega because of the treaty," Juliana whispers to the Professor.

I guess she isn't listening either.

"So many factors were in play," he whispers back. "So many ways it could have gone but lately I've come to think, maybe, just maybe some things end up the same no matter what."

The guide has to hear us but he pays no mind. He stops his tour-guide-speech, opens the left most of the four heavy doors beneath the Marquis and leads us inside. Afternoon sun streams through rows of dirty windows just below the ceiling some thirty plus feet above us illuminating sloping rows of orchestra seats between us and the stage.

A section of the seats near the front have been ripped out. New ones wrapped in plastic are waiting against the wall beneath the windows. A lone black grand piano with the top propped open is on the stage.

"Oh, wow. May I play," I ask the guide. He's delighted by my interest.

"Oh, no. Don't," Juliana says. "We're guests."

I dash through the aisle, climb the riser onto the stage and sit behind the piano.

There is no dust coating the keys. Someone's been playing. My pinky and thumb land on the low notes. The octave is not quite in tune. I roll notes of a chord with my right fingers. The intonation doesn't quite hit the hum I expected but a melancholy sound fills the hall. Something is shaken away as I begin.

I start out with the melody of a thing I was tinkering with once upon a time then quickly find myself hitting the chords of the Costa Rican pop song we heard when the tour bus was stuck in the mud and we all had to pull it out. Then I'm making something up. The improvisation is familiar though I can't put my finger on what its inspired by. I close my eyes. The hulls of bombed out buildings greet me. I slow the tempo. Let the notes at the end of the phrases ring out, hoping the sustain will chase the images away.

My mind goes to my instruments Antonia had me put in storage. The guitar I bought myself when I was accepted into law school. The amps and electric piano I've had since I was a teen. We're getting married there's no room and we're going to be lawyers, she said.

Here, this stage is nothing but empty space and the piano. Beneath the ruin and clutter and reconstruction there is nothing but the possibility. My fingers find extra notes; fat seconds and thirds augment the chords, trying to reflect this epiphany in sound.

Juliana and the Professor and the Guide have come to the stage. I glance then close my eyes again. I can feel them staring and brace myself for Juliana's snark. It doesn't come. I hit a low key attached to a broken string. The knock and clang throws me out of it and I stop.

They applaud. Julianna too. I'm flush with warmth. It's been too long since I connected with the truth of fingers on keys, of keys on hammers, of hammers on strings, of the resonance of notes with bones.

As I climb from the stage the guide takes my hand and helps with the care of an usher helping a concert virtuoso.

"Where I grew up there were beaches," he says. "I want to tell you this. It had the most beautiful sand. The most beautiful blue, you could see them all from the terrace of our house. I am the middle son of many brothers. Growing up, on Sundays. We always ate dinner together. My father worked all day long, six days a week. Sundays he spent with us- after dinner. He stood on that terrace and as the sun went down he would sing to himself. I don't know what he sang. I don't know the names of the songs or if I'll ever hear them again. The way you play makes me think of him. Makes me feel the way I did when he sang. I haven't felt that since I was a child."

I plant my feet on the dusty floor.

"Are you studying to be a concert musician?"

"No, a lawyer-"

"He's one of mine," Professor Armstrong interrupts.

"Oh, yet he *is* a musician too..."

"My students are many things," the Professor says.

"You are full of surprises," says the guide.

What am I missing? I didn't think the Professor knew this guy but it feels like they're continuing some god-damned competition.

"I'm going outside for a cigarette," I say but I don't smoke.

Doesn't matter, neither man is listening to me. I go outside. I stand outside the marquis letting my eyes adjust to the sun. Down the street I see a pay phone.

Juliana pushes through the doors and comes next to me.

"What the fuck kind of dick measuring was that," she says.

"I haven't felt invisible like that since I last saw my guitar teacher, Mister Shannon, as an undergrad."

"Boys never feel invisible," she says.

I'm not sure if she's being sarcastic or not.

"I asked him for a letter of recommendation for my law school applications," I say. "And he told me not only would he not write me a recommendation he'd never speak to me again if I applied."

"Nice, real nice," she says.

She takes a sorry looking cigarette out of her bag and lights it up.

"I told him I wanted to go to law school because I didn't think I could change the world through music. That I didn't think I could make a difference.

"That sucks."

"Yeah, otherwise he was a really cool teacher, that's the sad part. He did keep his word and never spoke to me again."

She flips her hair out of her face and takes a deep drag. "I didn't know you could play like that."

"Like what?"

"Like, well I don't know," she says.

I wonder if I have time to go to the pay phone before the Professor comes outside.

"I thought we'd been discussing structure," I say. "I'd just told him I thought a song is what you say a song is, theory or no theory, no matter what anyone says. I thought that was what offended him. Or that maybe he was mad that I believed that I couldn't make a difference. Now looking back, I think the opposite was true, that he believed *he* couldn't make a difference.

And me moving on, me taking a shot at something, at anything was what he couldn't take."

"Hey, you don't mind that I'm smoking? Do you?"

"I don't care. I'm going down the street to make a call. Just tell the Professor if he comes out before I'm back."

She flips her hair and doesn't say anything. I go to the pay phone and dial Antonia. I put in the country code. Area code. Her number. My number.

How do I even begin to tell her what I've seen?

The phone rings and rings. Then the answering machine picks up. I've already been charged for the call so I think of a message to leave.

"Hey, I'm outside this cool theatre they're rebuilding..."

And I feel like I sound like such a dope and wish she'd pick up.

"...but, um, yeah thinking of you."

I see the Professor and the guide come outside and join Julianna. I stand there listening to the static, watching them look around before Julianna points to me.

I hang up the phone.

LO SPAZIO TRA

The Space Between

THE BUS DRIVER leaves us at the shore where we're supposed to meet the Kuna. The only building around looks like it was once a garage but is now some kind of a makeshift pub. Three thick concrete walls support a tin roof. The fourth wall or what might have been garage doors are long gone leaving the place open to the air. Inside a few dozen men, Panamanian men in work jeans and white shirts covered in varying levels of sweat and grime, are gathered around two, long picnic style tables with attached benches. Their attention shifts from the two men arm wrestling in the center of the nearest table to us. They look like a couple of work crews changing shifts, but for what job, I can't discern. There's a pay phone along the side.

Kim is first off the bus and heads right inside. She walks past the staring men to the bar along the back wall and asks for a beer.

"Seco," the bartender replies.

The bartender looks like the rest of the guys. I'm guessing he's one of them and it's his turn to tend the bar.

"No whiskey? Rum, maybe," Kim says.

"Solamente, Seco," the bartender says.

"Hey, Phillpe! TJ! Julianna, everyone! They've got Seco," Kim yells. "Come and get it!"

The bartender lines up shot glasses and starts pouring. Kim walks to the men still embroiled in their arm wrestle and slaps an American dollar bill on the table.

"I've got next," she says.

I groan.

The arm wrestling men lean into each other trying to break the stale-mate. The rest of the men look around uneasily then pretend to focus on the match.

I head to the payphone instead of going in with everyone. I get Antonia's answering machine, again. I don't leave a message. I hope I've hung up without recording any of the cheering coming from inside. I return to the front to see Kim seated at the table across from and locked in an arm wrestle with the apparent winner of the last match. The guy appears to be struggling in earnest. She works his arm, down and down then slams it to the table with a roar of approval from everyone. He doesn't look unhappy with the loss he's smiling along with his pals who are jostling to take his place. I join Professor Armstrong, standing with the rest of the guys in our class looking on with befuddlement. The Panamanians seem to be having a grand time. They don't look terribly drunk. Maybe it's the novelty of it all. The joy of the absurdity of coming upon all of us here in their place that I'm seeing.

Julianna, Bren, and Nina squeeze onto the bench on either side of Kim. The Panamanians break into a whirlwind of clearing the tables and fervent discussion and I realize I'm watching an arm wrestling tournament come into being. "Our" girls versus all of them.

Kim throws back a shot with one of the men and everyone shares a big, happy laugh.

I don't sense a lecherous edge to any of it. Despite the alcohol it feels like good clean fun. An unexpected whirlwind of fun and good cheer that blew into their routine.

But I'm just not feeling into it. And apparently neither is the Professor. I can tell something's on his mind. More than that our Kuna representatives are late, and more than the fact that the rambunctious group of students he's responsible for are carrying on like this. I walk outside with him and we stand looking out at the water and listening to the roars and cheers and chants as the sun goes down.

WHEN THE PROFESSOR finally stands I have the feeling he's contemplating telling me something important.

"What," I ask.

He steps toward the shore. Something's out there. A shape silently moving through the water. A boat. A canoe. Two men paddling through the low tide. One in the front one in the back. Two more canoes become visible behind it.

The Professor walks to the bar to collect the class. Julianna notices him first. She stops speaking in Spanish with the man across the table from her and finishes the drop of alcohol remaining in her shot glass. Phillipe and Brenda look like they're about to make out but they notice Julianna staring and they stop, then a silence cascades through everyone allowing that Central American pop song I've been hearing everywhere, the one with the lyric that translates to "it's stuck," to be heard.

The three large canoes, and two boatman in each, are waiting a few feet off shore; they are much too big to pull onto land. One of the Kuna men disembarks into the knee-deep water, and motions to the professor to throw him the first of our packs. He's wearing cut off blue jeans and a faded and threadbare Thin Lizzy tour jersey with the white sleeves that looks authentic. The group of workmen come outside and watch us load up. They stand on the shore as we are paddled out. I feel them watching even after I can no longer see them. The Kuna man in the back of our canoe lowers a motor into the water. Kim gives a yell then all three motors kick in and we are speeding through the night.

WE MOTOR THROUGH the dark water for what feels like a few hours. Somehow they know where they're going and where to stop. When the motors finally cut we glide for a moment until the nose of the canoe hits something solid. Flashlight beams light us up. The water is calm and crystal clear. In the light of the roving beams I catch glimpses of the sloping bottom choked with aluminum cans and trash. A rusted tricycle tops the man-made reef of cast away things spreading from the island's edge.

Dozens of Kuna men and even more children are crowded on the dock waiting for us. Most of the men are dressed like our boat guys, in random pairings of styles of old clothing I recognize from my past; rock and roll tour t-shirts, La-Coste collared short sleeve shirts, t-shirts advertising brands I'd forgotten. The children are curious. I don't like the way the men are silently staring and that there are no women present.

Our boat guys shepherd us off the dock without acknowledging the group who has come to see us arrive, which makes me feel more uncomfortable. They take us along a sand street and the "welcome crowd" follows along on either side of us. We pass small, low buildings with tin roofs and walls made of a patchwork of materials.

We're herded into a small courtyard that I take to be their futbol court. Two of the boat drivers tap Kim, Phillipe, and another student, Ron Washington and motion for them to follow.

Kim looks green from the alcohol and ride but manages to say something groan-worthy.

"If you don't hear from me again tell my Mom I love her."

Over the next hour we're escorted from the futbol court in groups of twos and threes. I'm taken to a long building with a canvas flap between a frame of wood as an entrance.

The space inside is one large room dimly lit by embers in a stone fire pit. Tendrils of smoke circle upwards and escape in a vent in the vaulted ceiling. At least a dozen hammocks are slung between many the roof support poles. People are sleeping.

The boatman leads me to an unoccupied hammock, then exits. I glance around at the benches built into the walls and the cooking utensils on the stones around the smoldering fire.

I say, "hola" and regret it when no one replies.

I put my water bottle on the packed sand ground beneath my hammock and climb into it with my pack as my pillow. As soon as I am horizontal the adrenaline I've been running on leaves me and I feel fatigue waiting. I fall asleep to the crackle of embers and sounds of people breathing. In the night I'm woken by whispers very close to me. I crack my eyes open; a bunch of young children are inspecting me. One has my water bottle. Another is trying to untie my boot lace, I've forgotten to take them off. One boy puts his face right up to mine. I close my eyes and pretend to sleep. Despite the strange visitors I'm so tired it isn't hard.

LIGHT STREAMING THROUGH gaps in the patchwork walls tells me it is morning. The room is alive with the motion of people cooking and coming and going. My sleeping hammock is the only one still slung up. A young boy zig-zags through the bustle to me and he rustles my shoulder with a smile.

"Come," he says in Spanish.

I grab my pack and water and follow him outside. I don't understand why no one acknowledges us. As we're walking I wonder where the rest of the class is. Still sleeping, maybe. It can't be too long past sunrise. The boy takes me a short way to where the little island ends in a rocky edge only a few feet above the sea. A short, old man is standing there looking out to the ocean, a tin pail at his feet. The newly risen sun has made the flat water opaque.

"My grandfather. El Cacique," the child says. "In English. The Chief."

I approach and extend my hand. The pail next to him is jammed full of colorful fish.

The chief's skin isn't weathered as I expected and he seems remarkably fit. When we shake he says something in a language I do not comprehend.

"He says you make funny sounds when you sleep," the child translates. "Loud enough to wake someone deep in the nine worlds."

The chief laughs and motions for me to pick a fish from the pail.

"Deseauna," he says.

Healthy, bright, multi-colored angels, triggerfish, and orange, yellow, and white striped fish I've never seen before swim in a tight circle.

"He must like you," the child says. "He let you pick. Which one did you pick?"

"The orange ones look nice. How about you pick for me?"

"Can I?"

The chief laughs again. I like the way his grandson brings him joy.

The child lifts the pail with both hands and hauls it back the way we just came from.

The chief leads me to a nearby cluster of houses. There's a narrow alley in the space between two of the patchwork-sided buildings, just enough space to walk single file. I follow him into the shade of the in between space. We walk along the outside wall of the neighboring house to a set of stairs and go up. At the top is a platform made of boards about a story above the crowded island. A table and four chairs takes up most the small retreat. There are two plates, two glasses, and a pitcher of water set on the table. A line with clothes drying on it partially obscures the view of nearby island and the mountains beyond the water.

We sit. The Chief produces a cigar, lights it up and offers it to me. I think I tell him I don't smoke in Spanish. He says something but his Spanish isn't so good. Mine is terrible. I know enough to comprehend he's telling me he's leaving to go to Panama City. I don't need to know Spanish to know he is concerned.

Somewhere nearby a generator chugs and clangs as it kicks in. The refrain of an old Rolling Stone song crackles to life and joins the morning sounds of birds and people talking not too far away.

"Not everyone wants you here," says the Chief. "My people are divided about opening to tourism. I made the decision to let you come. We are building a place for visitors. I know fishing is difficult and will not last forever."

The child returns at the top of the stairs carrying a third plate and glass. Julianna is behind him.

"See, my grandfather is here," he says to her. "Breakfast is almost ready."

"What are *you* doing here," Julianna says to me.

"My grandfather is telling him how he is not afraid of the Bull," the child says.

The Chief introduces himself to Julianna and repeats everything he'd been saying to me about the Bull and tourism. It is easier to understand everything hearing it second time around.

"Why did he just ask me what a nice young couple such as you and I think of their island," she says.

I can just hear the Professor laughing when he hears about this.

The child comes up the stairs with sizzling fish. "Breakfast!" he says.

We all eat. The Chief smokes. He says nothing else and we do nothing to fill the space. There's something peaceful about listening to the din of the island with him in his secret spot. I'm grateful for the moment and then it is time to depart.

When the Chief, Julianna and I arrive at the dock the Professor and the rest of the class are waiting, all ready and loaded into three canoes. Two Kuna men wait in a fourth canoe.

The Chief loads into the fourth canoe and pushes off. I sit in front of Kim in the third boat. As our boats head into open water, the Chief's veers the opposite way towards the mainland.

"I would say welcome to San Blas, because that is what your map says," the boatman in the front says over the noise of the engine. "But we are Kuna and this is Kuna Yala."

His engagement with us is a welcome change. We speed past tiny islands, most no larger than a few acres.

"Take this," Kim whispers in my ear and passes me a vitamin-like capsule. "For the hunger."

"What is it?"

"Diet pill," she says.

"I don't need it but thanks," I whisper and pocket the pill.

Our boatman slows our canoe as we pass a tiny island shaded by a grove of tall palms. Every inch of sand is covered with long-clawed crabs jostling for space. The boatman in the back makes I joke I do not hear then hits the engine.

The morning passes and the sun rises higher; I find myself wishing we had some cover from the heat. Brenda opens a bar of almost-melted chocolate and tell me to take and pass it back. I give my bit to Kim.

Around noon the boatmen cut the engines again. Ahead is another idyllic, little, palm-shaded island ringed with white sand beaches and a barrier reef with meters and meters of turquoise shallows in between. Beneath the palms are three thatch huts with a cleared path leading from them to the beach.

The boatmen steer through a small break in the reef. We get out of the boats halfway through the shallows and bring our packs to shore. Even being waist deep in the warm tropical water is a relief from the heat. The Kuna drop the anchors. Phillipe and Kim and a couple of others throw their packs on the beach and splash and roll around in the water with their clothes on.

I walk with the Professor and one of the boatmen to the center of the three huts. It is a storage hut full of bags of rice and beans and a couple of cases of bottled Balboa Beer. Outside the hut is a shower hooked up to a rain catch with white plastic piping. To the left is the hut for the boys, to the right the hut for the girls.

We walk to the boys hut. The space inside is broken up with thatch dividers that offer very little privacy. The Professor counts the cots.

"You okay bunking with the girls to make this work," he says.

"I could just move a cot over," I say.

"You could but I trust you."

"Enough to tell me how you really broke your wrist?"

"Let's get through the review session first before talking about that, alright?"

"Okay, Captain," the boatman says to the Professor. "We see you back here this time tomorrow."

The Professor thanks him and we return to shore to see him off. The other boatmen are playing Frisbee with the class in the water.

We spend the afternoon sitting in the shallows in the shade of a big overhanging palm with a trunk curved like a scimitar, drinking warm beer and reviewing all our coursework. The International Monetary Fund. The Panama Invasion. Central American Environmental Conservation. As the sun gets low the Professor tells us we're finished and the rest of the time is ours. He offers bonus points on the exam for anyone intrepid enough to cook the rice and beans but no one takes him up on it.

Dinner is more warm beer and a potluck made up of our remaining snacks supplemented by a few coconuts that TJ has harvested from the big, curved palm.

"I never met a tree I couldn't climb," TJ says as he hacks a coconut open with the machete from the storage hut.

Kim and I lay back in the sand watching the stars come out. The sheer amount of them is incredible and the configurations add to my feeling of being nowhere.

"This is a place deciding what it is going to be," she says. "It is a where that is not a where yet. A place of intentions. An intentional place. You know?"

"I know you're drunk."

Brenda and Nina run past us, naked and holding hands and screaming as they splash into the water.

"I'm not drunk," Kim says, "*They're* drunk."

"Marco," Brenda yells from out in the water.

"Polo," a bunch of voices answer.

"What a stupid game," Kim says. "Hey wait, where's TJ? I should go out there before anyone gets any ideas with my man."

"Your man?"

"Shut up. I know you and Julianna had breakfast with the Chief. What was that about?"

"Not sure. He's concerned about his people's future. He's thinking about tourism and wants to know what we think of *this*."

"What *do* we think of this?"

A scream drowns out the rustling of the palms and the laughter. It's TJ.

Kim's on her feet and splashing through the shallows before I can make any sense of things. Is something attacking him out there?

I run after Kim. The scream finds new intensity in each passing second. Kim swims the remaining distance to where everyone is clustered around TJ. Stones and coral jab my feet as I try to move fast. When I reach them the water is deeper, my feet no longer able to touch bottom. I slide between Bren and Nina so I can see what's going on. Kim and Phillipe are treading water while holding TJ, keeping his head from bobbing under. His mouth is wide open, his eyes wide open. Kim splashes water on his face. He doesn't respond. But at least he's stopped screaming. Everyone is asking if he's okay. They're drunk as hell. They mean well but need to back off and give him space. I place my hand on his shoulder to help keep him afloat.

The instant I touch him everyone becomes silent. I look around to see why but everyone is gone. No, I'm gone. I'm in complete darkness. There's only perfect black. My hand on TJ's shoulder is all I can see.

We're floating together in this dark, lifted by what feels like a swell; gently up then down again. A current has us and is carrying us along. The sense of motion is the only thing I'm sure of. I can't discern direction; only that a smell of something like burnt ozone and leather is growing stronger, which might mean closer. I catch a whiff of brine and a cloying orange sweetness. Then that sensation is gone too and there is only the sound of a voice in the darkness.

"WAVES.
Darkness.
The space between."

The words are English words. The voice is old and scratchy and speaking slowly with a heavy Italian accent. Their sound is everywhere. There is meter to the intervals of space between them. I sense a time signature present but cannot comprehend it, I cannot gauge when the next word will come.

"The world is the world.
The worlds of nothing between worlds
are the world too."

I feel my hand on TJ's shoulder but I can no longer see it, or him, or anything. The swell lifts us again and I realize I've lost track of which way is up or down. I try to focus on something to orient me. The voice is all there is and it is emanating from everywhere.

"They will tell you there is only chaos
but there is order.
To go against order is despair.
We glimpse it,
slivers of understanding through human minds.
Most fold over and over and over and snap."

The whirs and hums and buzzing sounds of the jungle fill the emptiness framing the words. Then the rhythmic lapping of the ocean on wet sand and an electronic whine of a familiar reggae-laced pop song joins in. I'm above the beach looking down at the sets of rolling waves and surfers and all the people on the shore from two nights ago. I catch a hint of burnt fish, cigarette smoke, salty-wet skin, and surf-wax before that ozone, citrus-and-sea reek eclipses all else.

My sense of up and down returns. I know because I'm rising. And moving from over the beach to over the ocean. The shore touches only a tiny part of its vastness. Beneath is a reef. A colossal shapeless-shape the size of the continental shelf running along the edge of an unfathomable crevasse where the ocean's colors have faded to sun-less black.

In the dark-purples and deep sea ultra-blues I see shapes and I think I see, no somehow I *do* see a man down there. He is tumbling. Sinking through the strata of water where the light struggles to reach. He divides into two men, snaking ropes of intestines shared between them. The intestines turn a seaweed green and become toothy faced, beady-eyed moray eels. The dividing men divide and divide again. Morays snake out in all directions, their maws biting into the faces of the underwater men while the screech of the coatis fighting for Theron James' ripped bag of food drowns the gentle sound of the ocean kissing the shore.

The dark ocean colors become grey. I'm surrounded by sleek metal and molded plastic. Kim is next to me stirring a plastic cup full of ice. This is our flight down. No. Something's different. There's the weight of experience and sorrow in her eyes that wasn't present before. This is the plane ride we're going to take home.

The plane is flying through a vast empty blackness. It divides into two planes. Then the field of black folds in upon itself forming a mandala, a folding and unfolding kaleidoscope of cosmic snowflakes composed of vistas of ocean waves, intestines, coati and airplanes. The mandala breaks apart. Four, then eight, then nine pieces, nine directions. Then more and more. Countless more.

Is this the meaning of the word infinite?

"Waves."
"Darkness."
"The Spaces Between."

The voice has lost its scratch. Lost the accent. The words are tones. Humming gong-strikes resonating into each other becoming words again.

"Countless mirrors reflect each other.
Each a dream of another.
Words beneath words beneath words.
Worlds beneath worlds beneath worlds.
When you are taken by the undertow
if you are lucky you realize that you are but a river in this dark sea
and you fight,
you hold on,
and then you are some sort of you again.
Fighting.
Holding on this way
is both the path and the victory."

The countless aspects of the mandala fold over and into each other; countless duplicates and divisions collapsing into one panoramic visage, a vista of mountains and water. I'm seeing the Kuna's island, water, and mountains. I'm no longer merely feeling these things. I am floating over the mountains looking down at the actual island. I'm rushing earthbound. Rushing toward my classmates, to where they and I are gathered around TJ...

"...*Waves.*"
"*Darkness...*"

The sequence of words begin again but the voice speaking is Julianna's. The voice is also mine. I am speaking the words along with her...

"...THE SPACE BETWEEN...," the Professor says.

The Professor wasn't with us a second ago. He's got his tiny flip notebook out and open and is scribbling in it and muttering.

We're all in the shallows not far from where we were just keeping TJ afloat... was that a few seconds ago? The feeling I've forgotten something gnaws at me. I reach for it like a song name on the tip of my tongue but whatever it was has slipped away and there is only the sense of emptiness where it once resided.

"What the hell are you doing," Kim says to him.

"Writing it down," the Professor says.

"What?"

"The words he's been screaming."

"Now?"

TJ wheezes and leans forward trying to pull free of us.

"Easy," the Professor says. "It's going to be okay."

"We got you," I say.

"I'm okay. Get off me."

"You were drowning," Kim says.

"I wasn't drowning. I'm fine. It's nothing."

"…you will know you are a river," the professor mutters.

"He's okay," Phillipe announces. "He's fine."

"Yeah, I'm okay now," TJ says.

Phillipe swishes back out into deeper water and calls, "Marco."

Laughter and calls back answer him but there's something hollow in the revelry.

⚓

Innumerevoli Specchi Che Riflettono Tutto
Countless Mirrors Reflecting Each Other

TJ drapes his arm around Kim and allows her to help him wade out of the shallows.

The Professor's notebook is a mosaic of illegible wet smears of ink.

"So much for turning in early," he says and closes the book. "Back to sleep for me."

He swishes through the shallows to shore and ambles onto the path to the huts.

Kim and TJ turn the opposite way. Kim drops her arm and cups TJ's behind with her hand just before they disappear from sight.

"Kuna," Phillipe calls from the water.

"Yala," a chorus of voices answer.

There's splashing and a playful scream. Then more laughter in the dark. A bathing suit flies past me and flops onto the sand.

"Hey, are you the only one with clothes still on?"

Brenda and Nina splash out of the darkness and grab for my arms. Brenda reeks of Seco and sweat and doesn't let go when I tell her to stop. Nina grabs my free arm and tries to pull me into the shallows. From out of nowhere Phillipe crashes out of the water and gets his arms around me. The three of them wrangle me into the water.

Brenda pulls at my swim trunks. As I try to hold on to them Phillipe pushes my head under. I accidentally swallow water and push up. I gulp air and yell "Enough," but I'm met with drunken laughter. I stop resisting and let them shimmy my trunks off so I don't swallow more water or worse.

"Now you're ready to play," Phillipe says. "You're the *Cacique* now. Call it, call Kuna."

"Yala," voices call from different points out in the dark.

I do a half-hearted paddle towards the nearest voice and bump into Nina and Ron kissing as they tread water. A few droplets of rain patter on my head. The hazy sky and light rain reflect the starlight into a glow. I'd be enjoying myself if Antonia was here; if I were seeing this with her instead of going through the motions of this stupid game.

"Kuna," I call.

No one answers. There's only the sound of people moving away through the water and what I take to be Ron and Nina sort of moaning while they kiss. The energy of our crazy day has gone. Night and time has worn it away. I don't bother to call out again and make my way to the shallows instead.

Julianna is on the shore putting her swimsuit back on. She sees me and halts tying her bikini top.

"I'm going to bed," she says. "Are you coming?"

Someone whistles a cat call.

I drop my hands to cover myself and glance around the beach hoping to spot my swim trunks.

Julianna swishes a few steps into the water and takes my hand.

"I said, are you coming," she whispers.

She gently shifts her weight coaxing me to follow. The mountains are dark presences in the starlight.

Her invitation hangs there, its echo carries over the water with the sounds from the mainland, and becomes one with the night.

END PART I

198   *D A N I E L   B R A U M*

∾

I DON'T SAY no. I don't have to. I remove my hand from hers. We're standing there face to face in the ankle-deep water with only the light rain and starlit darkness between our nakedness.

"I don't think you're sure. You don't sound sure," she says.

"No. I'm not coming," I say.

"Que lastima," she whispers.

After a second she wades back to the beach and puts on her bathing suit. Then she slowly makes her way towards the huts.

"You must really love her," she says without turning to look back.

Her shape merges with the darkness. I look around for my trunks but only spot TJ's sarong. I grab it instead and wrap it around me.

Nina and Phillipe wade in and pass me hand in hand. The rain patters on the calm water.

I hesitate as long as I can before walking back to the hut hoping I can slip inside quietly and without a fuss. I slide open the white sheet that is the door and softly step in. With the big windows it's not that much darker inside. I can discern the thatch walls dividing the cots. Julianna's bag and flip flops are on the ground by the second wall. Across the room I notice motion in the almost dark; a large shape gently undulating. It takes me a second to realize it is the silhouette of Kim and TJ together in the farthest-most cot. She's on top of him with her hair down and back arched. They're trying to be quiet.

I try to remain quiet and gently step to the right behind the first thatch wall. I sit on the cot. Juliana's is on the other side of the divider only a few feet away. I can hear her breathing; heavy un-metered breaths not the soft, steady rhythms of someone sleeping.

A rumble of thunder masks TJ and Kim's heavy breathing for a few heartbeats. The deep crackles are the inherently the same yet somehow distinctly different than the sounds of the New York storms I grew up listening to; reminding me I'm so far from home.

A hermit crab is digging at the base of the thatch wall between Julianna and I. The thunder rips again, the kind of boom that could convince you that the sky is really breaking. A heavy rain hits the roof.

I lay down, close my eyes and feel sleep waiting for me. I fight the drift because despite my exhaustion I've taken so much in and I'm not ready for the day to end. I must have slipped into a dream because I wake up thinking I just searched the island looking for a way to call Antonia. I wonder how much time has passed because the sound of the rain is gone and there's only the gentle dripping from the windows.

Motion at the foot of the thatch catches my awareness. The hermit crab is still digging in the sand. There are a few tunnels leading back and forth to the other side of the divider.

I listen to see if I can hear Kim and TJ breathing together or if Juliana's breaths have taken on the rhythm of sleep. There's only the scratching of the crab burying itself in the sand.

IN THE MORNING the Kuna boatmen wake us by singing and banging on the sides of the canoes as they arrive at the island. The Professor clanks empty beer bottles at the entrance to the hut and rousts everyone out of bed then makes sure we clean up every bottle, every candy wrapper and every stray bathing suit before we are allowed to load into the boats for departure.

Out on the water our boats are the only man-made things in sight, a fleet of hungry, sun-burned, hung-over students all alone in the pristine waters of the archipelago. Over the sound of the motors I discern Phillipe belting out Pana-ma, Pana-ma-ah, from the other boat, trying to get the others to join in. My thoughts are all of Antonia. I don't have the gumption to sing; I'm barely taking in any of the beauty surrounding us.

Our bus is waiting at the shore. The garage-turned-pub is empty with no sign of our arm wrestler friends. Back at the Casita Libuela I head straight to the pay phone while everyone else is heading straight to crash out. Kim's holding the door letting everyone file past her. She's watching me. I contemplate the best way to tell Antonia the difference between sleeping in the strange room of hammocks and being out under all the stars as I dial the numbers and codes. It's early in the morning before work and should be a good time to catch a moment with her. The line rings forever, then connects with a static-click.

"Hello," a man answers.

"Antonia?"

"I told you not to pick up," I hear Antonia say.

I let the receiver slip through my fingers.

I hear her calling my name as the black plastic speaker spirals and sways on the silver cord. What a marvel that her voice can reach me here from the phone next to her bed, halfway across the world. How could it be that in the very place where we slept and shared so many moments a man just answered at five in the morning. I fixate on the phone rather than face the answer.

I leave the receiver swinging and walk away. Kim lets the door close, comes over and flops her arm around my shoulder without a word.

New York City. Two Months Later.

I LOOSEN MY tie, unbutton my top shirt-button and push the glass door open. The restaurant's air conditioning hits me; a welcome respite from Manhattan's humid Indian Summer. Kim's at the bar, her case of briefs and tote on the stool next to her. She's flipping through a pile of mail and sipping an iced drink in a tall glass.

"Hot enough for you," she says. "Almost like the summer."

"Indian Summer's always brutal. Happens every year."

"Technically, it's not Indian Summer unless it is November."

Despite her usual snark, she's being kind. She never said I told you so. When we got back home she helped me move my things from Antonia's place without a word too.

"Think they have any Seco here," she asks.

I'm not sure if she's serious. The bar is lined two to three people deep with people dressed like she and I; probably half of the staff of interns from the Federal Defender and Prosecutor's offices and more lawyers and young professionals than I can shake a stick at.

"If I call out "Marco" think the bartend will come," I reply.

"Good luck," she says. "Getting a drink is rough. Helps being a girl. Helps more being a girl with a twenty on the bar."

I look around to see if any of my supervisors or opposing counsel are here and catch Kim watching me look.

"I know what you're thinking," I say. "She'd never come here. And no. I haven't called her. I never want to see her again."

Kim says nothing though I know she has plenty to say. I've heard it all before and she knows it. Her disapproving expression references everything she's said before to me with as she takes a draw of her drink through her straw.

"I think this would taste good with Seco in it," she says.

"I'm just going to say I still believe love is real," I say. "Even when it's over. I know it was with Antonia, while it lasted."

"Who's playing tonight," she says. "My fiancé's watching at the Pub next door with his friends and invited me. I have nothing against Irish Pubs or even his friends but I don't drink beer. You think he'd get this already."

"You don't even like football," I say.

"So. I gotta know about the game. At least the highlights. Otherwise I'd have to actually talk to people tomorrow..."

She shakes her head in an exaggerated shudder and drains a quarter of her drink through the straw.

I want to point out that she never says her fiancé's name but think better of it. I'm surprised at even this rare mention.

"You ever think about TJ," I ask. "I know you have to."

She sets her glass down firmly.

"Keep the monkey in the jungle," she says.

"What?"

"That's my answer."

"What kind of answer is that?"

"A good one. And also a good solid bit of advice. I don't remember who first told me. But it doesn't matter. So, that fellow you mention, TJ, and outside of this conversation we don't speak his name, got me, is a monkey. *The* monkey. When in the jungle, well then out there it is perfectly fine to cavort with monkeys. My fiancé is my man. When not in the jungle... you see what follows... Not much more to say about this."

"Wait. Do you literally mean the real jungle?"

"Hmmm, in this case, yes," she says. "In general, no. That's not the point. The point is, the question you should have asked is does he think about me? Answer. No. He doesn't think about me, he freaking *dreams* about me with the burning passion of a dying star. You never forget your first. And I'm not only his first, I'm his best. He'll be reliving that night with me every time he's alone and horny. Which won't be very often, he is a fine one, so he won't stay alone for long."

"Do *you* think about him, hmmm?"

"Yeah, so what. I looked him up," she says. "And I couldn't find him. So I ran his name at work. Nothing."

"How sweet."

"It wasn't. Stop."

"I will."

"Okay, a real question is this. What I want to know is do you think about Julianna?"

I can't help but picture her on the beach. In the starlit darkness tying her bathing suit.

"Are you coming?"

If my answer would have been different would it have made a difference? With Antonia? Or with anything at all?

"It doesn't matter," I say. "Why?"

"I bumped into her in the clerk's office. You should call her."

Before I can say I don't have her number she holds up a piece of mail with Julianna's info scribbled on it.

"Don't ever say I don't give you anything," she says.

⚓

SOGNO DEL MONDO SOTTERRANEO

Underworld Dreams

THE ENERGY OF our crazy day has gone. Night and time have worn it away but the game of Marco Polo Kuna Yala is still careening on. I don't bother to call out again, instead I make my way to the shallows.

Julianna is on the shore putting her swimsuit on; her silhouette an elegant dark shape on the white sand lit by starlight through the rain. She sees me swishing through the ankle deep water and halts tying her top.

"I'm going to bed," she says. "You coming?"

Someone whistles a cat call.

I drop my hands to cover myself and glance around the beach hoping to spot my swim trunks.

Julianna wades a few steps into the water and takes my hand.

"I said, are you coming," she whispers.

She gently shifts her weight coaxing me to follow. The mountains are dark presences in the starlight.

Her invitation hangs there, its echo carrying over the water with the sounds of our classmates calling Marco Polo.

"No," I say.

"You sure? You don't sound sure."

"I'm sure."

After a second she releases my hand and says, "Que lastima."

She wades to the beach and puts on her bathing suit. Then she slowly makes her way towards the huts.

"You must really love her," she says without turning to look back.

Her shape merges with the darkness. I look around for my trunks but only spot TJ's sarong. I grab it instead and wrap it around me. Nina and Phillipe wade in and pass me hand in hand. Rain patters on the calm water.

I hesitate as long as I can before walking back to the hut with the hope I can slip inside quietly and without fuss. With the big windows it's not that much darker inside and I can make out the thatch walls dividing the cots. Julianna's bag and flip flops are on the ground by the second one. Something's moving in the almost-dark across the room; a big patch of shadow undulating above the farthest-most cot. It takes me a second to realize it's the silhouette of Kim and TJ together in the cot. She's on top of him, her hair down and back arched.

"This all ends," she's muttering in time with her grinding motions. "This all ends. This all ends. This all ends."

I feel like I'm witnessing the reciprocal of the moment she told me about on the bus when questioned if she would live again. A manifestation of the opposite iteration of the "her" who once thought this. The her who was shaken so badly on our flight down.

They're not trying to hide or they've forgotten to or lost the will to be quiet. Still, I quietly step behind the first thatch wall as if I don't hear and lay on the cot. Juliana's cot is on the other side of the divider only a few feet away. Her heavy sighs are not the rhythmic breathing of someone sleeping.

At the foot of the divider a hermit crab has climbed out of its shell. The strange lobster-shaped crustacean is scratching at the sand beneath the thatch. There's a split up its back.

"I know you hear them," Julianna whispers.

TJ's moans join with Kim's muttering.

"I do," I say.

"I know you want to feel like that. Right now. Don't you?"

She's right. But I wish it was Antonia here with me. I wish the endless blue sky and all the colors and crazy times we're having were the stuff of real life, of life back home, not something to be stumbled upon in a far away corner of the world.

"I do," I whisper.

Julianna's already come around the divider and standing there as I speak.

She puts her finger in front of her mouth in the universal signal for silence then unites her top.

The crab wriggles from its split carapace. For an instant it is an even stranger shape comprised of two almost-identical writhing, shaking forms. Then it climbs free of its exoskeleton and burrows under the thatch leaving its hollow molt next to the empty shell.

Julianna gently slides into the cot, next to me, the motion smooth as if practiced a thousand times. The heat of the day radiates from her sandy, soft, salt water coated skin. Her weight pushes me into the scratchy-roughness of the canvas cot but I don't care. A rumble masks the sounds of TJ and Kim. The resonating crackle is of the kind so deep that can make you really believe the sky is breaking. When it passes I can hear the Spanish words Julianna is gently mouthing on my neck below my ear. A heavy rain comes and the sound of it eclipses all else. In the distance I hear an echo of the thunder or just the sky breaking again, somewhere farther away.

THE PROFESSOR AND the Guide push through the weathered and city-grime coated doors of the Balboa Theatre and walk to Julianna who is standing under the Marquis. She points up the street to where I am standing at the pay phone. Antonia's line rings and rings and rings

"Hello," a man answers.

"Antonia," I say.

"I told you not to pick up," I hear Antonia say in the background not to me but to the man.

I drop the receiver and let it hang there spinning on the tarnished, silver cord.

THE RESTAURANT'S AIR conditioning is a welcome respite from Manhattan's Indian Summer. Kim's already staked out room at the bar and is ignoring the after-work crowd by flipping through papers while sipping an iced drink in a tall glass.

As I weave through the business-suited crowd I tell myself I'm not going to talk about Antonia and will relax like I agreed with Kim. But the place is full of the push and pull and circles and orbits of people pairing up or trying to and I can't help myself.

"I mean, love is more than something you decide, isn't it," I say to Kim a few minutes into our banter.

To avoid steering into the subject and listening to me talk about Antonia, Kim tries to catch the attention of the busy bartender and says, "Excuse me, I think this would taste better with Seco in it."

The murmur of a hundred conversations and music and buzz of cars outside swallows her words.

"Come on," I say. "Don't you think love is real? Even when it isn't?"

"If you say so," Kim says.

"I do."

I'm surprised that she's replied.

"This may not feel like any consolation, but it is," she says. "Here it is. Know what I think? There are no soulmates. There isn't any meaning to anything so how could there be?"

"Nothing?"

"Only what we bring."

"How do you know?"

"I don't. I mean I just do. Why does it even matter, right? I just don't buy all this fate and destiny stuff. No one is meant for one other. Nothing means anything. There's only choice. We're stronger that way. So I don't know, maybe love *is* something you decide, nothing more."

"That doesn't feel right. I feel like Antonia and I *were* meant for each other and us falling apart is just wrong. Cosmically wrong. Big picture wrong. This. Me. Everything is wrong and I'm going through the motions of a life but there's no reason for me to be here. I'm living out the not-happily-ever-after of this tragedy. That's a mistake. My life, this life is a mistake. Just a series of events with no meaning, playing out, events that just shouldn't be."

"If that's what you think, then that's what you think. I think a more likely explanation is you're not getting laid. And this is the "not getting laid" doing the talking. I believe in that."

"Come on. So tell me this. Be honest with me about you and TJ. Do you ever think of him?"

"Doesn't matter if I do or don't. I think what matters more right now is do you think of Julianna?"

"Why? Why go there? Why rub it in now?"

"I'm not. I ran into her. You should call her."

"You think so?"

"If you're asking me, I say don't be that guy. You *can* if you want, but why? Who'd want to?"

THE MOUNTAINS ARE dark presences in the night; indifferent to me abandoning the game and wading to shore, indifferent to all of us, to everyone.

Julianna is there on the shore. In the starlit darkness tying her bathing suit.

"I'm going to bed," she says. "Are you coming?"

If my answer would have been different would it have made any difference at all?

"Julianna? How're you doing?"

"Wow. I didn't expect to hear ever hear from you. How *are* you, doll?"

"Hanging in there," I say.

"So I heard. I ran into Kim the other day. I'm so sorry to hear-"

"Well all's fair in love and war. God, now I sound like Kim. I just had drinks with her yesterday and she passed your number along."

"I love Kim to death. How the hell is she?"

"Kim is *Kim*," I say. "She tried to order Seco at the Sexton, so...you know."

There's the sound of running water on her end of the line.

"Hold on a sec," she says. "Let me shut this."

"Did I call at a bad time? I can ring you back."

"No, perfect timing. I'm just getting into a hot bath. Getting myself squeaky clean."

"A bath, yeah. Taking it slow when you can is key to making it through third year," I say.

"For sure," she says.

There's an empty silence while I think of something to say. I think I can hear the acoustics of her bathroom, the echo of water in a small enclosed space. It wasn't so long ago we were on Panama's shores, with the vast ocean laid out before us but those nights feel so far away.

"Hey, I know it's last minute but I was calling to see if you want to get a drink tonight?"

"Tonight, hmmm," she says. "I am getting squeaky clean for-"

"Saturday night *is* date night."

"A date? Funny you should say. You're right that relaxing is so important. There's nothing like cleaning up, getting all ready to see someone special."

"Special?"

"He's about to find out how special when I see him."

"I'm so glad you said that. I wasn't sure if I should call and I'm so glad I did I was thinking we could-"

I listen to the sound of the water running on her side of the line.

"Oh, doll. Did you think? No. No, no, no. Sorry, no… I have a date tonight. I'm sorry."

"No, I'm the one who's sorry. I should go."

"Hey, wait. I want to say hang in there. And take care of yourself."

The phone clicks. The sounds of her bathroom are gone and I'm listening to my breath. Panama is so far away. Her sighs in the dark on the other side of the thatch wall are so far away. I close my eyes and I'm right there. But the past is moving farther and farther away with every second. I'm sailing farther and farther along the course my choices have brought me with each heartbeat.

Kim would say what happened with Antonia is not about me. I hate that I'm still thinking about her. That I'm still that guy. I want to call Kim. She'd say that whatever happened with Antonia was not my fault and it was going to happen no matter what I did. I want to believe that right now.

I don't bother hanging up. The room fills with the repeating staccato tone of the disconnected line.

TU SEI UN FIUME NEL MARE

You are a river in the sea

THE HUMIDITY HAS lessened a bit and the tropical night, cooled by the waves is just right. Sand stretches from the shore to the jungle; a tangle of tall, crowded palms, their hundreds of shapes a unified wall looming in the almost dark. Waves roll in, neat orderly sets breaking before the shallows.

The barefoot man sets his guitar down on the sand and leans it against one of the partially buried surfboards forming a circle around an open fire. Nearby, the two blonde surfer girls stop dancing and leave the spot on the beach under the wall-less thatch roof the surfers call the dance floor. A bouncy pop song continues playing as the young surfers dance, then it slows and slurs into a deep thrumming tone. The girls walk across the beach to the circle of surfboards and sit leaned up against longboards with the barefoot man. The man touches the patchwork of old, healed-over scars on his face.

The three of them watch a young man and woman leave the sandy dance floor. The young man and woman are Theron James and Kim. When they step off the beach and onto the road they disappear.

The pop song starts over again. It slows and slurs again, over and over. The scene they just observed plays out again. It plays out over and over. Sometimes Theron James and Kim leave the dance floor alone. Sometimes they leave with another young man and woman. Sometimes the four young people leave two by two. Countless combinations and iterations play out as they watch.

"If you stay perfectly still you can see the stars," one surfer girl says. "I can see them moving. I can feel *us* moving."

"We can't feel any of that," the second girl says. "If we stay perfectly still we can see the waves. Or is it if we stay perfectly still we can see while *in* the waves?"

"You *could* go out there and tell those people they reached *Il Pesce Danzante* after all," the first girl says to the barefoot man. "Or at least that they found what they were looking for."

"We should go dance with them," the second girl says.

The man shrugs.

"It doesn't matter," he says.

Past the shore in the surf someone yells. People are out there. In the dark. On their boards. Half-blind trying to time the break.

"They thought they were steering," the man says. "Thought they were holding on. But the waves had them all along."

"Isn't there something that can be done?"

"No. To surf is to understand this," the man says. "The best surfers know."

END PART II

∽

IL PASSATO SI STA SPOSTANDO SEMPRE PIÙ LONTANO
The past is moving farther and farther away.

DRIVING IN MIDTOWN Manhattan on a weekday is its own special hell. Daytime traffic brings out the worst in people, or maybe just the truth in people.

Yellow cabs swerve in and out of lanes inspiring choruses of horns. I grasp my steering wheel, roll out of the garage, and kiss my office goodbye. I say the day before Halloween means it's perfectly okay to leave early, middle of the afternoon early.

Some days are emptier than others. I wonder if being busy really helps, or if some days I'm merely masking the hollowness better. I know Professor Armstrong will have something enlightening to say on the subject. I've been meaning to look in on him for the past year. Yeah, I've been telling myself I want to see how he's doing, and I do, but more than that I'm hoping something he'll say will help me feel okay. Or to just… anything at all. Anything other than…empty. Maybe now that I'm no longer a student he'll have something more than his wry smile to offer.

The traffic ahead isn't letting up; I remember the United Nations is in session which means the roads are closed from 41st Street. So my jaunt uptown, at long last, isn't happening today. I figure I'll head to the Sexton instead of sitting in gridlock. Maybe I'll give Kim a call when I'm there. It's been months but maybe she'll want to play hooky for an afternoon or catch up. I don't blame her for not wanting to be around me. I'm trying but I'm sure people know what they're seeing is me trying. It's just not the same.

I know the Professor will be proud of what I've done since school. At least something is off to the right start. After a few months with the District Attorney's office I interviewed and received an offer from Trook, Benson, and Shahar. Senior partner Shahar brought me in to work with him on a new kind of environmental case they were taking to trial and the verdict went our way. I stood up for the environment and made a ton of money for the firm. Would Mister Shannon still not talk to me even if I bothered to contact him?

My instruments are home, in my loft. It's nice to have them around, even if they're only gathering dust. The last time I picked up my Fender desire was no-where to be found. I still think of Antonia but at least it's different. I hate it that I'm thinking of her now. I'm not pining, like this time last year. Everyone says that time heals. I think what they're describing is that some pains change from sharp to dull. At least I know now what we "had" was a figment of my perception and not something true, not something worthy of all my lament. Epiphany or not, everything still feeling so bland. Seeing Kim might help. If a drink with her will get me through another day I'll be grateful.

THE SEXTON's AC is a welcome respite from the late season blast of humidity. The place is humming; the mid-day-drinking-during-the-day crowd around the bar already two deep.

I navigate through the business-suit-wearing bodies telling myself I'm not going to think about Antonia. I'm going to relax and have a good time with my own company.

"I'll have a Seco. Uno Seco, por favor."

For a second I expect to see Kim but no, it is the woman on the bar stool in front of me who just ordered. After a moment the bartender brings her a shot and a clear drink in a tall glass. She drinks the shot and chases it with the drink in the glass, then coughs twice, intentionally spraying a small alcoholic cloud.

She's tall like Kim and dressed in a conservative skirt and blazer and yes she did just order a Seco but despite the attitude on display that's the end of the similarity. The woman's black hair is tied up in a bun with one of those stylish sticks holding it in place but she's not another of the clones the place is filled with. She's not from around here; there's a bit of all the world in her face, a face too young to be sitting alone at a bar clenching her jaw. I carve out a bit of space and stand between her and the next stool.

"You look unhappy. Can I help?"

She pivots her lean frame and looks me over with an icy expression for a second before returning to gaze at her shot glass and drink with disdain.

"I'm sorry," I say. "I thought I might be able to help."

"Why would you think that? I don't have a problem, I'm not paying for this shit."

She's not drunk, she's furious. It can't be over just the drink.

"You know, that's a crime around here."

"Sovereign. Immunity. Muchacho," she says. "Let them come to arrest me."

She says Muchacho with the Panamanian accent I heard all of last summer and I place her. Is she here for the UN Meeting? Maybe with El Toro? Part of his staff?

"Seriously, can I get you another drink? Around here not paying *is* a crime."

"Around here? Around. Here. Why would you say something like that-"

"I've been to Panama," I blurt. "I've been to El Chorillo."

And with that she turns and looks at me again. The TVs are blaring football highlights and several basketball games. One is tuned in to one of those new 24-hour news stations. Footage of a black US stealth plane fills the screen behind the dapper newscaster. We both watch the bat-like machine of impossible angles silently cross the sky, the miasma of sports and all the loud conversations as its sound track.

"You know what's a crime," she says and glares at the screen with the stealth planes. "Look how proud your country is."

I lean in close to her.

"I know about them," I say as near to a whisper as I can while still being audible. "I've been there. I've seen."

"What is it that you think you've seen?" she replies and places her hand on my shoulder.

I smell alcohol on her breath. Not Seco but really strong rum. My heart races from her proximity and the scent of cigarette smoke and something sweet and flowery in her hair even though I know my response was not her intent.

"Do you know what it's like to see a light that removes flesh? Not your clothes. Not your house. Your car. Only flesh. Skin starts to fade away and just when you think there's going to be so much red, more red that you can handle, you disappear. Just you. Everything else remains."

"The light is purple," I say. "One from each plane."

"Are you telling the truth? I can't tell."

"I told you. I was there."

"Tell me about something about Panama City. No, tell me about El Chorillo."

"Well, Panama City. Some places can be nice. Like downtown, near the shore. Nothing like San Blas though. El Chorillo? El Chorillo's hard to describe. What I remember most is the shore. There was an almost naked man climbing on the biggest heaps of trash I've ever seen outside of a dump."

"Maybe you are telling the truth."

I don't know why it's important to have her believe me. All around us people are moving like parts of one big choreographed dance. Buying drinks.

Forming and leaving and reforming little groups all in close proximity but separate. She's thinking something as she glances around the bar and then back to me.

"You are only talking to me because I am a woman," she says. "Because I look like this."

"I'm not gonna lie about that. I will tell you though, I starting talking to you because for a tiny, tiny second I thought you might be my friend. Someone I'm missing a lot right now."

"You're just saying that."

"No. She's the only other person I've ever heard order Seco in New York City."

"So, where is this *friend* you miss so much?"

"Not far, but too far away all at the same time. This can't be a thing that only happens to us New Yorkers. Moving on. Not because we've settled down but because we're... growing up... at our own paces. It feels like growing apart. She's...we're going through that now."

"For a liar that sounds like a true answer. You're not the one for settling down?"

On a reflex I start to reply that life is long and Antonia and mine is only starting but I catch myself. Sometimes in life you miss your chance. I decide not to say either thought.

"In El Chorillo there's a crater the size of a small parking lot that neatly stops right along the line of-"

"Rueben Blades house. Yes. What does it have to do with settling down?" she asks.

"Nothing. I don't know. I just want you to believe me."

"I believe you. Most Americans can't even point to Panama on a map. You know San Blas."

"San Blas is what you call it, what *we* call it, but *they* call it Kuna Yala. Man, those islands full of palm trees and crabs. Those reefs in the shallow water warm as bath tubs. Sand dollars as big as your hand, not the dead ones the live ones. I'm never going to forget it. Oh, oh when I was there I met the Cacique. Well, we had breakfast when he was on his way to meet with El Toro."

She laughs.

"Surely you must mean the esteemed President Ernesto Perez Balladares Gonzales-Revilla. Didn't think you Americans called him that other name."

"I'm sorry. Do you work for him? You work for him."

"I'm not here to talk about work. This is where you Americans go to not talk about work, correct?"

"I guess. In theory. You're right. What are we doing here? Let's go find some Seco. You want to go? I can show you a lot better places than here."

"Let's go and find some Seco? Is this what you are asking me? Hold out your hands."

I comply.

"No ring? No wife," she says.

"No and no."

"Ah, but you didn't say no girlfriend."

"You didn't ask. No. I have no girlfriend."

"So what's wrong with you?"

"Other than being a ghost in the life I once had, nothing."

"That's so sad, I almost feel sad for you."

"Don't. My friend taught me there's only one way to make sure you don't live a life that's sad."

"And what is that?"

"I can't tell you. Well it's not that I *can't* tell you, it's just no good to tell. I can show you. I mean. I mean the showing you is taking you to go find some Seco."

"Now I know you lie. There isn't a bottle of Seco in this whole city."

"You're probably right. But if there's any on the East Coast it will be in this place I know in Atlantic City.

"Atlantic City? What is this?"

"It's a place American people go. To have fun. For vacation. It's a nice drive. About three hours south. You can see the oceans along the way. There's a boardwalk. And a lot of Casinos with people up all night. It's where I'm hoping we can find some Seco."

She rubs her finger on her chin absently and her eyes are staring through me. I get the sense this contemplative expression is seen a lot by those close to her and a pang of desire shoots through me. I want her to say yes. I want to know her.

"I'd rather see your ocean than any more of here," she says. "Three hours? Can you promise have to have me back for my flight tomorrow?"

LATE AFTERNOON HAZE transforms into a white sparkle on the water under the Verrazano. The city buildings are all lit up with sun. It isn't anywhere near as extraordinary as the skyline at night. She's polite. But not impressed.

We roll into New Jersey and my mind is swimming with questions. About the Bull. About her life in Panama. But they seem unimportant weighed against the relative quiet of the car vibrating on the road and our hypnotic forward motion. The silence isn't uncomfortable; I don't see fit to break it. She flips through stations on the radio and isn't satisfied with any of the music. She settles on one of the classical stations and leaves it playing low. She nods her head, smiles diplomatically from across the divide of the armrest middle of the front seat which feels a million miles away. The Garden State Parkway's view isn't as nice as I remembered. I was hoping to drive back into the memory of water and sand dunes and sleepy towns of a road trip forever ago with my high school friends but how could anywhere remain so golden.

High above a jetliner streaks through the sky towards New York leaving a long, white contrail. heading for New York leaves a long white contrail. A wedge of geese in a perfect V formation cross its path, southbound, like us.

I hear an echo of Luis from El Chorillo telling us his mother's account of seeing a giant bat with purple eyes.

She laughs

"What?"

"I know what you're thinking," she says.

"That I was hoping the drive was nicer?"

"If everything was the same Panama I'd be disappointed," she says.

"I wouldn't. We're almost there."

We get our view of the ocean as we near Atlantic City. The boardwalk's summer bustle is gone. Tired light illuminates the last few families still out walking before dinner time. The Casino lights are already on, a futile rally against the dusk. I spot a carnival in the distance as I pull into the "In" ramp of the parking garage of the Silver Schooner Hotel and Casino Resort. I've been here before. I'm betting that they have Seco. Inside the garage is all concrete and boring grey level upon level of ramps housing the vessels everyone used to transport to this vacation-land.

We decide to head straight into the Casino, one of the benefits of traveling with no luggage. The covered walkway is long and gray and remarkably unimpressive. When we finally push through the double doors at the end an explosion of electronic color and sound greets us. Music and lights and bells and whistles. The novelty doesn't last long. There's emptiness everywhere. I know she sees it. I don't know why anyone happy and fulfilled would come here.

"Okay," I say. "Are you ready for Seco?"

"Ready," she says.

She's trying, like I'm trying. And I *am* trying to have fun. Despite the tons and tons of empty faces all around us. I'm trying not to let on that I'm empty too. I'm trying to find something here, with her. I hope she doesn't see this and that she's having a good time.

I smile and laugh as I lead her to a bar called the Octopus Garden, the place I'm betting that has the Seco. The Garden's rich, darkly-stained wooden doors are un-marked except for a door-knocker sized brass octopus on each one. Inside the space is all wood paneled and built to resemble the inside hold of a wooden ship. We're shown to a table for two in one of the eight-sectioned-off nooks radiating from the central bar. Aside from a few dressed-up couples I take to be high-rollers the place is very empty.

When our server arrives I promptly ask if he has Seco, from Panama I add, which sends him marching back to the center bar to ask. He returns promptly to tell us they do not. We order cocktails with nautical names from the menu instead. She's not impressed. Neither am I.

And just like that we're inside a fake ship, drinking drinks with stupid names we didn't really want in the first place. I wonder what it would be like to be on the open water in Kuna Yala with her right now instead of here. This bar and places like it that I once thought were something special are nothing; it was the sense of belonging and having experiences together that held the power.

She gets up and walks to the restroom, unsteady on her feet. She grasps a chair for balance and steadies herself.

The drinks come. They sit on the table, sweating as I wait for her to return. The ice in mine has melted. She returns and does not sit.

"I know its only dinner time," she says. "But I'm ready to call it a night."

"Is everything okay?"

"Everything is okay. I am exhausted. From traveling. From work. From being here in America."

"I understand. Okay, I'll get us rooms."

"There's no need. I've already arranged for two."

"Is there anything I can do?"

"Breakfast at dawn? Say 6:30, before heading back to New York?"

The wait staff are kind and pretend that they do not hear.

MY ROOM IS a nice one, with a terrace facing the ocean. I sit outside listening to the night wind, wishing I could sleep. The carnival's Ferris Wheel lights have gone dark. Its shape remains visible in the distance. After an hour I decide to go to the casino rather than remain sitting. I figure I'll buy a pack of cigarettes from a vending machine, kill an hour to get me closer to breakfast time, then walk back.

I squint when I enter the artificial brightness. I wander slowly, feeling like I'm in a waking dream drowning me in light and sound. There's a small crowd gathered around one of the craps tables. A young man rolls the dice. The old man next to him leads the table in cheering him on. I recognize the voice.

Waves.

Darkness.

The spaces between.

I've heard the voice before. The man is TJ's Uncle. His Uncle Tino that he told me about in Panama. I've never met the man. I've never seen him before and haven't thought of TJ's anecdote since Panama, yet I am certain that he is TJ's Uncle and that I have heard his voice just as certain as I am that the beach outside is made of sand.

Tipsy people in the crowd place their chips in the number boxes on the table. I approach the man.

"Constantine?" I say. "Uncle Tino?"

"Blow on those dice," he says to the young man. "And fight for it. The fight is both the path and the river."

"Your name, Constantine, right? I know your nephew, TJ, Theron James."

"You talking to me?"

"Yes, sir."

"Name's Jimmy. Pleased to meet ya. I'm lyin' I'm not pleased to meet anyone unless that man's come out roll is a natural."

People near him pat him on the back and respond with a flurry of "hell yeahs" and approval.

The young man scoops up the dice. People place field bets on the table.

"What do you mean by that? The fight is both the path and-"

The old man places chips on the table, takes a swig of a drink someone hands him, and resumes chanting a cheer for the shooter.

The young man rolls. The crowd hoots in approval of the number. I walk away certain that I am not mistaken.

THE DARK AND quiet is waiting for me in my room. I sit on the bed next to the night table and pull out the yellow phone book. I'm going to locate TJ and call him and ask him what his Uncle looks like.

I pick up the phone and figure out how to dial out. I hang up. Then dial room service and ask them to bring me a pack of cigarettes. I don't want to smoke. I want to have them delivered. During my high school trip it was so hard to get packs for the drive. Driving. Smoking. The ocean. Everything about here had felt so magical. I never could have imagined I'd be back here, like this. Directory assistance helps me find a ton of "TJ's" and "Theron James'" I call the first few and wake up people who are not TJ.

I go outside on the terrace and pace, then come back inside and pick up the phone. I ask the operator for Professor Armstrong's phone number.

"Professor Reginald Wallace Armstrong, please."

The operator reads me a number and puts me through.

"Hello," I say. "Professor? Professor Armstrong?"

"No," a man's voice that could be the Professor's deep baritone responds.

"Have I reached 212-448-9845?"

"Yes, you have."

"I'm sorry, so have I reached Professor Armstrong's home? Or his office? Reginald Armstrong professor of law, right?"

"This used to be his office."

"Used to be?"

"He's moved on."

"Is he okay?"

"He's moved on to teach in California?"

"California? Where?"

I write down the numbers he reads.

As I DIAL the California number I wonder who I just spoke to. Who would pick up an old office phone so late at night? An answering service? The line connects.

"Hello Professor?"

"No," a woman's voice replies.

"Who is this?"

"Excuse me? You phoned me. Who is this?"

"I'm one of Professor Armstrong's students. Ex-students. Is he teaching here?"

"We're closed for the night. But no he's moved on. To private practice."

"Private practice? Doing what?"

"Trucking."

"Trucking? He's a law professor."

"Interstate commerce," she says as if I'm supposed to know what that means.

"Interstate commerce?"

"Yes," she says in a condescending tone.

"Who is this?"

"Are you sure you have the correct number," she says.

"Wait? What? You just said he's moved on-"

I hear whispering and a rustling of papers.

"Have you tried this forwarding number?" she says.

I DIAL THE number the woman gave me.

"Hello Professor?"

"No. Who is this," a male voice replies, definitely not the Professor.

"One of his students."

"Honey. It's one of his students again."

"Again," I say. "Who is this? Have I reached his home?"

"No. Yes you have, but no he doesn't live here anymore. We're... watching the place for him. Well really we've just moved in. He's not expected back. Didn't you call not so long ago and speak to my wife?"

"No."

"Yes, honey. Another one," the man says.

"One of who? Where did you say the Professor is?"

"He's... gone south. To help the coral reefs."

"Coral reefs? Why?"

The man laughs. A woman's voice in the background is telling him to hang up. There's a knock at my door. Room service with my cigarettes. I put the phone down and go open the door.

My friend from Panama is standing there in the hall. She's pacing and has a bottle of Seco in her hand.

"Hi," she says.

"Hi."

"This is not what you think," she says.

"What do I think?"

"Doesn't matter. This is not it."

"Um, want to come in?"

"I shouldn't. I mean I'm not staying. Can we just talk here?"

"Whatever you like. The room has this nice patio. I was just thinking what a waste it was."

A young couple enters the hall from the stairwell. They drunkenly amble our way arm in arm. She comes inside. We cross the room in the dark, open the sliding door, and sit outside.

"I just came to thank you," she says.

"For what?"

"For this trip."

"It's barely been a trip," I say.

"Well for this time. It was just what I needed."

I glance at the clock on the bedside table inside. We've barely been half a day.

"It's not the amount of time," she says. "I finally took the time to stop. And I figured things out."

"I guess that means celebrate?"

"Oh this?" She puts the bottle of Seco on the table. "This is for you."

"Wow where'd you… shall I open it?"

"If you want. It's yours. For you. I'm not staying. I'm heading back."

"Now?"

"I'm on the next bus."

"Aw, you don't have to. I'll take you. It's not a prob-"

"No. I want to go alone."

"I don't understand."

"There isn't a lot to understand. I do this a lot."

"This?"

"Yeah, this." She gestures at me and the room.

"You know the Kuna saying," she says. "The one that starts out when you're lost in the nine worlds…"

"No. How does it go?"

"Oh, it doesn't matter. I mean I never tell it right. I travel. I meet people. I go places with them. I don't expect you to understand but what would you do if you could get away with something and not get caught?"

"Why would you ask me that?"

"I'm trying to do the right thing. Please don't make me spell it out."

"I get it. You're married or with someone. It's okay, I get it. But tell me, please, why would you ask me that question?"

"I used to do things just to get away with them. Because I could. Tonight, I know I'm done with all that."

"Used to?"

She takes both of my hands in hers.

"Don't be disappointed. I'm sorry you're disappointed. I should have just left but I wanted you to know this was important to me and to thank you. And now I have."

"Um, you're welcome."

She stands.

"Are you sure I can't take you?"

"Sure."

We walk to the door. I didn't think anything was going to happen. I had no expectations but there's no way to tell her that. Now that she's seconds away from gone I am disappointed. She's beautiful. We're here. The night feels so empty. Having breakfast with her would have made the time pass bearably. And if she had come for another reason I wouldn't have said no.

"If you're ever in Panama," she says, then stops. "I was going to say look me up but what's the point in saying that? Good night."

I watch her maneuver past the drunk couple who are still in the hall, ambling from door to door using the walls to keep themselves from falling; then she disappears into the stairwell.

I SLEEP LATE. I eat breakfast. I don't let the office know I'm not coming in. I've decided to go to Kim's house in Brooklyn.

News radio gives updates on a big storm. The skies are grey for my drive. I take breaks at a few rest stop to stretch. The quiet is as empty as last night was.

I park down the block from the Brownstone Kim and her fiancé have purchased. Yesterday's false summer has fled. Wind is blowing. Brooklyn parents are out Trick or Treating with their young kids dutifully holding umbrellas for the rain they are pretending won't come. Maybe they're not pretending.

Kim's house is decorated with a paper skeleton on the door; the kind with the articulated joints I haven't seen since I was a kid. Someone has placed one of its hands over its pelvis leaving me no doubt the place is Kim's.

Kim's fiancé opens the door when I ring the bell. He's wearing a skeleton tee-shirt of rib cage bones over a black turtle neck.

"Trick or Treat," I say. "Nice shirt."

He looks around for kids.

"Okay," he says. "Aren't you a bit old?"

"I'm a friend of Kim's. From school."

Worry replaces his diplomatic smile.

"Is she okay?"

"I haven't spoken to her in months and I was in town and thinking of our professor and-"

We're interrupted by a group of young Trick or Treaters rushing up the stairs.

"Look twin skeletons," a young girl in a dinosaur onesie says.

"Looks just like you," I say to Kim's fiancé.

"Spitting image," he says as he drops candy in each of the children's bags. A group of parents on the side walk look on.

"You live long enough eventually you realize you're the imposter. Tee shirt or no tee shirt."

"That's depressing," he says.

"Not as depressing as not being able to eat candy anymore."

The trick or treaters bound down the stairs to their parents and move on to the next home. Kim's fiancé and one of the Moms exchange nervous glances. I haven't changed my clothes since yesterday but I'm fine. They have nothing to worry about from me.

"So, you scared me for real there for a second," he says. "Kim's stuck in Nashville. The storms' got her flight grounded, she's not gonna make it home tonight. When you came to the door-"

"Nashville?"

"She's got a consulting job with a media start up. She's down there and Atlanta twice a month now."

"Oh, Media. She'll be good at that."

"So right, you're Kim's friend. I knew I knew you from somewhere I just couldn't place it.

"We never met."

"Feels like we have though. There was that one time in the city we almost did."

"Sharp memory on you."

"Kim keeps me on my toes. You're still in... law and order?"

"Oh god, no. There's no making a living in that."

"I hear you. I was so glad when Kim decided on private practice. Your wife must be happy."

"Oh, no, no no. No wife."

"Sorry. I can't keep up. Kim doesn't talk much to start with..."

"No. It's just me."

"Ever think about settling down?"

"Maybe."

Maybe there's a me like that.

"I was like that. Before I met Kim," he says.

How do you tell someone you are a shadow? The manifestation of a life that did not happen. I wanted a life like his. There comes a point you realize you are the failed iteration, not meant to be, but playing out, moving forward in time anyway.

"You okay? You don't look so good. It's getting cold why don't you come on inside?

"It's getting late."

"Nah, it's never too late."

He's relieved when I turn and walk down the stairs. I should have never come. I don't see fit to tell him about TJ or that I bet Kim is with him now.

TRAFFIC BE DAMNED, I head back to the city, to school, to see if I can figure out what's going on with Professor Armstrong. They'll be plenty of students around in the library, someone will tell it to me straight.

Thick, gray cloud cover hangs over the city. Heading uptown I pass groups of people my age, in costume en route to parties and gatherings I'll never know about.

By the school there are no party goers, only a few students coming and going and a homeless guy I used to see every day I'd forgotten about until now. As I'm looking for a spot I see the Professor walking across the faculty lot. He's carrying a banker's box pressed up against his side. His arm is in a sling. Not his left, like in Panama, it's his right this time.

If he's still around? Who did I speak to last night? And why did they tell me he was gone?

I think about circling over to greet him but I keep my window rolled up and drive past. I watch him get into a blue Jeep Cherokee. I wait, double-parked, until he pulls out. I follow him. After a few minutes I realize he's heading onto the expressway and I'm following him for real.

We pull onto the expressway heading north. Keeping him in sight isn't hard. He stays in the middle lane and stays right around the limit. After about twenty minutes he pulls off onto a park and ride.

A dozen or so cars and three tractor trailers are in spots. A man is walking his dog. A trucker stands outside the restroom smoking a cigarette. The Professor parks in a spot next to an old Russian Fiat. It looks just like the one he drove in Panama. It very possibly could be the one he was putting around in down there. I don't know how, or why or what the hell he's doing. He gets out of the Jeep and into the Fiat and pulls back onto the road.

I follow him onto the Taconic Parkway. There's a lot of land out here. The leaves have turned and are past peak color. Autumn reds and yellows are everywhere. The Professor takes an exits onto a narrow road. Its winding and only wide enough for one car going each way, so we've slowed. There's no other traffic and I wonder if he's noticed me. He has to see me. I hope he thinks nothing of it. We pass a house from a time gone by on a lot cleared from the trees. There's a quintessential red barn, a lot of overgrown grass then there's nothing but trees on both sides of the road again. A possum and a line of babies dart across the road. I wonder why they're up during the day, despite the overcast gray; in the boroughs I only see them at night.

We approach another house on a lot surrounded by trees. The Professor slows and pulls into a long driveway. There's a pond on the land next to a building that reminds me of that three walled garage in Panama standing where the driveway ends about a half-acre in. This building has a metal, roll-up door and looks well maintained.

I stop at the foot of the driveway. The Professor has to have noticed my vehicle. He gets out of the Fiat, and I half expect him to wave. He takes a five-gallon plastic pail out of the Fiat's trunk and enters through a door to the left of the bunker's roll up garage door. If he's noticed me he's given no sign.

I wait a long while. I tell myself to turn around and drive away. I wonder where I'd go. To work on Monday? Back to Kim's?

I get out of my car and walk. The bunker-garage appears freshly painted. A blackish-gray. Little flecks of silver stand out almost luminescent despite the day. The air smells clean, with a hint of burning leaves somewhere along with a tinge of what I take to be industrial glue or braising metal. The door the Professor entered is built into the concrete to the left of the metal roll-up. I pull it open. The metal creaks and clicks and is all kinds of loud.

Just inside is a line of metal electrical boxes on the wall, each with a heavy T-flip switch inside their open front panels. Industrial lamps hang from the space's ceiling beneath two trunk-lines of square industrial ventilation ducts. The cold fluorescents illuminate only the front half of the cavernous space.

There are two parallel metal rails built into the concrete floor leading from the roll up door and disappearing into the far half of the space where the light does not penetrate. I didn't notice any rail lines outside. Another grey Fiat, just like the one the professor left outside is lined up on the subway-line thick rails, parked in the light just outside the area obscured by darkness. It's dirty and covered in what looks like black soot.

DANIEL BRAUM

The Professor is sitting on a folding chair next to the Fiat. He's counting something I take to be a pile of cash. From the colors I can tell it is not US currency. There's a five-gallon plastic pail next to him. Something is in it is moving and splashing water over the sides.

A man is on his knees scrubbing at one of the Fiat's tires with a rag and soapy water from another pail. There is a shiny silver finish beneath the black coating he scrubs away. Something about the dents and pounded-out angles of the vehicle makes me think of the stealth planes.

"Professor?" I say.

The man scrubbing the Fiat looks up.

"You?" he says. "Professor. It's him."

I know his voice. Recognition dawns on me. The man is TJ. A year has changed him. His hair has grown in, long, like a rock and roller that's in style now. He's put on weight and his arms are muscular. His boyish face has filled out into a man's but he's still got his model good looks

"What's he doing here?" TJ says. "He's not strong enough. You said he's not meant for this."

"Take it easy," the Professor says. At first I think he's talking to TJ, then I realize he's talking to me. The Professor stands and walks towards me, slowly, as if I'm someone dangerous.

"What's going on, Professor? What are you two doing here?"

"How'd you find me," the Professor asks.

"I didn't know you were hiding," I say. "TJ, I tried to call you. I think I saw your Uncle last night in Atlantic City."

"You said he couldn't find this place," TJ says. "You said no one could."

"I'm handling this, Theron James," the Professor says.

"How'd you break your arm," I say.

"Oh this?" the Professor says. "Well. I was coming from-"

"No, tell me how you broke it down in Panama."

"Let's just talk first."

"No, now. On the island you said another time. Another time is now."

"I always liked you. Trusted you," he says to me. "Somethings I think maybe are just going to happen no matter what."

"Professor, no," TJ says.

He walks around the car putting it between us. He opens the driver side door.

"Theron James, do not enter that vehicle," the Professor says.

TJ doesn't move.

"What is this place?"

"It is much easier to show you."

The Professor walks to the wall by the door and flips the first of the heavy switches up. The rails in the floor thrum for an instant then lights in the back half of the space turn on. But the space remains in darkness.

I can discern the rails. They lead to something spanning ceiling to floor. What it is can't tell. It is as if the light is struggling.

The Professor flips the second switch. The pitch of the hum tunes up and something is different about the air. TJ turns the lights of the Fiat on and I remember touching his shoulder in the shallows. I remember the sensation of being pulled by a current with him.

The Professor flips the next switch in the row. And the next. A low-pitched drone joins the crecendoing hum and the crackle of the struggling overhead lamps.

"This is how I broke my arm," the Professor says. "There are worlds of nothing between worlds."

I knew he was going to say that. I've heard him say it before and a pang of sadness overcomes me. How did it come to be that I'm standing here, in this place? Instead of holding hands with Antonia or someone for me, somewhere warm and nice, or just somewhere?

I hear the last switch on the wall clack as the Professor throws it up. The lights seem to have what they need to shed light again and I think the darkness is leaving. The Professor is speaking the lines of something, something very familiar.

"Waves."

"Darkness."

"The spaces between."

TJ's saying it along with him. I try to make out the shape of what is there in front of us. The rail lines lead right to it.

The Professor and TJ go quiet and the kinetic thrum fills what would otherwise be silence. I wait for them to speak. I think they're about to speak again. The last of the shadows clear from the corners of the room. My chest catches the rhythm of no-longer forgotten words. I think the overhead lights are going to burst but they win their struggle. I can hear the Professor and TJ breathing in. The pattern blooms in me. I remember what to say next.

RUM PUNCH IS GOING DOWN

Beli⁊e. 1986.

I'M IN A water taxi speeding away from Belize City, catching spray, sitting shoulder to shoulder with a dozen travelers licking the Caribbean Sea from their lips. A young woman with stringy, almost white blonde hair on the bench next to me is the only one craning for a glimpse of the sinking sun. Her boyfriend Brett, a shaggy-topped guy with jailhouse tattoos too faded for his baby-face is chatting with everyone but her. A wild-eyed, grey-haired man named Andy listens to Brett's rambling about an aquifer, while the fit, tall old woman holding his hand stares past me, euphoric about something the rest of us are missing. Everyone's a bit off. You have to be some kind of crazy to take this little boat to a little island in the middle of nowhere. Tropical air heavy with humidity and the vanishing scents of the places we've each left behind unite us.

Our driver's in a hurry, steering the engine at the stern to keep us on a path inside the buoys and out of the shallows beyond that will stop the boat cold. The sun's got the calm surface all opaque and shimmering with the last of day. I picture morning light through my apartment's dirty window on Stefania's lithe form in my bed, a frame of glowing white outlining her contour.

We speed into a patch of mangroves; their waxy green leaves drink the retreating light.

The trees form a maze of channels. Their bulbous roots hang in the water, miracles of nature that filter salt and provide shelter. The wake we leave catching a turn briefly submerges the nearest cluster of tendrils. A trio of large dark shapes are visible beneath the surface in a growing patch of shadow. I want to dive in.

Stefania only wanted to pass through the living world below on the way to *her* dream of diving the Blue Hole, not to touch life but to get to the bottom, where it all goes black. I see now how *my* dream was merely a curiosity adjacent to hers, one she entertained for a while. I shared with her one of my most cherished memories; a grade school presentation of how impossible little things like sea horses and whole worlds live protected and hidden in mangrove forests like this. I wanted to see them myself. My secret dream that never went away. I'm almost done feeling sick over how I revealed something so meaningful. I should have known she'd never leave her life for me.

I tell everyone sea horses are why I've come. Running away feels more like truth.

THE DRIVER SLOWS us to a stop where the channels return to open sea. With the sun below the horizon I can see the shapes under the water converging on the boat. The driver takes off his cap revealing half-grown-in dreads, unhooks a pole from the boat's side and dips it off the bow. It's met by a round, whiskered face. A manatee. The big peaceful animal playfully grasps the stick with webbed flippers. The driver speaks affections to it in creole.

"Oh look, how cute, Baby," the woman next to me says to Brett.

"They're everywhere, Silver," he replies flatly, to her disappointment.

Silver can't be more than twenty. A tan line on her shoulder reveals just how white her skin was before all the sun she's seen. A paper bag holding bottles of hard liquor clinks at her feet.

For a second I think she is going to try and catch Brett's attention again. Instead she strikes it up with the tall gray-haired woman she addresses as Ranit.

"How'd all these channels get made?"

"Hurricane Hattie," Ranit says. "She ripped her way through. Even tore the Caye right in half."

"The Split looks worse than it is," Brett remarks to Andy.

His voice is dry and too loud. I recognize the hardness lurking in his eyes and the way he speaks as the same. He's much too stiff and wound up for me to believe his projection of being an easy-going guy.

"Can't wait," Andy replies. "I hear there are sharks and crocodiles."

"You a fisherman too?" Brett asks.

"Sort of," Andy says.

"There are some sharks, yeah," Brett says. "Most of 'em are no worry, too tame from being fed all the time. Crocodiles? No. Nope."

The passengers move to watch the driver and the manatee. Brett and Andy go to the stern and examine the outboard motor.

"The Caye wants to be a tourist place someday," Ranit says to me, though I'm sure she wants Silver to hear. "Can't have crocodiles in a tourist place. But they're here. Be careful if you swim."

"Brett's gonna buy land," Silver says. "We're going to build houses on the North Side of the Split. With real plumbing because, ya know, Brett knows how to do it. He worked construction back home."

"Oh, now I remember him," Ranit says. "He's Harlan's boy."

Silver returns to silently minding the bag of alcohol.

"The government's in the middle of cleaning up the 'undesirables' who live at the Split," Ranit says, this time for me. "Homeless, Rastas and ex-pats. Gang members. Not all of them have been run off yet. Keep your head up."

"Thanks," I say. "If I go, I'll keep it in mind."

"You'll go. It's why you're here."

"What makes you think that?"

"When you come long enough to remember Hurricane Hattie you get to know things."

"Like the way your man 'knows' that engine?"

"Andy?" She laughs. "Just met him. I let him come along."

"Then he must be special."

"He isn't. I was up the coast saying my last goodbye to a dear friend. So was Andy. Fate would have it the three of us, in another life, worked for the same employer. I decided, uncharacteristically mind you, to indulge in his affections."

"Hattie was when, Sixty One? What keeps you coming?"

"Let's see. How do I put it...?"

The driver is done with the manatee and notices Andy and Brett at the stern.

"The Caye's still an empty place," Ranit says. "Empty as in, not full of what it might ultimately come to be, just yet. I find undecided places conducive to the liminal. It's a great place to practice being not attached."

Brett and Andy return to their seats. The driver returns to the motor.

"I'm here to see sea horses," I blurt.

Ranit responds with a kind smile and disinterest.

"No sea horses at the Caye," Brett interjects. "No. Nope not at all."

A military speed boat passes in front of the channel opening. It slows to have a look at us. Our driver gives a familiar wave before it speeds off.

Its wake rocks us causing the bottles between Silver's feet to clank. Brett notices and finally puts his arm around her. Our engine's chug eclipses the sound of birds and lapping water.

THE CAYE IS a tiny, palm-filled oasis less than a mile wide. A few buildings, brightly painted homes, and hotels dot the beach where docks reach into reef-sheltered waters. As we slow to tie up I see where the island is split in two by a channel wide enough for a few boats to pass through side by side.

Passengers are waiting on the dock. Bicyclists with baskets on the front of their rides, are on the beach waiting to be hired. A young man and woman release from an embrace as we disembark. My boat mates head to land and pair up with cyclists to pedal their luggage. The new passengers board. I remain, watching the couple wave as the boat pulls away. The woman continues waving long after it is out of sight. At thirty, have I missed my last chances to experience a connection like that again?

I leave the woman and head for the beach. Our boat driver is waiting for me with a smile and the last basket-fronted bicycle.

He introduces himself as Ras Nicholas but implores me to call him Nico. For a small fee he will take me and my bag to a place to stay. I'm tired and without choices. I hadn't planned anything beyond getting here and trusting it would all work out.

"Looks like you are my captain on both sea and land," I say.

"I do everything and anything I can for work," Nico says. "What do *you* do back home?"

"Nothing anymore. I quit my job to come. I used to fix cars but I don't think that'll do me any good."

"I'm glad you're here. Twelve of you came today, this will be good for business."

We laugh.

"This is Front Street," Nico says. "I'll take you to the best place. I know them all."

There isn't much besides palm trees, flowering bushes, and a few small houses on the sandy road. There are no cars. Nico pedals slowly. I walk next to him. The salt air is tinged with barbeque smoke. Bats flit across the road between lime trees.

A bell dings. Ranit and Andy pedal past, each on their own bike. They wave, ride ahead, and cut across a small seaside graveyard consisting of a few white wooden crosses and sinking headstones before disappearing into a group of well-maintained beach huts farther ahead.

"See you are fitting in already," Nico says.

We pass through the graveyard and stop on a spot of mangrove-lined shore. A dozen huts raised on stilts overlook the water between two rickety docks. Nico arranges a room for a week for me. I'm amazed at how inexpensive it is. I really might stay forever.

I climb the wooden stairs to my hut pausing for a look around. I spot Nico pedaling towards the back of the island. He stops at a small house raised on cinder blocks and stows his bike. Instead of going inside he climbs into the space beneath it.

I enter my hut, flop onto my narrow cot and fall asleep in my clothes. Images of the lush mangroves and the white seaside-crosses wash through me. I dream mangrove roots are growing into my throat. I rip at my neck and mouth and pull out thin, pink fishing line. I keep pulling and pulling leading out more and more line. Laughter wakes me. I lean out my window and see Silver and Brett are walking on the beach towards Front Street. Silver looks up and sees me.

"Hey, we're going to dinner and the party," she calls. "Come on."

"Only one place, if you wanna eat you better listen," Brett says.

I hurry down. On Front Street we pass a few cleared lots with wooden buildings under construction. A couple of families sitting outside watch us curiously.

The "party" is at the only bar, an open-air three story building of thatch and timbers. Wet suits hang from the second and third floor railings. A Chinese food place is next door, which remarkably is the only other establishment I've seen. Rastas, weathered tourists, and ex-pats are lined up out the door. On the beach across from it is a matronly Belizean woman tending a smoking BBQ in the center of a crowd. On the pier behind them are two dock houses painted with dive flags.

Brett says hello to seemingly everyone, swigging from their drinks and taking bites from their plates while Silver and I stand around, unintroduced. I notice Front Street ends not far away in darkness that I take to be the Split.

I notice an attractive dark-haired woman, right out of my dreams, standing alone under one of the palms. Before I can muster the courage to go over to her Silver takes both Brett and I by the elbow and ushers us inside. Brett finds this funny. Most of the space is a dance floor, surrounding a small round bar. It's so crowded I'd believe everyone on the island is here. Brett makes space for us. Two things are on the menu. Rum and Rum Punch. I offer to buy the drinks and realize just how inexpensive everything is. The money I allotted to spend for today will last at least all week. I decide to buy a round for the people near us. The rum is strong. I feel drunk pretty fast and wish I'd eaten something first. I notice tall, gray haired Andy dancing with a young woman. Ranit is nowhere to be seen.

"Dance with me, dance with me," Silver says to Brett.

Brett ignores her and proceeds to introduce me to a young Belizean man he calls "Douglas the Fisherman, his fisherman friend." Douglas remains deadpan through Brett's wordy introduction. He's clean cut, wearing a plain-white tee, khaki shorts and sturdy brown boots. Brett suggests I buy rum punch for Douglas, and all his friends, and one for Douglas's dad who is somewhere outside. I agree. Douglas chimes in with the idea I should buy a round of rum punch for everyone. I have enough money to do so several times over so I say what the hell.

I hand my money to the bartender. Brett and Douglas pass out drinks and chat about what a good idea it would be for me to hire Douglas's dad for a fishing tour.

I tell them I want to look for sea horses. They regard me with puzzled expressions.

"You're a decent guy Rum Punch," Brett says after a second. "Word of advice to you, beware of Hitler."

"What?"

"He's a nasty Rasta," Brett says.

"No, he's one of the homeless ex-pats," Silver says.

"Whatever," Brett says. "Listen, man. He lives in the bushes at the Split. He's probably outside begging and hassling people around now. Whatever you do don't let him eat your food he's got AIDS. I've seen him try to bite people when he's pissed."

"That's terrible," I say. "Doesn't anyone do something?"

"He's gonna die soon," Douglas says.

"That's fucked up," I say.

"I've had enough of this. Dance with me," Silver says, pulling at Brett's arm. "If you won't, I'm gonna recruit Rum Punch."

Brett doesn't seem to care. He resumes talking with Douglas as if I'm not present. I feel dizzy from the alcohol.

"So let's do this." Brett throws his arm around me. "Ready to see tame rays and sharks?"

I think I'm going to say something smart to buy me a way out. All I manage is a slurred, "When?"

"Now," Douglas says.

Andy emerges from the dance floor.

"Hey, I didn't realize you're such a popular guy," he says. "Can I get one of those rum punches, buddy?"

"We're doing business," Douglas says. "Go away."

Andy responds by pushing him with fierceness I didn't expect.

"Whoa, oh shit," Brett says.

He takes Silver by the hand and they disappear onto the dance floor.

"Rum Punch and *I* are having a moment here," Andy says. "You get the fuck away."

There's the same hardness I see in Brett present in Douglas as he stares at us before turning to the door.

"Don't fuck with Rum Punch," Andy says in a sing-song tone and drapes his arm around me.

"Another round for my pal, here and you know what for everyone," I tell the bartender.

I realize I've been stupid. I'm still being stupid. I need to figure out how to start over. Only I'm way too sloshed.

Andy's sloshed too. Now I'm stuck with his arm around me instead of Brett's. He's gripping my shoulders like a pervy uncle. His aggression and sing-song tone are more disturbing together.

"You okay, Andy," I say and try to move his arm. He's a head taller than me.

"You ever lose a friend, Rum Punch? You don't look old enough to know what I'm feeling."

"I know..."

I'm too drunk to communicate the loss I've known.

"Ranit and I, and our mutual dearly departed, we all worked in the Bureau once. Our friend offed her ailing husband when his pain got too bad, then offed herself. She was the smartest friend I ever had. Oh I could tell you the things she's done and the sights we've seen out here."

"That's freaking awful," I say.

"Awful is right," he says. "What's the point of anything?"

He leans on me as if we've just exchanged some profound truth. I'm trying to figure out a way to peel him off when Nico edges his way to us.

"All my friends are here talking about death and darkness and drunkenness," Nico says.

"Yes, we are," Andy says. "Don't even think about feeding me any of that Rasta peace and love right now."

"Did I say anything? I came to join you."

They engage in a sloppy, drunken hug. I take the opportunity to push my way outside.

The crowd around the Chinese Food counter is even larger. It takes me a bit to orient myself and determine which way is back to my hut. I navigate through the people milling around eating, talking, and smoking.

"Buy me food from the China Man," a hoarse, creole-accented voice yells near me.

Someone pushes my back, sending me stumbling.

"Come over here, Rum Punch. I said buy me food from the China Man."

I turn and face a lanky young man who has come up behind me. His skin is mottled with patches of depigmentation. His hair is matted. Some of the mottled patches are red and inflamed. There's what I take to be half of a swastika scratched raw on his forehead. His eyes are not focused.

"You've got the wrong guy," I say.

"No, I know you're you. You're the one who's been Jewing up the place."

I walk as fast as I can. How far do I have to go? I know all the way up Front street. Then through the Cemetery to the beach, to my hut.

He's following. A few paces behind him I see Douglas and an old man I'm guessing is his father. Hitler catches up to me in a snap and pushes me again. His hands are on me. Patting me down. My shirt. My shorts. A hand is rifling in my pockets.

I twist and turn and throw wild blows and manage to pull away from him. I try to run and only manage to swerve and trip. I wish I had walked back to the crowd instead of trying to make it to my hut. Hitler's coming up on my side. I brace for a blow.

When I look again, he is on the ground holding his mid-section. He stands fast and comes at me. Someone jumps between us and throws a kick that connects with his head. It is Andy.

Hitler collapses to the ground. Andy slowly and purposefully paces around him. The angry ex pat tries to stand. Andy kicks him in the face.

"Hey, Rum Punch, you okay," Andy asks in the same sing-song tone he used in the bar.

I'm reeling from the violence. How can he be so calm?

Hitler rolls to his side, reaches for Andy's leg, and tries to bite him. Andy kicks him square in the face. There's an awful crack.

I crawl over and check his pulse. His mouth is full of blood and his neck is not right.

"Holy shit, you killed him."

"*I* killed him?" Andy says.

"I didn't kill him. What the fuck?"

"He was attacking you. Let me think for a sec."

"The guy has no pulse, man. We should... call the police. That was self-defense, right?"

"There's no police here. There's one soldier at the bank, when it's open. Let me think. Think. Think. Think. Okay I got it. There's only one thing to do."

"What?"

"Help me lift him. We're going take him to Anna Lucinda."

"Anna Lucinda's a doctor?"

"No, she's a crocodile. We're going to the dump."

"How the hell do you know so much? Ranit said you've never been here before."

"Yeah, I did tell her that. Doesn't matter now, come on."

Andy grips him under each shoulder. I hold his ankles and we lift. There isn't much heft to him. I can't stop replaying Douglas the Fisherman saying how he's going to die anyway.

The dump is three streets away at the back of the island and over a bit, effectively a world away. A short wide dock leads over dark water reeking of waste and rot. A chair is floating in the murk. We take the body to the end of the dock.

"Good. She's out there," Andy says. "I see her eye shine."

I don't see the crocodile or her eyes. I'm struggling just to keep up my end of the body. Andy swings the body back and forth. I catch his rhythm.

"Let go," he says.

The body hits the water with a big splash, spraying us with filth.

"Good," Andy says. "She's coming."

I look where Andy is pointing and I see a reptilian head moving through the water, a triangular wake spreading behind it.

We head off the dock onto Back Street and silently return to the front of the island.

"This sucks," I say, as we turn onto the beach.

"It's going to be okay."

Back at "our" beach, gentle waves lapping on the mangroves feels like home. Ranit is on the nearest dock, holding a pose, balanced on one leg, silhouetted by starlight. Brett and Silver are on the other dock throwing out fishing line.

Andy and I approach Ranit.

"You boys stink," she says. "What have you gotten into?"

"Nothing," Andy says.

While maintaining her pose, Ranit rolls her neck instructing us to jump into the water.

Andy takes a running leap.

"Ow," he says. "It's shallower than it looks."

I'm too tired to do anything other than sit on the edge. On the other dock Brett's pink fishing line has gone taught. I cannot keep my eyes open and I'm asleep before I see what he pulls in.

"Gonna get burned bad if you sleep like that in the sun. Wake up, brother."

I open my eyes to Nico gently poking me with his foot. The sun is almost ready to rise.

"You smell like you bathed in rum and nasty garbage," he says.

He helps me to my feet and off the dock.

"My prescription? A shower. Burn those clothes. Drink a lot of water and go back to sleep," he says.

"I don't have any water."

"That won't do. Come on, then."

We walk to his little house. I follow him under the steps into a cellar only as big as my hut. A cot and a bucket are the only things I can see.

He hands me a red plastic cup and we sit on the cot. Nico leans forward, pats the ground, grasps a round metal handle and pulls, opening a wooden trap door over a dark hole. Cool air wafts into the humid dank space. Nico removes rope coiled inside the bucket, ties it to the handle, and lowers it into the darkness. After a few seconds there is a splash.

He retrieves the bucket, dips my cup in, and prompts me to drink.

"It's fresh," he says. "Underneath the Caye is one big cave. It is mostly filled with salt water. When it rains, run off filters through and floats on top."

He takes a swig from my cup.

"See, sweet and fresh."

"An aquifer," I say.

"What?"

"That's what you call that, I think."

"You learn something every day," he says.

I gulp my water. It *is* clean and fresh.

"Yeah, Brett don't shut up about it," I say.

"Brett be talking about the cave?"

"The aquifer, I think, yeah."

"His father, Harlan was one of the divers who died down there trying to map it."

"Holy shit. You can go in and dive?"

"There's a way in at the dump. And at the Split. And a few people have figured out how to set up their basement like this."

I drink the rest of my water and thank him. He pours me another glass.

"What's it like being a Rasta?" I say breaking our silence. "Back home, people don't talk about it."

"Fuck if I know? I'm from Detroit. Came here chasing my wife who ran away with our kids. Never found her. I never left. Not yet, anyway. Ha, Rum Punch, I just let you in on *all* the secrets and you're here not even a day."

"Fuck. What's the point of anything?"

He throws up his hands.

"I'm sorry to be trouble."

I stand to leave.

"No trouble, brother. Helping each other is the one thing I know to be true. Wait. Before you go one more thing for you."

He produces a sauce jar full of water and hands it to me.

"Oh, thank you. I'm gonna drink this later-"

"You better not. Look. Found that little guy this morning washed up on the beach. Now I figure he's meant for you."

I hold the jar to my face. Inside is a little sea-horse, its tail gripped around a stick floating in the salt water.

I SLEEP HALF the morning and I'm still hungover. I glance at the yellow seahorse in the jar and wonder what it eats. I decide I'm going to take him to the Split and return him to the ocean. I carefully put the jar in my bag along with my mask and snorkel. On Front Street I purchase a fresh soursop juice from a cart vendor, which helps my head.

The Split is shaded by tall palms and home to lush hibiscus bushes alive with butterflies and hummingbirds. Beneath the greenery are foundations of abandoned buildings. Mangroves grow along the shore. There's the frame of a new building going up. Fifty yards away across the channel, the North side is ringed by more mangroves than I can count. Palms and brush have claimed every inch of space.

The water's edge before me is littered with broken shells, fishing hooks, cigarette butts, nasty dried up bait and dead fish and all sorts of trash from the boats that tie up there. I find a decent place to take off my flip-flops and jump in with the jar in one hand.

Warm water greets me. A slow current pulls towards the back of the island. I take a big breath and go under. The shore slopes steeply. Mangrove roots reach into the deep, drinking the ocean and sheltering the resident fish.

I surface and kick out allowing the current to have me. I dive and surface. There are plenty of crabs and fish. No seahorses. After a few minutes I've been carried to where the channel opens to the sea at the back of the island. I return to my starting point and go again. I choose a nice set of roots to release the seahorse into. I open the jar. Instead of going into the roots it darts past me into the channel. Sea horses aren't strong swimmers. Its dorsal fin oscillates madly to move it. Will it make it across? The tiny fish disappears from view quickly.

I notice something large in my peripheral vision. A crocodile is entering the channel. Twice as long as me, at least. With limbs pulled in tight it swishes its large powerful tail side to side, propelling it through the split. Is this Anna Lucinda returning from sea? The reptile meets my eye. It does not stop and exits the other side of the channel as quickly as it came.

DANIEL BRAUM

I make a final attempt to find seahorses. I spot pink fishing line waving in a dark area beneath the mangrove roots. Is this one of the cave entrances? I surface for breath. When I descend I cannot spot the line again and decide calling it quits is for the best.

ON MY WAY back to my hut I come across Andy heading my direction. He's carrying a bag of bananas and has an un-lit joint in his mouth.

"Hey, Rum Punch," he says. "Come smoke a joint with Ranit and me."

"Man, what's up with that? You're in public."

"What? There're no cops here. And everyone's smoking. There was a drop this morning. Where've ya been, sleepyhead?"

"Don't smoke. No, thank you."

"Really? What's wrong with you?"

"Nothing. I like to be... clear. I'm trying to figure shit out."

"Fooled me last night."

"Hey, quiet. What's wrong with *you*?"

"Easy, there's nothing to worry about."

"You sure?"

"Positive. The big guys made their drop. Their guy on the island fished it out and got his share. Now it's time to enjoy."

"No I meant about-"

"I know what you meant. I told you everything's okay. You sure you don't want ?"

"I'm gonna crash. I just went for a swim."

"Suit yourself. Be sure to come to the party later. We're going to celebrate."

"Celebrate what?"

"The drop? Being alive? Not sure. I don't make the parties I just go to them."

It dawns on me that days and nights are a repeating pattern here. Sun and salt water. Darkness and drinking and dancing. Repeating. Repeating.

Repeating. Surely there is a pattern to the way the seahorses live too. I just have to figure it out to find them.

I go to Nico's house to return his jar. He's not in his cellar. I check upstairs. His door is open. Inside is empty and broom clean.

I WAKE UP late from my nap. A warm tropical rain has moved in and it is dark. I hurry to the bar.

I'm soaked when I arrive. A few people are dancing outside on the sand. I avoid the first floor and climb the exterior stairs to the second floor, which is full of people. There are swings tied to the rafters and a single, thick rope coming from a square hole above. The rope disappears into a square, open trapdoor in the floor. It descends into the center of the first floor bar and into another trapdoor. I don't remember it from last night.

I glance around and notice the attractive dark-haired woman ascending the stairs to the third floor. Silver is on one of the swings, an empty space beside her despite the crowd. I make my way over.

"Hey, where's Brett?" I ask.

"Grabbing drinks. Rum Punch, you buying again?"

"I hope not."

Some bearded ex-pat guy in a Hawaiian shirt claps me on the back as he passes and says, "Thanks for yesterday, Rum Punch."

"What's with the rope?" I ask.

The music stops.

"Oh, it's about to start," Silver says. "Nico's going down."

"What?"

"Watch," she says.

A chant of Ni-Co, Ni-Co, has started on the third floor. Silver and the people around me join in. The rope sways. There's a cheer from above. Nico is climbing down, hand over hand, his legs gripping the rope as he slides.

Everyone rushes to touch him.

"What's going on," I ask the Hawaiian-shirted guy next to me.

"Nico's going down," he says matter-of-factly.

A gust of wind coats us with warm rain. I squeeze to the center of the room to get close to Nico.

"Hey, Nico," I call, "What's-"

"Hey, Rum Punch! How's my seahorse?"

"She's good. With friends now, I hope."

"I'm glad. And I'm glad you came," he says.

He descends to the first floor. We crowd closer to watch him. He lowers himself into the center of the bar and through the trap door there, into darkness. The bartender closes a hatch over him.

The music comes back on.

Brett returns with two cups of rum. He pauses when he sees me.

"Hey, no hard feelings, right Rum Punch?" Silver says.

"Um, right, Rum Punch, no hard feelings," Brett repeats.

"Yeah, sure, of course."

"Okay, good," Brett says.

They down their drinks.

"Dance with me, Brett," Silver says. "In the rain! Let's go in the rain, come on!"

Brett ignores her and is talking to everyone else, again. Silver grabs me by the elbow and leads me down the stairs.

SILVER GUIDES MY arms as she spins. I follow her splashing steps in the wet sand.

"Really, no hard feelings towards Brett?" she says.

"I was shaken up a bit, but it's all good."

"Okay, good. Thank you. It's hard for him. He lost his Dad down there trying to map it."

"I'm so sorry. How did it happen?"

A bunch of people descend from the stairs and hurry into the Chinese Food place.

"When Brett was a kid they'd come here," she says. "It's the biggest underwater cave. In the whole world. It's easy to get lost or stuck. One day he never came back up."

"That sucks."

"And it sucks that no one really knows about it. Just the people here and hard core cavers."

I notice tiny lines around her eyes. She's older and probably seen a lot more than I thought.

"What was all that with Nico?" I ask. "Isn't it dangerous?"

"Nico knows what he's doing. There are places to get out, through the ground. If you know where."

"Why though?"

"Nico was never here to stay," she says. "I bet he's back to looking for his kids."

"What's the other bet?"

"That he wanted to be the life of the party one more time. Or is just... gone. But enough. I want to know about you, do you like it here so far?"

"I went looking for sea horses today."

"Find any?"

"No but I let one go."

"You said-"

"Nico gave it to me."

Tears well in her blue eyes.

"What happened to my life, Rum Punch? I never asked for anything special. A life. A house. A fence and a dog and maybe kids, like Nico. And look. I'm here instead."

"I'm here too. I don't know. I woke up one day and realized nothing fit anymore. Maybe it never had at all."

"What are we supposed to do?"

"Don't know," I say. "Can I buy you some Chinese food?"

"Oh, yes, please."

"What's good?"

"Conch and garlic sauce."

The rain stops. Silver and I sit on a log on the beach and eat.

"Is this where you tell me to leave Brett?" she says.

"No. I don't know. I will tell you, anyone, myself, not to travel on paths that don't serve you. You can't move towards and away from something at the same time."

Brett and Andy and Ranit and the attractive dark-haired woman descend the second floor stairs together onto the muddy street.

Silver smiles and waves her fork. They come to us.

"You're the one looking to find the seahorses," the new woman says.

Ranit winks. I stand.

"Yes, I am. Thank you it's a pleasure-"

"Don't be formal, Rum Punch. I'm Maya," the woman says. "Finding seahorses is easy. You just go to the Split at the crack of dawn when they're waking up to eat. You want to do this?"

Brett looks up to the moon.

"I'm in," he says. "Be easier to stay awake until morning at this point."

WE'VE GATHERED A bunch of snorkel masks. And cigarettes. And bottles of One Barrel rum. We sit under the construction frame. Maya is from Baton Rouge, back home. She says she can't go back. Warrants and missed court dates from years ago.

"Your travel family is cool," Maya whispers in my ear.

"I just got here yesterday," I whisper back.

"Why don't people go across the Split to swim and sun," Maya asks Ranit. "Can you?"

"You can," Ranit says. "You're allowed. People just don't."

"Why?"

"They just don't."

The sun is almost up. We get our masks on. The channel comes alive with flying fish. For a few seconds the Split is lit with hundreds of clicking, silver bodies skipping the surface. Something has passed between all of us. No one acknowledges the feeling with words. No one needs to. I don't want to be in a world where people don't do things like stay up all night like this.

We jump in. The current takes us diagonally instead of a straight shot across.

Near the thickest cluster of mangroves we dip our heads under. The newly risen sun illuminates particles in the water. The particles are thousands of little living things. Colored fish dart around feasting on them. In the roots are yellow sea-horses. Just like that, we've found them. Six-inch long, strange yellow fish gripping mangrove roots with their prehensile tails as they feast.

I surface for air.

"There. Done, easy," Maya says.

"Thank you," I say.

I breathe and descend again. There is sun lit blue until visibility fades. Miles away is the Great Blue Hole that Stefania dreamed of. The chasm in the sea so deep no light reaches the bottom. The ocean is such a mighty thing. I try to get my mind around the sheer magnitude of it. The improbability of spots like this. How easy it would be for Anna Lucinda or anything bigger to make a meal of me. It would be so easy to let go. Stop caring. To give in and seek an end.

Was this dark fascination what Stefania succumbed to? Did the weight of everything, of simply existing, get to her? And take her down to where she craved only black? Was it a closer journey to seek oblivion than to try to find her way back to a semblance of happiness? Or did she merely just not love me, or herself anymore? I'll never know.

I try and guess if any of the little seahorses are the one Nico gave me. They all could be. Ah, if my ten-year-old self could see me now.

WE DRY OFF as birds are singing and the homeless in the bushes are waking for the day brushing the remnants of their sleeping spots off their clothes. Our alcohol has been finished off. Maya takes me by the hand and whispers to me if I want to come with her to shower up and then get some breakfast.

Over her shoulder I see Hitler turn the corner onto the Split from Back Street. I stare as he walks towards the bushes and mangroves. I'm certain it's him. His matted hair. Blotched skin and lanky frame. He reaches a low, green bush, drops to his knees and crawls into the leaves and branches.

"Friend of yours?" Maya says.

"No. Quite the opposite."

"You gonna stop staring?"

"Sorry I... didn't expect to see him."

"See, Rum Punch," Andy says. "Everything's okay."

I'm not sure I believe him.

He's found an inflated inner tube and jumps with it into the channel.

"Please don't disturb me, I'm mourning," he says.

"Is this why you keep coming back," I ask Ranit.

"I might change my answer tomorrow," she says. "Today I say I come back because I like that pirates once used the reef and shallows to hide from unwanted company."

"Thwarting unwanted company sounds good to me," Maya says. "You'd make a great pirate."

"Why thank you. I do admit the non-extradition policy is something I find more and more attractive as the years roll on," Ranit says.

"I knew there was something I really liked about this place," Maya says

"It's a great place to hide," Ranit says. "Great place to run away. Mostly everyone is a criminal. A seeker. A mystic."

"Which one are you?" Maya asks me.

"None of the above," I say.

"You sure?" Ranit says. "I think I know."

"No. I'm not sure," I say. "What makes you say that?"

"When you've been coming here a while, you get to know things."

Maya and I head to find breakfast. She takes my hand. I'm far away, daydreaming of the cave beneath us.

PUBLICATION HISTORY

"How to Stay Afloat When Drowning"
Pareidolia, Black Shuck Books, July 2019

"Goodnight Kookaburra"
A Walk on the Weird Side, Necronomicon Press, August 2017

"The Monkey Coat"
Nightscript 4, Cthonic Press, October 2018

"Tommy's Shadow"
Kaleidetrope #5, October 2008

"Rebbe Yetse's Shadow"
Space and Time Magazine, Winter 2017

"Cloudland Earthbound"
The Audient Void #4, Fall 2017

"Between Our Earth and Their Moon"
Original to this collection.

"Palankar"
Nightscript 3, Clthonic Press, October 2017

"Sogni del Mundo Sutteraneo / Underworld Dreams"
Original to this collection.

"Rum Punch is Going Down"
Nox Pareidolia, Nightscape Press, October 2019

STORY NOTES

HOW TO STAY AFLOAT WHEN DROWNING

One of the inspirations for this story was my desire to write an homage to one of my favorite short stories, "Because Their Skins Are Finer" by Tanith Lee. I knew the story was going to contain an interaction between something from the sea and someone who takes from the sea as (in very rough strokes) happens in the Tanith Lee tale. I wanted to avoid the elements of the "repentant hunter" and "vengeance" present in "Because Their Skins." When developing and doing the pre-writing I landed on presenting a tension to be in both the reveal and discovery of what is going on in the seaside town and presenting tension between whether our narrator's experiences are real or imagined, a psychological or supernatural phenomenon.

While deciding on the characters and their emotional truths, I was asked to write a story for the Pareidolia anthology. Pareidolia is defined as the tendency to interpret a vague stimulus as something known to the observer, such as seeing shapes in clouds, seeing faces in inanimate objects or abstract patterns, or hearing hidden messages in music.

I had an image in my mind of the scene where the main character sees the sister's face for the first time and her mouth is full of "shark" teeth. Is he seeing things? Or is he observing something objectively real? I intentionally crafted the story to work whether the answer or "explanation" a reader latches on to was either psychological (a reaction or effect of the main character's grief) or supernatural (that these shark-people were real), without definitively landing on one way or the other. I wanted the entire story to operate as a kind of pareidolia where the reader is not certain if what they and the characters are observing is a psychological or supernatural phenomenon. No matter what my intent was in presenting the speculative element the most important thing in creating an engaging story is the emotional truth as brought forward in the details of all the character relationships. What do you see in the story?

GOODNIGHT KOOKABURRA

What do you see when you close your eyes? Can you visualize your thoughts in that darkness?

Around the time when I was asked to contribute a story for the *Walk on the Weird Side* anthology to benefit Necronomicon 2017 I had been thinking about a unique phenomenon attributed to aboriginal sacred sites in Australia. I spent a few months in Australia in 2007 and observed some unusual occurrences on my travels. I learned that aboriginal sacred sites are gender specific, male or female. Each place is said to act as a boon to the matching gender and a bane to the opposition gender, in rough generalization. Do you see this phenomenon happening in the story? Or maybe something else is happening.

In the genre of Weird Fiction there is a long tradition of the natural world being connected to unexplained, supernatural, and other-worldly phenomenon, running all the way back to Algernon Blackwood's short story "The Willows," where two men are experiencing a phenomenon on their canoe trip in the wild. Here it could be interpreted that natural setting and the weird fiction speculative elements are converging with the emotional reality and conflicts of the main character (if one lands on that something supernatural is happening at all.)

TOMMY'S SHADOW

"Tommy's Shadow" is another story where I wanted tension between the possibility of a psychological and a supernatural explanation to be in play. As in "Goodnight Kookaburra," the name of the possible supernatural element is not mentioned. Do you recognize what it could be? I felt the name would call too much attention and risk tilting the balance of the focus of this modern, suburban, rock and roll "fairy tale."

Unlike fairy tales which rely on well-used tropes and character types, when writing this story it was my intention to play with and subvert some of them. I also thought about how to depict the violence in the story- something I am not comfortable with and was even less so at the time.

One strategy is to "cut away" from the violence and to allow the implication to carry the scene. This can sometimes be effective. Author and editor, the departed and greatly talented Gardner Dozois noticed me doing this, "cutting away" from things in the story when he reviewed my work as part of a workshop. It amazed me how he astutely was able to hypothesize part of the real-life happenings and inspirations for the story from what I did not put on the page. He challenged me to take my most personal and close to home fears and most awful situations and to put them to paper. I am still working on his advice to this day.

THE MONKEY COAT

I was writing this one during a time when I was fortunate enough to be spending some time with author Jack Ketchum. When we'd hang out, drinking of course, the conversations always weaved into topics on the craft fiction. "Don't look away" was one of Dallas' go-to lessons and a phrase familiar to any of his students. And it fit in perfectly with Gardner Dozois' challenge. "Not looking away" was very much on my mind when writing the "Monkey Coat."

As with Tommy's Shadow I wanted the "The Monkey Coat" to be a story that could be seen as either psychological or supernatural. depending on which elements any given reader is picking up on and giving merit to. I wanted there to be a sufficient amount of elements present for a reader to hang their hat on either possibility while still maintaining a balance without the scales tipping definitively one way or another. It was my intent to reach a rendering where both tracks of possibility would be unable to be discounted.

Both the song "Shock the Monkey" by Peter Gabriel and Tanith Lee's story "Because Their Skins" are two works that continue to stay relevant for me even after all these years. While neither was a direct inspiration for "The Monkey Coat," I always wanted to write a story that put the cruelty of the fur industry on display too. However, I wanted to be sure to stay far away from anything on the nose or preaching. I feel stories must be entertaining and immersive first and being heavy handed with theme or a message can easily erode effectiveness and suspension of disbelief. Upon drafting the story quickly evolved away from the fur industry, despite a fur coat being present front and center.

Also when writing the story I learned about object-oriented ontology and how it might relate to fiction. Friends and colleagues were discussing stories where the story of an object or non-human thing continues and goes on after the story of the humans ends or is separated from it. Some of these are found in horror such as "Monkey Paw" stories or stories where a Talisman or cursed or haunted object is passed on to another user or victim. I was not thinking of this concept when drafting the story but it is interesting to think about it through this lens. It is a logical leap that the story of "The Monkey Coat" goes on after we leave the story of Ivy, just as it went on after the coat left Grandma Estelle and June.

REBBE YETSE'S SHADOW

Real world things and anecdotes, (such as the Asylum in "Tommy's Shadow") often are starting points. Often these real-world elements are eliminated in the crafting process, as the advice "kill your darlings" advocates. The inspiration for this story was an experience one of my relatives had when traveling to New York. However, a recounting, even a good one, without character stakes is merely a recounting and not much of a story. Often the task for me is how to embody the ideas in an inspiring anecdote in dramatic structure.

Because the ghosts are presented as real and unambiguous, this story is perhaps the most traditional and the most fitting inside the genre lines of horror of the collection. It is fun to contemplate how the story might have turned out if it were crated as a strange tale. With some revision the supernatural could readily be presented as possibly being a psychological manifestation. This direction and the tension and opportunities that come with it were not developed. It was written before my self-education on strange tales and weird fiction and before I started consciously thinking about genre structures in my creative process. While the ghosts here are intended as literal it is a nice juxtaposition to have it appear alongside strange tales and stories playing with intentional ambiguities.

CLOUDLAND EARTHBOUND

Setting is the aspect of story that often comes to me first and inspires me to write. The characters and their conflicts are then born out of these settings. While the Cloudland Ballroom, a historical music venue in Brisbane Australia was a real place the characters and situations in the story are fictional and fictionalized. Considering this, and that Cloudland has been long gone, it can be said that the Brisbane and Cloudland presented here are alternate ones.

One of the things I find powerful about fiction is how the passage of time can be depicted. Progress and development are full of inherent conflicts. I find myself coming back to aspects of these two notions in my stories. Even when unintended writing in great detail about a specific place can serve as a time capsule.

"Alternate universes" and "multiple worlds" and "multiple realities" are concepts common in genre fiction and have been presented in myriad of ways over the decades. In our real world I sometimes see development as a (simplified) battle between two sides, those wanting it and those against it. I often think about the ways of how this kind of battle could be presented as a literal and supernatural battle. It has been pointed out to me that several of the stories in this volume operate as depictions of an "alternate" present scene or a depiction of the alternate or timeline that "lost" or was "left behind." I guess this way of looking at it could depend on which character a reader identifies with and is rooting for, if any. In any event I like the resonance this kind of alternate world presentation has with the other stories in the volume. Are there any specific places that exist no more that are closely associated with a cherished time and place for you? This world is so full of them for me.

BETWEEN OUR EARTH AND THEIR MOON

I love stories that on first glance appear to be one thing or appear to be following "standard" tropes but then turn out to be another thing or subvert the trope(s). I'm fascinated with how structure and expectation can effect category and or perception of a story. Ultimately, I feel any of this, and everything is secondary to delivering an entertaining and enjoyable story; yet if that is established I am just so excited

263

about subverting and transcending category and expectation.

What I am talking about is more than mere bait and switch. These kinds of stories often are both the "standard" iteration of the story and also more than it or also operate in the far corners borderlands of the source. An excellent example of this is the film "It Follows" which on one level appears to be and operates as a "standard" teens in peril versus a stalker story but is also something more and is operating both on different levels and playing with the tropes presented. I was pleased that my novella the Serpent's Shadow elicited this sort of feedback and reaction from readers. One of the rewards of crafting a story this way is the supernatural can operate not (only as) antagonist but as a catalyst. When the story is less about or no longer about or not about "defeating a monster" (as in having to find a "silver bullet" and then hunt and slay the beast) there is more room for a story to be about the real worlds (the underworlds I spoke of) of the characters presented and their emotional conflicts and truths.

At first glance the story has the trappings of a (supernatural) noir story. We have a detective character assigned to solve a problem. While that external level is present there is more to it. The story also plays with the element of what if something that is perceived as supernatural is just something that is not understood? The element of alternate worlds and specifically one's alternate selves are in play. What would a character do if they met themselves? When offered a choice to "solve" one's own problems at the expense of an alternate self what choices would a character make? What choices would you make?

This is a stand-alone story and not a sequel yet it features a character from my short story "Across the Darien Gap." The loss and memories that are in play here are the present scene of the previous story. There is plenty of conflict to explore when a character has experienced such loss and has the opportunity for such choices.

PALANKAR

In fiction sometimes the conflict, the struggle, is against another's choice. How far will we go to "save" our loved ones? How far do we have to go to learn what choices are not ours to make at all?

Stories about "doppelgangers" have a long history of appearing in weird fiction and horror but I did not know that at the time I was writing "Palankar." It was the first short story I wrote after reading "The Swords" by Robert Aickman and beginning what I call my education about strange tales and the genre of weird fiction.

I've you've read this far you know that I love stories with intentional ambiguity and a tension between supernatural and psychological explanations for the strange elements in play. The Yucatan Peninsula, in this case the Palankar Reef is a source of inspiration that compels me again and again. The challenge I gave myself was to present ambiguity if Steven really was replaced when down in the depths of the continental shelf, or not? I was my intent that everything presented was open to and worked with and fit with either "explanation."

With the plot not beholden to explain nor solve this question or problem it was free to explore move with and delve deep into the choices of characters, into the "here and now of the story." It is the emotional realties and the choices of the characters which are of the ultimate importance and the heart of the story. The supernatural element, if it really is supernatural at all, is the catalyst.

UNDERWORLD DREAMS

The original inspiring idea for this story was to depict what I call a "crossroads moment" (a moment, a choice where a life could have gone one way or another) and to show both outcomes in the story. One of the characters asks another "What would you do if you were on a "desert island" and could "get away with being unfaithful?" I became less interested in following through with this focus on this element and more interested in the meanings of the choices to the characters. If there are a multitude of universes that branch out and explode from all of our choices who is to say which ones are right and which ones are "wrong." Wouldn't it be a matter of perception and perspective? Embodying this notion in a character quickly became the focus of the story as I wrote it.

This story features some un-orthodox structural elements to achieve the sense of a "crossroads moment" and "multiple universes." The "chapter headings" are also lines that are found in the story. (They also appear in other stories in the book, have you noticed where?) Do you notice where some of the characters from this story appear in other stories in the book?

RUM PUNCH IS GOING DOWN

This is the second story I wrote for a pareidolia themed anthology. Yes, there is a sense of whether something supernatural or not is happening on or with the Island throughout the story. What I intended as the defining "pareidolia" moment is not revealed until the end scene of the story. A character we believed was dead is seen in the end scene. Did we the reader see him die or not? Was he dead or not? Did he come back to life or not? Depending on which answers (if any) one assigns to these questions determines whether one is perceiving the story as a psychological or supernatural phenomenon. It is my intent that both explanations are equally supported and one is not wrong nor right. Does it make a difference to the characters and their stories? Is the universe reactive or uncaring? Are the meanings the characters find in this underworld the same no matter what? To band together. To be good to one another. To enjoy and connect with one another and the natural world. Even in broken states and remote dark places they all (and we all) might find themselves.

ACKNOWLEDGMENTS

Thank you to:

Steven Berman, publisher of Lethe Press;

To the editors and publishers who first published some of these stories:
James Everington, Dan Howarth, Steve Shaw, Joe Pulver Sr., Niels Hobbs, Fred
Coppersmith, C. M. Mueller, Hildy Silverman, Obidiah Baird, and
Robert Wilson;

To my friends and colleagues on my writing journey: MM Devoe, Nicholas
Kaufmann, John Foster, Ben Francisco, David Wellington, Lee Thomas, Sarah
Langan, Victor LaValle, Chandler Klang Smith, Peter Ball, Chris Lynch, JJ Irwin,
Kelly Link, Dallas Mayr, and Gardner Dozois;

To my friends on the road;

To Lucius Shepard and Tanith Lee;

and to my family.

ABOUT THE AUTHOR

DANIEL BRAUM is the author of the short story collections *The Night Marchers and Other Strange Tales*, *The Wish Mechanics: Stories of the Strange and Fantastic*, and *Yeti Tiger Dragon*. *Underworld Dreams* is his third collection. *The Serpent's Shadow*, his first novella released from Cemetery Dance eBooks. He is the editor of the *Spirits Unwrapped* anthology from Lethe Press and the host and founder of the Night Time Logic reading series in New York City which can also be heard on the Ink Heist podcast.

His work has appeared in publications ranging from *Lady Churchill's Rosebud Wristlet* to the *Shivers 8* anthology.

He can be found at bloodandstardust.wordpress.com and on Twitter @danielbraum

CPSIA information can be obtained
at www.ICGtesting.com
Printed in the USA
LVHW012322240221
679846LV00006B/1179